I KNOW YOU

GUERNICA WORLD EDITIONS 61

RUSSELL GOVAN

I KNOW YOU

TORONTO—CHICAGO—BUFFALO—LANCASTER (U.K.)

2023

Guernica Editions Founder: Antonio D'Alfonso

Michael Mirolla, general editor
Paul Carlucci, editor
Cover and interior design: Errol F. Richardson

Guernica Editions Inc.
287 Templemead Drive, Hamilton (ON), Canada L8W 2W4
2250 Military Road, Tonawanda, N.Y. 14150-6000 U.S.A.
www.guernicaeditions.com

Distributors:
Independent Publishers Group (IPG)
600 North Pulaski Road, Chicago IL 60624
University of Toronto Press Distribution (UTP)
5201 Dufferin Street, Toronto (ON), Canada M3H 5T8

First edition.

Legal Deposit—First Quarter
Library of Congress Catalog Card Number: 2023930049
Library and Archives Canada Cataloguing in Publication
Title: I know you / Russell Govan.
Names: Govan, Russell, author.
Series: Guernica world editions (Series) ; 61.
Description: Series statement: Guernica world editions ; 61
Identifiers: Canadiana (print) 2023013310X | Canadiana (ebook) 20230133142 |
ISBN 9781771838047 (softcover) | ISBN 9781771838054 (EPUB)
Classification: LCC PS3607.O93 I2 2023 | DDC 813/.6—dc23

For my mother, Helen Govan

August 6, 2019

1.

MY PHONE BUZZES. I reach and grab it from on top of my bedside drawers. It's a WhatsApp from Alice on the group chat. *Anyone else awake?* It's ten past five.

An immediate response from Morag. *Me. Can't sleep.*

I respond. *Me neither. Been awake a while.*

There's a pause. The three of us are waiting to see if there's anything from Lindsey or Seonaid. Fifteen seconds—forever—passes.

Morag breaks cover again. *Guess it's just us three then.*

Alice: *How long have you been awake?*

Me: *Must be half an hour.*

Morag: *About ten minutes.*

Alice: *I've just woken. Are either of you actually up?*

Me: *Are you mental? It's ten past bloody five!*

Morag: *I'm still under the covers.*

Alice: *My mum said that if I got up before seven, she'd kill me.*

Me: *If I get up, it'll disturb Gran. My mum would go ballistic.*

There's another pause. We said everything we had to say to each other yesterday. Several times over. We all know that, and I know Alice and Morag will be thinking the same. We'll get our results by text at eight, with certificates coming in the post later today. The UCAS website will confirm whether we've got our places at nine.

Alice: *I think I'll go back to sleep.*

Morag: *Good idea. Me too. Love you, gals. See you all later.*

Alice: *Love you both loads. And you too, sleepyheads!*

Me: 😴👌✌️✌️

I put my phone down. There's no way I'll get back to sleep, and neither will the other two. The four of them are my besties. I've been friends with Alice and Seonaid since primary school. This last year, we've become closer friends with Lindsey and Morag. Those of us that stayed for sixth year formed new friendship groups after so many others went off to uni last autumn. I might have gone then too, except I blew my exams. I was predicted straight As and ended up with four Bs and a C. The school said they'd support an appeal for upgrades on compassionate grounds and would write to the university. But I didn't want that. Mum was in bits about Dad, and so was I, if I'm being honest. Home wasn't in any fit state for me to leave it. And I wasn't in any fit state to leave.

So five of us ended up doing sixth year together. Seonaid had missed her place to do medicine by one grade. Alice wanted to stay on because her boyfriend was. Sensible Lindsey said she was too immature to leave home at seventeen. And Morag, in her own words, "made a complete arse of her exams the first time round." So that was us—"the dunderheads," we call ourselves. And now it's a year later. In just a few hours, we'll all have our separate paths determined for us.

It's another glorious morning. The sunlight arrowing into the room through the curtain gaps confirms it. The dawn chorus is fading, and the stillness that goes with the early quiet is returning. I slide my legs off the side of the bed and sit up. I reach into the drawer for the candle and place it on top. Then I reach for Dad's lighter, fire the wick, and sit back, looking at the flame. I used to do this a lot in the first few months after he died. Not so much recently. The minister said that some people find it a comfort. I was desperate and would've tried anything. I'm still kind of surprised I do it.

The flame's white and steady. I was a Daddy's girl. I still am, and I always will be. I was his favourite. He never said it, of course, but I know. The sly winks, the smiles, that time I overheard him boasting about me, the in-jokes we shared. The flame looks like it's fixed, almost solid but not quite. My eyes are moist. Today would've been important to him. He wouldn't have gone into his work until he knew my results, like he did when I got my National 5s. He'd want to be here to celebrate, or to comfort me. I wish he was here. So much. Tears roll down both cheeks, and the flame flickers ever so slightly. I watch it as it steadies and fix on it for long enough to see wax run down its length on all sides. Eventually, I know it's time to blow it out, even though I don't want to. *I love you, Dad.* A firm, gentle puff, and the flame is gone. The delicious smoke fills my nostrils.

I roll onto my back, head on pillow. I look up and see dust motes pirouetting in the sunbeams, energized by the draft from my movement. I hope there's a heaven, or some kind of afterlife. It's too painful to think that when someone dies, so does their love.

I've thought a lot about love this last year. Although my head said differently, my heart knew I'd never get over losing Dad. Then Findlay came along. He's not a substitute, obviously. But he's filled my heart and brought me joy and comfort and hope. I can still hardly believe we're an item. No, not that. We're more than an item. We're blessed to have met each other so young. We're perfect together. Perfect.

I've had a few boyfriends—well, seven to be precise, if we exclude anything before I was fourteen. None of them were serious, and the longest any of them lasted was a couple of months. I just get bored. They always seemed to become clingy or jealous or both. I got quite good at ending things without too much upset, mainly. Eventually, I'd get asked out by another boy that I fancied enough to say yes to and that would last as long as it lasted.

Anyway, Findlay had been going steady with Roxanne McAllister for nearly two years when they split up. She wanted to go to uni, and he wanted to stay on and do Sixth Year. And that was that. It was the talk of the school. They were the golden couple. She was beautiful and smart. A bit up herself, but okay to talk to when you got to know her. He was just heart-stoppingly handsome—tall, blond, and with a smile that melts glaciers. He captained the rugby and debating teams, and he was super smart to boot. He got five straight A's in his Highers. Too good to be true, except he was real, because I saw him every day.

Everyone was amazed when he and Roxy broke up. But not half as amazed as I was the following weekend when he asked me out. He just came up to me at the checkout on the Saturday afternoon and asked me what time I finished. Then asked if I wanted to go for a meal. And I said yes. We went for that meal. We kissed—and pow! That was it. I'd kissed boys before, but this was completely different. Within a few weeks, we were an item. We'd probably already fallen in love with each other by then.

Findlay had stayed on because he thought he'd have a better chance of getting in to study PPE at Oxford if he did Sixth Year. His heart was set on doing what he called "the world's most prestigious degree" there. But he's given that up for us. For me. When he realized the prospect of us being apart was bringing me down, he volunteered to go to St. Andrews as well. He really did that for me. I would never get into Oxford, probably. And anyway, I don't want to go that far south and be so far away from Mum and Gran, even my brothers. So Findlay said he'd stay in Scotland so we could still be together. That's how much he loves me. Sacrificed his dream for us. Oh, and he's great in bed! As in really, really great in bed. I mean I've never been with another guy to compare him against, and I never will. Because there's no need. It simply couldn't be better.

Now all I need is for my results to be good enough to get in, and we'll spend the next three years together in St. Andrews. We'll do the first year in halls. Findlay thinks it's the best way to meet people. Then we'll get a flat together for second, third, and fourth years. I just need to get those results.

2.

MY PHONE BUZZES again. Something's wrong. I've got a piercing headache. There are noises downstairs. I realize I've dozed off. I reach for the phone. One minute past eight. The text with my exam results is there! Crap! My chest and shoulders are tight, and I hold my breath. I can't swallow.

I open the text and close my eyes. I force an inward breath and open one eye. My index finger is trembling as I start to scroll. *Please, God, please, please.* Four A's. Four A's at Advanced Higher! I scream involuntarily, and the bedroom door flies open. Mum stares at me, face frozen with hope and fear. She tilts her head almost imperceptibly and raises her eyebrows, imploring.

"Four A's! I got four—" I don't get any more out, as she's on the bed hugging me harder than I'd ever have believed and planting a kiss on my cheek.

"Oh my God! Oh my God! You clever, clever girl!" She squeezes me even tighter, and I see she has tears in her eyes. "I was outside waiting. I didn't know what to ..."

Now it's my turn. I'm cuddling her so hard that she can't speak. "I can hardly believe it, Mum."

She wriggles free enough to catch her breath. "Dad would be so proud."

Tears well up for the second time this morning. I can't form any words.

"Ahem!" My twenty-year-old brother, George, probably not long in from the nightshift, is standing in the doorway holding his phone toward me. "I take it it's good news? It's not that I care, obviously, but I've got Archie on the line wanting to know." Archie is George's twin, travelling in Southeast Asia over summer before going back for his third year of civil engineering at Edinburgh. "Well?"

"Four A's! I got four A's!"

"Did you hear that?" George is talking into his phone. He pauses. "Aye, I'll tell her. Mind and not be picking up any of thon exotic diseases. Cheers." He switches the phone off. "Archie says well done, but he's still the smartest in the family. I haven't the heart to tell him that we all think he's thick." He comes over and kisses me lightly just in front of my ear. I can't remember him ever kissing me before.

"Yuck!" Scott, our wee brother who'd been hidden behind George, has stepped forward to the threshold. "Everybody's kissing and greetin' in here. I'm away down to get my breakfast."

My phone buzzes. It's a text from Seonaid. Mum looks at me, says, "You better take that," and gets up off the bed. "See you downstairs when you're ready for your breakfast." She and George close the door behind them.

Seonaid: *You okay?*

Me: Yes. *What about you?*

Seonaid: *Me too.*

I close the text app and ring her. "What did you get?"

"Three A's. What about you?"

"Four A's."

"Four! That's brilliant."

I know she means it. She's genuinely delighted for me, just like I am for her. I hear her giggling down the phone and dissolve myself. "I know, I know. We've done it. Off to Dundee for you now, Doctor MacDonald."

"Aye, and off to St. Andrews for you, Professor McVicar."

"How do you think the others have got on?"

"They'll be fine, I hope. Poor Alice forgot to register for the text service in time, so she'll have to wait for the post."

"I don't think I could bear that. Waiting and wondering when the postman's going to get there."

"I know. Still, we'll find out soon enough. Oh, hang on—message from Morag! Smiley face—brilliant."

"And another smiley from Lindsey!"

"Fantastic! We better message them as well, or they'll think we've failed. Best hang up. You'll want to see how Findlay's got on."

"Aye. Best skedaddle. See you at The Silver Tassie at eleven. Well done, beautiful girl!"

"Well done to you too, prof. See you later."

I can't stop grinning. This is a good, good day. Alice's results will be fine. We'll all have made it. I think about messaging *Dunderheads triumphant*, then think better of it. Best wait until we know for sure that Alice is safe.

I message Findlay: 🤍👍🏼🍾✉️🤍🤍🤍 Send.

I don't need to worry about him—his results last year got him an unconditional offer. I pause, waiting for his reply.

Instead, I get a text from Alice: *Congratulations!* 🎻🎻🎻

Me: *Aw! Thanks, hun. When's your postie due?*

Alice: *Any time now. I'm bricking it. All five of us can't get what we want. I'm going to be the odd one out.*

Me: *Rubbish. You're the smartest of all of us.* That's not true, and we both know it. *You'll be fine.*

Alice: *Thanks. I hope so. Best get back to looking out the window. If you don't hear from me … well, you know.*

Me: *You will will WILL be fine! Love ya.*

My phone buzzes. Findlay: *Congratulations.*

Me: *Thanks, Mr. 100% Gorgeous.*

Findlay: *Can we meet up?*

Me: *Everyone's going to The Tassie at opening.*

Findlay: *Before that.*

Me: *Okay, Mr. Mysterious. Meg's teashop at 10.00?*

Findlay: *See you there.*

3.

THERE'S AN ALIEN sitting across the little round table from me. It looks and sounds exactly like Findlay, but it betrays itself by talking gibberish. I can hear it speaking, but only just over the sound of the blood swish-swish-swishing in my ears. It's hard to focus because my eyes are like dams struggling to contain too much water. I feel like I might faint or be sick or both.

Don't be upset, it's saying. *I don't want you to be upset.* But if it doesn't want me to be upset, why is it saying this? Why is *he* saying this? I try to breathe in slowly, but snotters interfere. I take a tissue from my bag and clear my nose. Another to dab my eyes. I take a deep breath in, hold it, then out—long and slow. Repeat. Twice. Think. This is a nightmare. I need to make sense of it so I can banish it. Make the alien disappear and get my Findlay back.

"Why did you tell me you were coming to St. Andrews rather than Oxford?"

"I don't know. I meant it when I said it at first. Then, when I changed my mind, I didn't know how to tell you."

"When did you change your mind?"

"When the offer from Oxford was confirmed." His voice is low and matter of fact – almost casual, but his face is screaming his discomfort. He looks shifty.

"When was that?"

"Does it matter?"

"Yes, it fucking *matters*." My voice is a low rasp.

He breaks eye contact momentarily, then stilettos me: "January."

"What?"

"January," he says, twisting the blade.

Nausea batters my body like a huge wave. My left hand clutches the tabletop, my right squeezes my empty Coke bottle, desperately seeking something firm to cling to. Don't be sick. It'll pass.

"Eilidh, are you okay?" He's leaning forward. "I'm so sorry. Really, really sorry. I wanted to tell you, but I just didn't know how. What we had was so good. I didn't want to upset things. You have to believe me."

He reaches across to put his hand on top of mine, but I pull away.

"*Was?*"

"Sorry, what?"

"You said what we had *was* so good."

"Oh … well, I meant …" He's frowning and looking daggers at me, as if *I'm* the one at fault.

"You said *was*. You said it without thinking." There's a light in the fog, and I'm homing in on it. Alert. "When did you get your offer?"

"I told you: in January."

"So when did you apply, then?"

"Sorry?"

"You heard me. When did you apply?" He breaks eye contact again and looks down at the table, giving me his answer. The fog has gone completely, and now I see everything. "You never applied to St. Andrews, you bastard. It was just a pile of shite to keep me onside, to get inside my knickers." I'm gulping air now. I feel fire in my neck and face. "Roxy McAllister dumped you, and you needed someone else to shag. You thought, *There's Eilidh McVicar, she's a bit stupid, she'll do*. You fucking snake."

He leans over the table, grabs my wrist, and pulls me toward him. "Calm down, you're causing a scene."

I glance round the tea room. It's half-full, mainly mums with pushchairs. And they're all looking at us. I look back at the serpent, but it's me who's hissing. "Admit it, Findlay. Admit it, or I'll really create a fucking scene."

"Fuxsake, Eilidh! We're only eighteen! We're not meant to settle down and live happily ever after, you fucking nutjob. It's all just meant to be a bit of fun. There's no need to make everything so fucking heavy."

I'm on my feet. I've freed my wrist, and my other hand is swinging the coke bottle at his head. He's too quick. He ducks and pushes his chair back, launching the table into my midriff. I lose balance and fall backward. The back of my head hits something hard, and the pain is indescribable. Then blackness. Then nothing.

July 3, 1984

4.

"STOP!" I'M SHRIEKING. "Stop! Stop! Stop!"

We've gone barely two hundred yards from the village.

The pickup stops so suddenly that I fly forward and headbutt the cab. I see stars and flashing lights like they do in cartoons. My hand reaches instinctively to my right brow, then into vision, and I register blood. The harsh engine is still splutter-running, and the women and children, heaped and hurt by the violent halt, are shrieking all around me.

Donny's screaming my name. "Walt! Walt! What the fuck is it? Why are we stopping?" I turn. There's a tarpaulin stretched over a frame at head height to shade the bed of the truck. Donny's roaring at me from up front in the driver's seat. Through the window at the back of the cab, I can see his face is a wide-eyed mixture of anger and confusion. "Why have we stopped?"

I shake my head, seeking clarity, but that only makes the pain worse. I focus on the woman, Biftu. Huge, eloquent, impassioned eyes. Terrified. Her arms again make the shape of cradling a baby as she holds my gaze. Pleading. Desperate.

"There's a baby left behind!" I'm pointing furiously in the direction of the village. "Donny, we've left a baby behind!"

"What?"

"I said …" I make my way to the rear and jump out. "Biftu. We've left her baby back there."

"Fuck."

The noise of the bullet shattering the brake light is a hundred times louder than I could've ever imagined. The women and children are banshees, the canvas both amplifying and damping their wailing at the same time. Donny is on the ground beside me. Fear in his eyes. Shouting. "We can't stay here."

"I know. Get back in the cab. Drive."

"What?" Another bullet cracks off a rock in front of the truck.

"Drive! I'll meet you at the burnt-out farm two miles back."

"Don't be so fucking stupid, Walt." But he can see I am that stupid. His eyes fill, the only spare moisture for a thousand miles. "We'll wait for you."

"One hour, max. If I'm a no-show, go. I'll make my own way back."

He nods a lie. We both know he'll wait as long as he can, perhaps even until dark. "See you there. Or back at the camp. Take care, Dubya." He uses his old nickname for me, something he only does these days when he's worried about me, then scrambles back into the cab. I snake-belly through dust and stones to a squat, leafless bush, driven by primal instinct to seek cover, however inadequate. The throttle roars, and the synchromesh grates in protest as Donny forces the shift stick into first. The truck lurches forward. Biftu is gripping the tailgate with both hands, staring out at me. She holds my gaze until the pickup disappears from view.

Shit! Act first, think second. How many times? Okay, genius, what's the plan? Think. What would Daniel do? Think! Who the hell is shooting? And why? The TPLF are active in the area. Derg forces too. But what's the point? Who would want to shoot starving civilians? There are stories of armed groups raiding villages to steal any food reserves. But not here. One look at these villagers, and it's clear there's nothing here. Nothing. No livestock. No grain. Nothing. Nothing but emaciation and despair.

It doesn't matter who or why. What matters is the baby. I roll onto my side and twist my head so I can see the village. Two smaller huts sit some fifty yards to the left of the rest. The one furthest away is Biftu's—I remember her coming out of it when we arrived. She also nodded and pointed to it when she was telling me about the baby.

The village is deserted. Well, except for whoever's doing the shooting. But there's no movement in the trees behind either. Maybe they've moved on. Maybe they don't realize that I'm still here. Maybe I could wait for dark and then go back. But that's too many maybes.

What's certain is that there's a baby in that hut. There's a psycho or psychos around with a gun or guns. They've fired three bullets.

The first when we were loading people into the pickup, and two more after we stopped. Single shots each time. Not automatic. The baby is in danger. Donny will wait for me at the burnt-out farm. He'll wait until dark, despite what we agreed. That gives me three and a half hours. It's less than two and a half miles. I can easily cover that distance carrying a baby in half an hour, tops. I can afford to wait. There's plenty of time.

But the baby's in danger.

I start to slide-crawl forward. It's a couple hundred yards to Biftu's hut. I can get pretty much all the way there without having to break cover. Not the most direct route, but definitely safer. I say cover, but if anyone's looking, they'll easily see me. I'll still be exposed, but I won't be so obvious to someone who isn't actively watching for me. I keep low and get to the edge of the so-called cover in less than two minutes. Only twenty yards to the hut. I'm crouched, breathing slow and deep, senses supercharged. Silence and stillness, not the merest hint of a breeze, so it's like looking at a painting. No, it's more like being in a photograph. Everything seems real, but not quite. There's not even a smell, other than baked dust. My mouth is dry, and the cut over my eyebrow is throbbing. I can't see a soul. Maybe they've gone. Maybe it's just me. Maybe it's safe. I'm clutching at maybes again. Concentrate! Stay alert. No one anywhere. No sound.

Go! I cover the ground in a couple of seconds, deliberately light of foot to avoid sound, and spin through the open entrance, pressing my back against the internal wall. Freeze. Don't even breathe. Listen. Listen. Breathe. Listen. Have they heard me? The silence is unbroken. I think I'm okay.

I turn my attention to finding Biftu's baby. There's plenty of natural light in here, so my eyes adjust easily. The walls are adorned with mats covered in designs and patterns in earth tones, red clay, black and white. Metal cooking utensils, a kettle and plate, all hanging from the wall—a layer of dust testament to their lack of use. There's a low wooden table covered in upside down handle-less teacups, a white footstool tucked below. Beyond the table is a bed, a garish satin-green cover over the mattress. On top, wrapped in brown swaddling, is the baby. It's on its side, face toward me, eyes closed.

I tiptoe gingerly forward. I'm still afraid to make a noise, but not as fearful as I am that I'm about to confirm what I've already decided. The baby's dead. I knew as soon as I saw it. I've seen too many dead babies since I came to this godforsaken country. It's tiny. Looks about three months old, but it could be twice or three times that age. Just never grew for lack of food. And it's an it. Not a he or a she. Just an it. A baby. Dead. I've seen this too often before, but my stomach still heaves, and I have to fight my body's desire to shudder a sob.

I want to scream. For Biftu's baby. At the injustice. In frustration. The pointlessness of it all. At Biftu's selfishness. My stupidity. Everything. I lean forward and arrange the green cover over the baby. A tear reaches my cheekbone then drops, forming a bottle-green spot. I'll leave the baby here. This is its home. The camp is no place for a baby. I'll need to find something to dig a grave. I straighten up and turn, stepping to the doorway. I look at the other buildings. This is an agricultural village. There will be tools, something I can use. The larger huts toward the centre of the settlement are my best bet. I step out of Biftu's hut slowly. Despite the horror within, I'm conscious that whoever was shooting at us earlier might still be around. I scan for danger. All as quiet and still as before. I cover the fifty yards to the first of the larger huts in a matter of a few seconds, despite crouching as I run.

The entrance is open, but it's darker than inside Biftu's hut. As my eyes adjust, I see that I've struck lucky. I select a pickaxe from a row of tools propped against the wall and try it for weight. It'll do. I take it back to the entrance and survey Biftu's hut and the immediate surroundings, looking for a suitable spot. I need to get closer to see the makeup of the ground. I stride forward, pickaxe shaft in both hands, head tilted to let me check the surface. The bang and the blow are simultaneous. I'm hurled forward. The pickaxe pitches and lands in front of me. Before my forehead even hits the metal axe head, everything goes black.

I know I'm dreaming. I know because I'm back in the States with Donny and Daniel, even though Daniel's dead. It's the time when Donny and I told Daniel we wanted to come with him to help out. Our contracts had run out, and we thought, "What the hell?" We'd played soccer beside Daniel for three years and gotten to know him really well. Despite the fact he was ten years younger than us, we were all three equal buddies.

Daniel was the nicest guy I've ever known. He spent way too much money on clothes, trying to look like the coolest American black guys, but he just couldn't carry it off. He looked like he was trying too hard. And he had the goofiest teeth and biggest smile possible. Despite his strenuous efforts, he was the antithesis of cool. And he was always talking about home. How it was the cradle of civilization. That his people were noble, sophisticated. Abyssinia it was called, then Ethiopia. He'd talk about the temples and the culture and how it was the oldest country in the whole world. At least that was for the first couple years. Gradually, his stories changed. Letters from home told increasingly of the effects of war and famine. Life in the States was good, but his heart and soul were with his family. We knew he was going home for the off-season to help out with humanitarian projects, and we decided to go with him.

Daniel cried when we told him. He cried more easily than any other man I've ever known. He was also the toughest guy I ever played alongside. He was strong, brave, and fearless in the tackle. One time, he fell awkwardly and broke his wrist. Gritted his teeth but didn't scream out or cry. Tough, tough man. But random acts of kindness would make him blub. When the team visited the sick kids in the local hospital, he'd be inconsolable for days afterward, upset at their suffering, although he never showed it to their faces. When he saw a dog run over in the street, he couldn't speak for hours, and when he eventually did, it was through tears.

And he was funny. Always smiling, laughing, joking. The prankster in the dressing room, where juvenile humour isn't just encouraged but cherished.

He never had any money. He was the star of the team and well paid. But he spent it as fast as he earned it. Donny told me after Daniel died that every time his paycheque arrived, he'd wire half of it home and send a quarter of it to the local hospital. The rest went to clothes, living expenses, and good times. And to paying back what he'd borrowed to tide him over to the end of the month.

I loved that guy. Really, really loved him. So did Donny. He was just the kind of guy you wanted to be around. He made you feel good about life. Appreciate it. Enjoy it. He was the kind of guy that made you selfish for his company. So it was a no-brainer for Donny and me to say we'd go back with him to help out for three months. And we did just that. But three days after we got to Mek'ele, Daniel stepped out in front a truck—and bang! He was gone. Donny and I cried. We cried and cried. But we agreed we'd stay on for the full three months. For Daniel.

It's a funny thing about dreams. I know it's a dream, and I know that Daniel's going to die. But it doesn't matter. Because Daniel's here with Donny and me right now. And we're laughing and joking and it feels good. Better than good. It feels great. It's true bliss—there can be no better feeling

But then I'm made a liar as another dream chases the first away. And the new dream is even more wonderful. Patti's here. She's with me. I try to speak, but my mouth isn't working. Patti leans forward and presses something wet to my lips.

"Patti."

"Hello, you."

"Patti. How …" Too painful. Too hard to talk. She gently applies the wet compress to my lips. "How did you get here?"

"Don't worry. You'll soon be fine."

"Patti. I love you."

"Wheesht, now. Rest."

"You're the one, Patti."

Then darkness returns, and the dreams are gone.

July 6, 1984

5.

THE TAPPING ON my arm is gentle but persistent. I think it might be Mum trying to wake me. I wonder why she's not saying anything. My head feels woolly, and I can taste vinegar. There's a vague sense that someone or something has been following me, or chasing me. I don't know who or what, but I have a sense of unease. More tapping, slightly more urgent.

"*Reveillez-vous! Reveillez-vous!*"

I open my eyes and instantly shut them again to close out the strong sunlight. I raise my hand for shade and crack my right eyelid a fraction. A woman is looking straight at me, her expression urgent and beckoning. "What?"

"*Reveillez-vous.*" Gentler now she has a reaction.

"Eh?"

"English? American?"

"What?"

"Are you English? American?"

"Scottish." I sit up, trying to take in my surroundings at the same time as I work out who this woman is. She's probably around forty, hair scraped back from an honest, ruddy face. She has an accent that I can't place.

"Okay." Her expression changes to puzzlement. "And what is your name?"

"Eilidh. Not meaning to be rude, but who are you?" I realize the bed I'm on is uncomfortable and that the tight walls and ceiling are made of cloth. "And where exactly am I?"

"So many questions, Eilidh. I am Mathilde. You are in a relief worker's dormitory." She looks hard at me. I wonder if she can see my confusion. "I was told there were two new French girls, but you are not one of them, obviously. Not that it matters. You are here now."

"Yes, but where is here?"

"How is it you say? *Not meaning to be rude.* But I have already answered that, and now you must get up. You are late, and there is much work. Please get up and come with me."

I sit up and unquestioningly swing my legs out of bed. There's a pole holding up the cloth ceiling. This is a tent. And I'm dreaming. This has happened before. I've been dreaming and realized it's a dream. Not often, but often enough to realize it's happening again now. Usually when I realize, I wake up pretty quickly. But not this time. Not yet.

I duck down to follow Mathilde out through a flap in the tent. Bright sunlight, like really blinding, assaults my eyes. As they adjust, I take in my surroundings. I'm outside the tent we've just left. It's one in a row that stretches as far as I can see in both directions, with two more rows behind just the same. Each tent is kind of circular, or octagonal, coming to a point in the centre. In front of me is open ground, reddish-brown dusty earth, for maybe fifty metres. Beyond are more rows of the same tents, stretching into the distance until they become indistinguishable from each other, merging into a sea of whitecaps against a distant mountain range.

"It is overwhelming, yes? It would be dark when you got here last night. The first time you see it in daylight, well …" Mathilde opens her arms and gestures, eloquently demonstrating the inadequacy of words. "But you will soon be used to it. Come. You need to eat. Then work."

She's beetling off at some pace, not looking back. She's taller than me, maybe five-eight, and leans forward as she scurries. She darts left between the tents then continues straight. I'm walk-trotting to keep up. I see further along that there are larger tents. Mathilde ducks into the first of them with me in close pursuit. There's a clutch of people gathered, standing round a blackboard, maybe a dozen of them. Men and women, mainly in their twenties, casually dressed—almost scruffy. A few have stethoscopes for necklaces. They turn as we enter.

"I could not find the French nurses. But this is Eilidh. She is Scottish. She got here last night."

"Okay. We've just finished the briefing. Lloyd, you pair up with Haley and bring her up to speed. Mathilde, please have another look for those nurses. We need them." The speaker throws me a brief smile as she instructs Lloyd before immediately switching attention to Mathilde.

The gathering begins breaking up with individuals and groups moving in different directions. Mathilde is first out of the tent, without so much as a look in my direction. A tall, gangly guy with a straggly beard and huge glasses approaches me and offers his hand. "Hi, Haley. I'm Lloyd. Lloyd Harburton. Good to have you on board." His smile is kind, sincere.

"What?"

"I said it's good to have you on board."

"No. I mean what did you call me?"

"Haley. Is that wrong?" He looks crestfallen.

"Eilidh. No H at the beginning. Don't worry, though. It's an easy mistake."

"Ah, okay. Look, follow me and we'll get you some food."

He's nearly as quick off the mark as Mathilde. What is it with folk around here? I follow him outside and round to the back of the tent. Thin blue smoke rises from a fire beneath a suspended black pot. Lloyd lifts a small bowl and spoon from a pile on a mat to the side of the fire. He spoons mush from the pot to the bowl and offers it to me.

"What's this?"

"Oatmeal."

"Not hungry. Thanks."

"Eat it, Eilidh." His tone is severe. I sense he's uncomfortable. Doesn't like conflict. But determined. "You must eat it." Gentler now.

Not worth a fight. Anyway, I wonder if I can taste things in dream world. The texture is more like semolina or tapioca than porridge, and it's tasteless. No seasoning or sweetening. It's bland to the point of being unpleasant, but I spoon it down. I think I am actually hungry.

"'S okay," I concede. I want Lloyd to feel good about me, to like me. I sense he's one of the good guys.

"You get used to it pretty quick. There's not much variety around these parts."

"Are you American?"

"Sure am. Wyoming. And you're Scotch?"

"Scottish."

"Cute. Anyway, what's your background?"

"I don't understand. What do you mean?"

"I mean are you a nurse, a student doctor? You look too young to be a qualified MD."

"I'm just a student. Not a doctor or a nurse."

"Sure. Me too. Still got another year to go. Where do you go to school?"

"I've finished with school. I'm going to St. Andrews University."

"Sure. I understand. American English and English English. What year are you in?"

"I've not started yet. I go in the new term."

"You haven't *started*? Not at all? You've got no medical training?"

"Well, I'm a qualified first aider, if that helps."

"Sheesh. And that got you through the selection? Look, no disrespect, but I think we should deploy you on very basic care. Is that okay?"

I haven't got the faintest idea what he's talking about, but there's no point in upsetting him. This is just some super-weird dream. I shrug. "Whatever."

He takes the empty bowl and spoon, then places them back on the mat, separate from the unused ones. "We'll go to one of the infirmary tents. Stick close and ask me anything you want."

I walk alongside Lloyd, casting my eyes toward the serried ranks of tents. There's some activity over there, with people moving languidly in ones and twos. I can hear the sound of children playing some game. And there's a stench, like the biggest septic tank in the world is being emptied. The scene is surreal, just as you'd expect in a dream. "So many tents." I'm saying this to myself and don't even realize I've spoken out loud until Lloyd responds.

"There are thousands. Last I heard, we had over twenty-five thousand people in the camp. More arriving every day. The refugees are on that side, the relief workers, supplies, and other stuff on this side." We've stopped outside another of the larger tents. "Okay, Eilidh, we're here. I said we'd deploy you on basic care. By that I mean palliative. Now, that's a pretty shitty stick to be thrown on your first day. Do you think you can handle it?"

"I don't understand what you mean."

Lloyd strokes his beard with his right hand, his expression wistful.

"Palliative, Eilidh. There's nothing we can do for these cases. They're too far gone. All you can do is try to provide whatever comfort you can. We need to use the better qualified staff on the saveables. This will be really tough, Eilidh. Really tough. Do you think you can handle it?"

I have no idea what he's talking about, but I nod anyway. "I'm pretty tough."

"Okay." Lloyd pushes through the tent flap, and I follow him in. There are eight low beds, all occupied, each with an empty white plastic chair beside it. On some beds, pairs of eyes turn toward us. As we make our way through, I realize that there are two occupants on each bed, one adult and one child. We reach the farthest bed. The woman there nods recognition to Lloyd, rolls gently away from a scrap of humanity, and slowly rises to her feet.

"'Allo, Lloyd." I suspect she's in her mid-twenties, but she looks more than twice that. Jet black hair pulled back in a short ponytail, vacant grey eyes and chapped lips. I've never seen anyone look more exhausted.

"Marie, this is Eilidh. She's your relief."

Marie looks at me without acknowledgement, then returns her attention to Lloyd. "I don't want to be relieved. I want to stay with Kia. She needs me." She has a strong French accent.

"You know that isn't how it works, Marie."

"I can't leave her. It's not fair."

"I understand. Really, I do. But you're exhausted. You're no use if you fall asleep. Kia needs someone with her. You have to leave her."

It's like watching a minor domestic dispute on a soap opera. Except that it's played out in whispers and ends almost before it begins, Marie falling into Lloyd's arms. He hugs her close.

Eventually, she draws a deep breath, steps back from him, and turns to me. "Kia has been with us for six days. Her brother carried her here. He told us she is two years old. He died the next day. But she is a fighter. She fights hard. So hard." Her quiet voice has been calm, but now trembles. She takes a step toward me, places her hands on my shoulders, and looks right into my eyes. "You *stay* with her." Her ferocity unnerves me. She leans her head forward, and we're cheek to cheek. She breathes into my ear. "Her name means 'season's beginning.'" She steps back and we look into each other's tear-filled eyes in silence. Marie turns, goes to the bed, bends, and kisses Kia. She lingers before standing up tall and then walks straight past Lloyd and me and out of the tent.

I wipe a tear from my eye with my knuckle. I look at Lloyd. I don't know what to say.

"In here, we have eight children or babies. Seven of them have a parent or grandparent with them. Kia is an orphan. You have to stay with Kia."

"Just stay with her?"

"Yes. Just stay."

"What about medicine. Changing nappies? Food?"

Lloyd nods to a table at the side of the tent. "There's water and muslins there. And fresh diapers."

"Medicine? Food?"

Lloyd shakes his head. "Too far gone to eat or for medicine. All you can give her is love." A pause. "Eilidh, can you do this? You don't have to."

"I can do this." I don't know why I'm going along with it though. Why don't I just say, *No, Lloyd. If it's quite all right with you, I'm going to wake up now.* But I don't. I just climb ever so gingerly onto the bed beside Kia. I watch as Lloyd leans over and places his stethoscope against her tiny chest. He's pensive, concentrating. Then he stands up and steps back. I look up at him. "Well?"

"Her breathing is quite shallow, but her heartbeat is stable."

"And?"

"And that's all there is, Eilidh. It's just a matter of waiting."

I want to scream at him. To shout and demand that he do something. He's a doctor, for fuck's sake. Or nearly. But dream-me says nothing. I'm defeated, hopeless. I lie on my side, my eyes flicking from Kia to Lloyd as he visits each of the other beds. It's a ritual. He places his stethoscope against a child. Listens, then says a few words to the adult with them. Then on to the next. Pointless. It's such a waste of time. Such a sham. I should be furious. But there's no room for anger in my heart.

I look into Kia's sleeping face. We've all seen pictures on TV. The shape of the skull clingfilmed with skin, only the eyes not shrunken.

But those pictures don't convey the beauty. Kia is a beautiful, beautiful wee girl. I place my forefinger in front of her nose and feel the tiniest hint of breath. She moves her head ever so slightly and sighs. There's a mark on the cheek that she's been lying on. It's the impression of a button that's come loose from her blouse. I gently ease the button from under her face and slip it into my pocket. Her eyes open and fix on mine. Studious. "Hello. Hello, Kia."

Kia does nothing. No movement. No sound. Her lips part to reveal the tip of a pink tongue. Then gone. Then repeated. She's parched. The poor wee mite is completely parched. Gently, I ease myself up and off the bed, maintaining eye contact. "I'll get you a drink, Kia. Only be a second." I fill a tiny paper beaker from the dispenser and bring it back to her. I cradle her head in my hand and offer the cup to her mouth. Her tongue reappears, slightly longer, but doesn't reach the water. I ease her head forward, but still her tongue doesn't reach. I want to scream, but I ease her head back onto the mattress. I dip my pinkie in the water and drip it on to her. Her tongue absorbs it like a sponge. I repeat the action eight times, before her tongue refuses to reappear.

The woman in the bed closest to ours has got up and sat in the chair. She's been watching me with Kia, but now her focus switches back to her own child. There's another bed over which an old man hunches in a chair, sitting listlessly by his doomed grandchild. The other five beds are still shared.

I climb back onto the mattress and lie curled on my side facing Kia. Inches between our faces, light years between our worlds. She looks at me, and I have no idea what she's thinking. I suspect she's beyond pain, but maybe I'm kidding myself. Her eyes are huge, and they fill my heart. I would do *anything* for her. Anything. Is this how a mother feels? *All you can give her is love*. And I can. I can give her love more easily than anything I've ever had to do. I understand why Marie told me I must stay with her. She's going soon, and she mustn't be alone. She must know that she's loved. And she is. I love this tiny girl with all my being. Her eyes close periodically, and my heart stops each time. An hour passes, maybe two. Her eyes close again, and this time I know her heart has stopped.

A huge, silent sob causes my body to convulse. And again. A hand touches my shoulder. I sit up and look round. It's the woman from the next bed. A woman who looks younger than me. She leans over and pulls the cover over Kia's face. Then she puts her arms around me and holds me. Gradually, the convulsions stop, and my breathing becomes regular. The girl-woman steps back silently, turns, and takes her seat to continue her own vigil.

I leave the tent and stumble round to the rear and past the porridge pot, where I throw up. I drop to my knees, and the sobbing returns, not silent this time. I don't know how long it lasts. Long enough to hurt. The next thing I know is that Lloyd has his hand on my shoulder. I get up, turn, and throw my arms round him, bury my head in his chest and cry forever.

Eventually, his soothing restores a film of calm. "It's okay, Eilidh, it's okay. We all feel like this sometimes. The first time is the worst."

I break from him and step back appalled. I want to vent my fury at the injustice, and he'll do. But then I see the weariness and sincerity on his face, and my rage subsides. "I don't want to be here."

"I know. We all feel like that a lot of the time."

"No, you don't. I don't know how I got here. I don't want to be here. I thought it was a dream, but it's really a nightmare. And I can't wake up. I don't know how to wake up." I'm just on the speaking side of weeping.

"It's a nightmare for all of us. But worse for you because you're new to it."

I look at him. He understands completely, and completely doesn't. "What should I do?"

"Same as the rest of us. Work. We're here to help. Work is all we can do." He sees the fear in me. "But for you now, some different work. Come with me. I know what you can do that shouldn't be so ... so challenging. You've had enough crap for one day."

He takes me lightly by the hand and leads me to a group of four smaller, regular-sized tents pitched between larger ones. He stops and looks at me. "Can you still work?" He waits. "There's someone in here who needs watching over, but he's getting better. Can you handle that?"

I shrug and make a non-committal noise. I just want to wake up. Then sleep. Sleep a long, dreamless, nightmare-less sleep.

"Eilidh! Can you do this?" There's an edge to his voice that pulls me back. "I know you've had a rough start. But this is shit for all of us. There isn't time to feel sorry for ourselves. People here need our help. If we're not working, we're not helping. Can you help?"

"Yes. Yes, I think so."

"Good. Now wait here." He disappears into the tent behind the one we've been standing in front of. I hear voices, and after a moment, he returns with a short, glum-looking woman. "Eilidh, this is Louise. She'll brief you on what you need to do for the rest of your shift. I'll come back and find you when it's over. Okay?"

I nod and he does a kind of stupid salute, the wrong way that Americans do. Then he turns and heads off.

"Okay," I say, but I don't think he even heard me.

"Follow me." Louise is another American. From the deep south at a guess. I follow her into the tent. There's a single bed and a full-size man on it. Another of the white plastic chairs is positioned beside it, with a tall table bearing a water dispenser, paper beakers and muslins, as well as two boxes marked with red crosses and writing in a language I don't recognize. Louise nods toward the man in the bed. "This is Dubya. You're going to be keeping an eye on him."

"What's wrong with him?"

"He's been shot."

"What?" Utterly stupid question. "Why?" Even more ridiculous.

"Dubya's a volunteer. Some kids got here four or five days ago in a terrible state. Said they'd come from a village where they were the last ones not too weak to walk here. Dubya and another guy took a pickup out to see who they could rescue. The village got attacked by gunmen. After they evacuated, Dubya realized they'd left a kid behind and went back. Ended up shot. Wasn't found 'til the next day. We thought he wouldn't make it, but he's pulling through now."

"Sounds like a bit of a hero." I take a proper look at the figure in the bed. Long, lean, thick copper hair, prominent Roman nose, five o'clock shadow turning to beard.

"More foolhardy than heroic. But he's a real cutie."

"Dubya is an unusual name. Where's he from?"

"I think he's American. His buddy who brought him is a Texan. He kept callin' our patient here Dubya. It's a nickname, the Texan's way of pronouncing the letter W. This guy's prob'ly called William or Wesley or the like. His proper name will be in his records, but everyone just calls him Dubya."

I nod my understanding. "What do you need me to do?"

"I just changed his dressing, so that won't need to be done for another couple hours. I'll call back then. Meantime, just keep him comfortable. Docs say we need to get liquid into him, but there are no drips. So damp cloth to his lips is prob'ly best you can do."

"Okay, thanks." I fill a beaker, take a muslin, and sit in the bedside chair.

"As I say, I'll be back in a couple hours. Meantime, if there's any problems, just holler. There's bound to be someone close by." Louise makes a face that says, *Any more questions?* When I just smile at her, she smiles back and leaves.

I turn my attention to my patient just as he moves his head and winces, pain flashing across his face. I don't know what to do. I dip the muslin into the beaker and then pat his lips. He has stiches in a huge cut above his right eyebrow. His lips are badly cracked, and his right cheek is bruised and scratched. Maybe he fell on it. He's got a nice face. The face of a hero. I wonder if he really is a good person. Hard to tell when his eyes are shut. You're meant to be able to tell if someone's good by looking into their eyes. Not that I'm any judge.

I'm just starting to think about Kia when he startles me by opening his eyes.

I smile, trying to encourage him.

He's trying to speak.

I pat the wet muslin on his cracked lips.

His whisper is hoarse, barely audible. "Patti."

"Hello, you." Keep smiling. Keep encouraging.

"Patti. How ..." He winces sharply again. I refresh the muslin and apply more water this time. "How did you get here?"

"Don't worry. You'll soon be fine." Keep smiling. Reassure him.

"Patti. I love you."

"Wheesht, now. Rest."

"You're the one, Patti."

He's asleep again. I don't know whether to go for help. Probably best not. I can tell Louise when she comes back.

I don't know how much time passes. I know that I definitely haven't fallen asleep. I'm kind of intrigued by this mystery man. And thinking about him stops me dwelling on Kia. I watch him breathing, regular and shallow. Occasionally, there's a mighty intake of breath and a long exhalation, which I find comforting for some reason. There are also times when he flinches suddenly, and I can read pain on his face. I can't tell if he's suffering physically or whether dreams are allowing bad memories in. You'd think time would drag, sitting watching a man sleep. But it doesn't. I try dripping water onto his lips from my pinkie on a couple of occasions, but he just frowns and tries to move his head, which in turn causes him to flinch.

I wonder who Patti is. Wife? Girlfriend? And where's he from? He spoke in English. Hard to place his accent. Definitely some American in there, but I thought he sounded Scottish too. Probably just me projecting onto him. Maybe he's Canadian or something. I'll ask the others when they come back.

Of course, I forget to. Louise comes back and introduces another woman called Sophie, who Louise explains will relieve me. I tell them about his brief episode of consciousness and the otherwise uneventful passage of my watch. Louise says she'll update Dubya's doctor after she's taken me for some food and back to the dorm. Despite her protestations, she eventually accepts that I'm really not hungry and just want some sleep. We say goodbye to Sophie and walk slowly in what I think must be the direction of the tent that Mathilde woke me in this morning, a dozen lifetimes ago. I'm surprised to realize that dusk has already fallen.

Louise is a quarter of a step in front, leading the way, but at a relaxed pace. "It's not easy here, Eilidh. Not everyone's cut out for it."

I wonder if she's just making conversation. But her comment is too pointed for that. Normally, I would bristle at a challenge like this. But I don't have the heart. And she's right. "I'm surprised anyone's cut out for this, whatever being cut out for it means."

"You've had a really tough first day. A horrible baptism. There'll be better days." She stops and turns to look right up at me. She's more earnest than glum, and there's compassion in her tone.

"I don't know how I got here. All of a sudden, I was just ... I was just here. And I don't want to be. I don't know what I'm doing. I just watch babies die and people in pain." I'm babbling.

Louise reaches out and puts her hand on my shoulder. "It's okay, sweetie. You just need to have a good night's rest. Then we'll see how you're feeling in the morning." She steers me ninety degrees, and I realize I'm at the dormitory tent. "You're the first to bed down tonight, but the others won't disturb you. I'll see you tomorrow." She smiles and nods. She's kind. How can she have any reserves of kindness left?

I enter the tent and identify the bed I awoke in this morning. It's unmade. I climb in, fully clad, not even bothering to take my trainers off. I pull the blanket over myself. I remember thinking this was uncomfortable before, but it feels fine now. I wonder if I'll dream about Kia. Or Dubya? Or will I even have any dreams in this living nightmare-dream? Like a play within a play. I wonder if ...

August 6, 2019

6.

"Eilidh. Eilidh? Are you all right, love? Nurse. Nurse! She's waking up."

I feel like I'm being chased. And I sense that whoever or whatever is doing the chasing poses some kind of threat. There's a pain like an axe is embedded in my head. A huge axe. It's split the back of my skull, and the blade tip is just behind my forehead. The pain is unbelievable. Blinding, piercing lights. I squeeze my eyes shut. I can taste vinegar. I feel sick, like I'm ready to heave. "Mum? Mum!"

"Wheesht, darling, I'm here. How do you feel?" Even though my eyes are closed tight, I can picture Mum, compassion, concern, and reassurance all struggling for control of her kind, beautiful face.

"I think I need to be sick."

"Nurse! She feels sick."

I feel something landing softly on my chest and brushing against my chin. I open one eye, less than a quarter. There's a woman in blue scrubs over me, looking down. There's some kind of cardboard sick bowl just below my chin. The woman, the nurse, takes my wrist in one hand. "If you think you're going to be sick, just use this. If the pain's bad, we can give you something for it. Is it bad?"

"Uh-huh." I nod and regret it simultaneously, as the axe adjusts position within my brain.

"You've had a fall and taken a nasty bang to the back of your head. It hasn't broken the skin, fortunately, but you've got a bump like an ostrich egg. It's quite common to feel sick after something like this, but it should soon fade." She turns away, directing her speech toward someone else. "Awake for about a minute. Pulse is normal, as is temperature."

Another woman appears. Younger, in maroon scrubs. "I'm Doctor Naismith, Eilidh. You're in the cottage hospital. As Sheena—Nurse McLaren—said, you've had a fall and bumped you head. I'm sure it's pretty sore. Now, on a scale of one to ten, how painful would you say it is?"

I'm careful not to move my head. My mouth's dry, and it's hard to form words. "Ten."

"Okay. We can get you something for that. Sheena, can you get the pain relief we discussed earlier? Thank you. Now, Eilidh, you gave us all a wee bit of a fright. When you fell, you knocked yourself out. You've been unconscious for—" She looks to the clock on the wall. "For the best part of twenty-five minutes. Now that's quite a long time, so I need to check a number of things. Is that okay? Do you understand?" She's all big eyes at me.

"Yes."

"Good. First, I need to shine a bright light into your eyes. Are you ready?"

"Yes." Jesus! There's bright, and then there's blinding. I screw up my eyes involuntarily as she switches the light from one eye to the other.

"Pupils equal and reactive." I'm not sure if she's talking to someone or just out loud to herself.

"That's good isn't it?"

"Yes, Eilidh, that's a good sign. Now, here—take this. It'll help with the pain." She hands me a tiny paper beaker with a clear liquid in it, which I drink in one go. It's completely tasteless. Then she hands me a plastic cup with water. "Just take a few small sips of this." It's at room temperature. Disgusting. But I sip it anyway. "Well done. That should start to help with the pain soon. I just need to check a few more things."

Mum's hovering behind the doctor, looking over her shoulder at me. Apprehensive. Bizarrely, I remember the Munch painting *Anxiety* from the print in the school's art classroom. I smile at her. "Don't worry, Mum." She smiles back at me with that Mum-type reassuring *everything's going to be okay* smile that doesn't fool anyone. "Really, Mum. I'm fine."

The doctor has been moving around me, shining a light and looking into each ear. Now she's back in front of me. "Open wide." I open my mouth wide, and she shines her light inside, tilting her head at various angles as she has a good look around. "Good. You can close now, thank you. Now I'd like to sit you forward a bit. Are you ready to try that?"

"Yes."

"Good. Just bring your head forward ever so slowly. Yes. Yes, just like that. Good. Well done. Now, can you very slowly and gently turn your head from side to side for me? Good. Well done, Eilidh. You can lie back now. How did that feel?"

"I've got a headache. At the back and front of my head. It's really sore, but not quite as bad as it felt a minute ago."

"Good. How about your neck? Have you got any pain in your neck? Did you feel any stiffness when you were turning your head?"

"No."

"Good. That's good, Eilidh. And how about your vision? Can you see clearly?" I don't know if she keeps saying *good* to reassure me, Mum, or herself.

"Yes. I can see fine, thanks."

"Great. Can you raise your right arm slowly for me? Good. You can lower it now.

Same with the left. Good. Now your right leg. And the left. Perfect. Well done."

Doctor Naismith takes a pace backward, and Mum steps forward and bends toward me. She pauses and looks into my eyes, relieved and terrified at the same time. She leans in and kisses me gently on the cheek then sits beside me on the bed, laying her hand over mine. "So, doctor, will she be okay?"

"All of the superficial signs are positive. Breathing is stable. Eyesight and speech both fine. There's no wound or blood loss. No apparent neck pain, weakness, or paralysis. No obvious signs of concussion. Just an unpleasant headache, which isn't really a surprise after such a nasty bump on the head. But we can't be too careful with a head knock, particularly when you lost consciousness. I'm going to refer you to the city hospital for a CT scan, just to be on the safe side."

"Okay, we understand," Mum replies on my behalf. She's being the parent, taking control even though I'm an adult. That would usually be the spark for me to have a go at her, but actually I'm glad. "Do we need an appointment?"

"I'll phone ahead and make the arrangements. Now, how about transport? Do you need an ambulance?"

"Does she need an ambulance?" Mum's voice is going up with her stress levels. "I've got a car."

"Oh, that's fine, then. No need for an ambulance if you're happy to drive her, Mrs. McVicar. I'll just write you a referral note to take with you. I'll be right back." Then, almost as an afterthought: "You can give her more paracetamol for the pain later, if she needs it." She turns and disappears from my line of sight.

"Will you be okay, love? I'll drive carefully, really slowly. No bumps or sudden braking."

"I'll be fine, Mum."

"Eilidh." She's looking right at me. "Eilidh, love. What happened?"

"Mum, it was terrible. I don't know. There was this camp. Thousands of people. They were starving. A baby died. I had to look after this man who'd been shot."

Only slightly, but nonetheless perceptibly, Mum leans back. Bewilderment and concern battle for control of her face. "What are you talking about?"

"There was this camp. And a baby girl called Kia …"

"Eilidh." I feel gentle pressure as she squeezes my hand. "Eilidh. Are you all right?"

"Everything okay?" Doctor Naismith reappears over Mum's shoulder.

"Doctor, I think she's hallucinating. She's going on about some camp or other, and a baby dying and people being shot and …"

"Eilidh." Doctor Naismith has placed herself between Mum and me and is bent down, looking into my face. "Eilidh, are you seeing things? Are you seeing things right now?" Her voice is calm and gentle. Enquiring but reassuring.

"No. Not now. I'm not seeing things now. I was talking about what I saw."

"What you saw when?"

"Before." Is this woman stupid? "Before I woke up in here."

"Ah. Okay, then. I think that perhaps what you're remembering is a dream."

"It wasn't a dream! I remember that I thought it was. But I couldn't wake up. I couldn't wake up because it was real. And I was there."

The doctor is looking right at me. Mum is behind her, full on rabbit-in-the-headlights face. Fuck. It *was* a nightmare. How am I being this stupid? If my head didn't hurt so much, I'd feel embarrassed. "This is real, Eilidh. You know that, don't you?"

I know not to nod. "Yes." My voice has gone all small. "I had a nightmare. A horrible, horrible nightmare. But I'm awake now. This is real." I'm not sure if I'm telling Mum and the doctor or myself.

"That's fine, Eilidh. Dreams and nightmares can seem completely real sometimes. Perhaps more so after such a knock to the head." Her eyes are flicking between Mum and me. She's as keen to reassure Mum as she is me. Maybe even more so. She pauses and smiles, then holds out a white envelope to Mum. "Mrs. McVicar, here's the referral notice for when you get to the hospital. Just go to the A&E department and hand them this. I will give them a ring to let them know to expect you."

Mum takes the envelope. "Thanks, doctor." She places her free hand on the back of the doctor's. "Really, thank you."

I find my voice. "Yes, thank you."

Doctor Naismith smiles at both of us, turns, and heads off.

"Okay, you. Let's get you to the big hospital." Mum takes my hand as I get off the bed, like I'm five or something. And I don't mind. I don't feel much like a big girl right now. This is a time when I just need Mum to be my mum. And she knows it. We walk in silence, quite slowly, out the front door of the hospital to the car, parked outside Mum's office next door, and get in. Mum calls her boss and explains that she's taking me for a CT scan. She gets the car started at the third attempt, and we head off for the city.

We drive a few minutes before Mum tries again. "I'm almost scared to ask." She pauses. Sighs. "What happened, love? What happened?"

I remember what happened. My head is pounding, throat tightening, eyes filling with tears. I take a deep, deep breath. "Mum, I'll tell you. But right now, my head is hurting something awful. Is it okay if I tell you later?"

She fires a sideways glance at me. "Aye, okay, hen. We can talk about it when you feel like it."

The rest of the journey plays out in more silence, except when Mum curses a BMW that cut her up at a roundabout. The traffic is surprisingly light, and we reach the hospital and get parked in just half an hour.

Everything seems to accelerate. They're expecting us at A&E. It's quiet. They're able to scan me within another hour, and I'm free to go.

"When will we get her results?" Mum is controlled and still a wee bit anxious at the same time.

The radiographer gives a practised smile. "There's a gremlin in the IT today, although it should be fixed later on. We'll email the results to your GP, and she'll follow up with you."

We say our goodbye-thankyous and are back in the car.

I need to tell Mum. I don't want to. I don't know how. But I can't not. "Mum."

"Yes, Eilidh?"

"Mum." Then I lose it. Completely lose it. I'm full-on sobbing. Shoulder heaving against the seatbelt, tears streaming, nose running, choking, struggling to breathe, head pounding.

The car is stopped. Mum's leaning over me, hand gentle on my brow. Feather kiss to my forehead. "Shhhhhh. There, there now. Let it all out." She does her magic trick of making tissues appear out of thin air. "That's the girl. It'll be okay. It'll be okay." I love my mum.

My breathing's easier now. More even. I tell her about bastard-face Findlay. I tell her everything. The lying. The cheating. How I'm the stupidest cow on the planet. Sobs keep interrupting me. It makes me mad that the snake is still making me cry. And that's making me cry even more. He's not fucking worth it. Eventually, I'm finished telling Mum and finished crying. I look at her.

She looks at me. "The bastard."

I've never, *ever* heard her swear before except for the words *bloody* and *damn*. I really love my mum.

She starts the car up again (at the second attempt), and we begin the rest of the journey home. "Have we got any paracetamol at home?"

"Yes, plenty. But I'll get more when I'm out later. Is the headache really bad?"

"Bad. But not that bad." I lie. "I think I'll maybe go for a lie down when we get back. Is that all right?"

"Of course it is. Will you want me to make you a sandwich or something when we get in? It'll be half-one by the time we're home. You must be starving."

"I'm not feeling that hungry, Mum. Anyway, you'll need to get back to your work."

"No, no. I'll just ring Derek and tell him I'll not be back in today. He'll be absolutely fine about it. I want to be around in case you need me. And besides, it's probably best if I'm around to tell George what's happened when he gets up. Stop him going and giving Findlay a doing."

She's right, as usual. I can't help but smile at the prospect of George giving the snake-bastard a hiding. Mum catches me, and smiles too. We both know it's probably wrong, but it's a delicious thought. We drive the rest of the way home in silence.

When we get in, Gran gets up from her chair and comes toward me. She's wee and old and frail, and her brain's completely cooked. But something in there still works. She looks right into my face, and her eyes fill up with tears, triggering mine to do the same. She steps forward and puts her arm round my waist, pulling me to her. Her free hand draws my head gently down on to her shoulder, and she holds me as firmly as she's able. A huge, silent sob racks my body, but she holds me tight. She's whispering into my ear. "It'll pass, lassie. It'll pass." She knows me, even though she doesn't know who I am or how she knows me. She still loves me, but I don't believe her. This will never pass.

"Okay, Ma. Eilidh's had a knock to her head. She just needs to go for a wee lie down." Gran releases me on Mum's instruction and takes a step back. She smiles at me and nods before turning back to her chair.

"Thanks, Mum. I'll head up now. Is the paracetamol in the medicine cabinet?"

"I've put a packet on your bedside table, along with a glass of water. Oh, and I've plugged your phone in to charge as well." I make a puzzled face. "They gave me your phone at the hospital, when you were sparked out."

"Ah. All right." I pause. "Mum?"

"Yes?"

"How did you get to me so quickly? In the hospital, I mean."

"You know fine well I only work next door. Aggie Reynolds saw Meg McCartney's man carrying you in. I thought she was kidding me on at first, until I realized she was serious. Then I nearly collapsed with the shock." She comes toward me, kisses my forehead, and steps back.

"You gave me a real fright, Eilidh McVicar. A real fright. But you're all right now, thank heavens. Now! Away up the stairs and have that lie down."

"Aye. Okay, Mum." I turn and make my way upstairs. My head is still thumping fit to explode. I take two paracetamol with a couple of gulps of water. Mum's got my phone charging and set to silent. I'm not going to pick it up now. Plenty of time for that later. My nose is starting to run, but I don't want to blow it because it'll be agony. I'll just dab it. I reach into my pocket to pull out the tissues I took from Mum, and something pops out and bounces off my shoe. I crouch down, slowly to avoid jarring my head, to see what it might be. I reach out to pick it up, knowing already what it is. I stare at the tiny white circle on the tips of my fingers. Kia's button.

7.

THIS IS MENTAL. I'm here, in Scotland in 2019. I got up this morning. Got my exam results. Felt brilliant. Went to meet bastard-face. Had a fight. Got kayoed. Taken to hospital. Then to another hospital. Now I'm here. But this button says that's not right. This button says that Kia was real. The camp was real. Dubya was real. Mathilde and Lloyd and the others were real. And that I was there. I was *there*.

It's not the situation that's mental, it's me. Think, Eilidh, think! This is just a button. A wee, white button. Just like thousands and millions of other wee, white buttons. It doesn't say "Kia's button" on it. Or "Made in Africa." If it even was Africa that the camp was in. See! I don't even know where it is that I think I was. Classic. Exactly what you'd expect of a dream, or a nightmare. You can remember some details really vividly, but when you try to remember other bits, they're just not there. I mean, if I don't even know where the camp was, then how can I have been there? It was a dream. A nightmare.

Think about the physics. There's a continuous timeline from when I got up this morning until now. I was unconscious for about twenty or twenty-five minutes. But I was in the camp for a whole day? I don't think so! Couldn't have happened. I know what *could* have happened. I was knocked out. Unconscious. Asleep. What happens when people sleep? They dream. Or have nightmares. I had a nightmare. It wasn't real.

But what about the button? How did the button get here? Why is it the same as the one that came off Kia's blouse? I don't remember picking it up anywhere else. I don't remember putting it in my pocket. But I must've. There's no other logical explanation. I must've put it in my pocket and completely forgotten about it. But maybe in the back of my mind, I remembered picking it up somewhere, and that's how it came to be in the dream. That could make sense. More sense than me spending a whole day half a world away when I've been here all the time.

If I didn't already have a thumping headache, thinking about this crap would certainly give me one. It was a nightmare, and I just need to forget about it.

My phone vibrates on top of my bedside drawers. I reach for it just as the message on the screen fades. I activate the screen again and see five missed calls and fourteen unread WhatsApp messages.

Seonaid: *Where are you, gorgeous girl?*

Alice: *It's OK! I'm OK! I got the grades. You don't need to hide because of me.*

I smile. I'm so pleased for Alice.

Seonaid: *Where are you? EVERYBODY is here.*

Lindsey: *Hurry up. You're missing the party.*

Alice: *Come on you. This is the biggest party EVER.*

Lindsey: *Morag's blown it again. At school now discussing clearing.*

Shit. Poor Morag.

Alice: *Are you off shagging Findlay?*

Seonaid: *Alice thinks you're shagging Findlay? Are you?*

Seonaid: *Hurry up, you dirty cow.*

Alice: *Third glass of wine. Pissed. Not even midday.*

Seonaid: *Findlay's here. Asked him about you. Blanked me. WTF?*

Alice: *Are you OK? Is everything OK?*

Lindsey: *Gotta leave. Message me to say you're OK.*

Seonaid: *What's wrong? CALL ME.*

I'm crying. I'm fucking crying again because of that bastard. This should be one of the happiest days of my life. And because of that bastard, it's one of the worst. The fucking lying, cheating, conniving two-faced bastard. And he's gone to the pub! Like nothing's fucking happened! I fucking hate him. I really fucking hate him.

I text him: *I fucking hate you.*

Another: *I REALLY fucking hate you.*

Another: *I hope you die, you bastard.*

Another: *I hope you die soon.*

Another: *Bastard. Bastard. Bastard. Bastard. Bastard.*

I feel better.

I text again: *You fucking snake.*

I know! Web search. Snake. Images. Big cobra rising up out of its coil, jaws open and fangs showing. Save image. Back to bastard-face in contacts. Edit. Delete image. Save new image of snake. Good. Fucking snake.

I text him the snake picture: 🐍 🐍 🐍

Is this wrong? I don't fucking care. I hate him. This makes me feel better. I use a fresh tissue to dab my eyes. What else can I do to the bastard?

I don't know how long passes with me lying in bed thinking of terrible fates I wish would befall The Snake. I hear the doorbell ring downstairs and Mum talking to whoever's there. Sounds of people coming in.

After about five minutes, there's a gentle knocking on my door, and Mum pops her head round. "How are you feeling, love?"

"So-so, Mum. My head still hurts, but not as much as before."

"Are you up for visitors?"

"Who? Who is it?"

"Seonaid and Alice have popped round to see you. Are you up to seeing people? I can easily ask them to come back another time if you're not up to it just now."

I don't know what to say. Part of me wants to just hide from the world. But these girls are like my sisters. "I'd like to see them."

"Okay. But I'll tell them that it's just for a wee while." She smiles and disappears. I hear her footsteps going down the stairs. A pause. Some muffled voices. Sounds of people coming upstairs. I know it's Seonaid and Alice. But I'd have known it wasn't family anyway because their footsteps don't sound familiar. My strange train of thought is interrupted by a gentle tapping on my door, for the second time in a few minutes.

"Come in."

Seonaid is first through the door. Tall, long straight hair, chin tilted down, and eyes huge with concern. Alice is beside her—shorter, her beautiful, freckled face hesitant, tentative.

I can tell they don't know what to say, so I speak first. Except it isn't words that come out. It's more crying. Their images blur as my eyes fill and they move toward me. Seonaid's arm is round my back, and my temple is resting on her shoulder. Alice is sitting on the other side of the bed and is wiping tears from my cheek with a tissue. They're both making *there, there* noises.

Seonaid's voice is soft. Soothing. "Alec McDonald's mum told him she'd heard you'd been taken to hospital. He asked us what was going on and that was the first we heard anything. Obviously, we knew something wasn't right. When you didn't show at The Tassie and didn't answer your phone or messages. And then when Findlay just ignored us when we asked about you."

"I phoned the hospital." Alice has taken over explaining. "But they just said you weren't there. So we came here. Your mum's explained. That you had a fight with Findlay. About the bang on your head. That we're not to stay long and to be careful not to tire you out or upset you."

I laugh-sob.

"What is it?" Alice sounds worried she's said the wrong thing.

"You two could never upset me." I'm smiling. I love these girls.

Seonaid takes my hand in hers. "What happened, Eilidh?"

I tell them everything. The lies. The deception. He was always going to Oxford. He was never coming to St. Andrews. He was just using me. I am the most stupid, gullible cow in the world. He called me a nutjob. I was just a bit of fun. It was my fault for making everything so fucking heavy. I'm embarrassed. Ashamed. Heartbroken. I will never get over this. I cry a lot as I tell them, and they cry with me. They call him much worse names than I have.

We also talk about exams. Results. Uni. Who did well and who didn't. What happened at The Tassie. We speculate about Morag and what she'll do next. We're sympathetic. She's not academic, but she's lovely. Most of all, we talk about boys. One in particular. About how much of a shit he is.

We go over everything time and again. Because I want to. Because I want their reassurance. Their sympathy. Their confirmation of what a shit he is. Hours pass.

I tell them about the Coke bottle and trying to stove The Snake's head in. Alice looks a bit alarmed, but they both tell me they would've done the same. Banging my head. Waking up in hospital. Going to the big hospital. Having the scan. Coming home. How lovely Mum has been. They agree how lovely Mum is.

"How long were you unconscious for?" Seonaid is like a doctor already.

"Twenty, maybe twenty-five minutes."

"Do you remember anything about it?" Alice sounds earnest.

"It was like I was in another place. A camp. A huge camp. Far away from here. People were starving. Dying. A little girl called Kia died. There was a man in a bed. I was, like, looking after him." There's bewilderment and concern on both their faces. "But it was just a nightmare. Really vivid. And it felt like I was there for ages, a whole day. But it was just a nightmare." I smile with what I hope is reassurance, and they laugh, grateful. I need to change the subject, move things on. "There's something I wanted to ask."

"Sure, girl. Go for it." There's a hint of anxiety in Alice's voice.

"When you saw Findlay at The Tassie, what did he say?"

"I saw him on the other side of the bar." Seonaid's voice is low, and she's looking at me intently. "I waved. He saw me but just ignored me. Lindsey waved as well. And Alice." She looks at Alice, who nods confirmation. "But he ignored all of us. I was already worried 'cause you weren't there and weren't answering calls, so I went over to ask him where you were. He just looked at me like I was something he'd trodden in and then turned away."

"And how did he …" I'm struggling to understand myself what it is I'm asking. "How did he seem?"

Seonaid tilts her head, slightly quizzical. "On reflection, now that I think about it, he seemed like a snake with legs."

"Well, I was further away, course." Alice has her newsreader face on. "But he looked more like a six-foot pile of shite."

There's quiet laughter as we melt into a group hug. My eyes have filled again. I'm so lucky to have friends like these. Loyal. Trustworthy. Honest. Dependable. They're like anti-venom for The Snake.

Eventually, we break apart, and Alice makes a show of consulting her watch. "Eilidh, we've been here *hours*. We promised your mum we wouldn't stay long."

"Mum won't mind. She knows that time with you two is better than any medicine."

"Still, we'd best be going. I need to be getting home for my dinner." Alice gives me a squeeze and gets to her feet. She looks straight at Seonaid. "It's nearly half past six, you know."

"Shit! Really?" Seonaid seems as surprised as I am. She gives me a peck on the cheek and gets to her feet. "Eilidh, we really better get going. We'll speak to you again tomorrow." She pauses as her hand reaches for the door. "And if you want to talk again before then, just give me a call."

"And me. We can come back over, or just talk on the phone. Or even just chat on WhatsApp. Whatever you want." Alice is so earnest.

I smile. "I think tomorrow will be fine. Thanks for coming. I really, *really* appreciate it."

They both come back to me, and we have another three-way cuddle. I don't really want them to go, but we all know that they need to. "Go on! Skedaddle! Or I'll set my mum on you!"

After two or three more minutes of nearly managing to say our goodbyes, the door closes behind them, and I hear Mum talking to them as they go downstairs. Also, the deeper rumble of George's voice. Then the sound of the front door opening and closing.

George's footsteps on the stair. A tap on the door, which he opens without waiting for a reply. He stands in the doorway like he's surprised to find himself there. George is tall, broad shouldered, and in need of a shave, but he always looks boyish rather than manly. He doesn't know what to say.

"What is it?'

"Mum wants to know if …" He walks toward me and parks himself on the bed by my feet. "Mum told me."

"Told you what?"

He knows I'm at it. "About Findlay Fuck Face." There's a hint of a smile that vanishes before I can be sure it was ever there.

"Oh, that."

"Aye, that. And about you having to go to hospital."

"Oh, that too?"

"Aye, that too." He pauses. "Eilidh?' Another long pause. He looks down at his hands, then back up and right at me. But he doesn't say anything.

"What?"

"Did he hit you? Did he push you? I know what you told Mum. But you can tell me the truth. I won't say anything to her. Promise."

I sigh. "No, George. He never hit me. He never pushed me. The truth is that I went for him and lost my balance."

49

"Are you sure?"

"I was there."

"Aye, okay. Mum's made me promise not to go looking for him."

"She's right. George, much as the thought of you punching his lights out appeals, he's just not worth it."

"*He's just not worth it*," he says, high pitched and sing-song. "Why do lassies always say that? It would be totally worth it to rearrange his face."

I snort-laugh and George smiles at me. "George, you've promised Mum."

"I promised not to go looking for him. I never said anything about if I just bumped into him."

"You know what Mum meant."

"Aye, but—"

"Aye, but nothing. Promise *me* you're not going to hit him."

"You don't still care about him?"

"I fucking hate him, George. I hate him more than anything. I hope his whole life turns to shite. But he's *really* not worth it."

"Am I allowed to tell him what I think? If I see him?"

"Promise you won't hit him?"

"Promise."

"Then you can call him all the names you like, if you see him." George shuffles along the bed, leans forward, and kisses me on the forehead. "Bloody hell!"

"What is it?"

"You kissed me! That's twice in one day. Are you sure it's not you that's had the bang on the head?"

"Never did!"

"Never did what?"

"Never kissed you."

"You just did!"

"Any witnesses?"

I reach behind for my pillow and swing it at him. He ducks and I miss. "You are so annoying!"

He shuffles back on the bed, out of range. "Mum says Seonaid and Alice were here for a while."

I know where this is going. "Aye, they were here a fair while."

"I said cheerio to them when they were leaving."

"I thought I heard you."

"Alice was looking well."

"And Seonaid?"

"What? Oh, aye. Seonaid was looking well too. So what were the three of you blethering about for so long?"

He's the worst fisherman in the world. Completely transparent. And oblivious. "Oh, this and that. Relationships, obviously."

"Of course." He pauses.

I'll wait. He's still got no idea that I've got my hook out for him.

"So," he says, "what exactly about relationships?"

"Well, my disaster with the bastard snake, obviously. Are you thick?"

"Oh, of course. Sorry."

"And poor Seonaid's still not got anyone. But she's hopeful she'll find someone when she goes to Dundee. You know she's got in there to do medicine."

"Has she? Good for her." He pauses. *Soooo* obvious. "And what about Alice? Is she still going out with what's-his-name?"

"What's-his-name? You know fine well she's been going out with Sandy Waddell for the last three years. What's-his-name indeed!"

"Oh, that's right. Sandy Waddell. I'd forgotten." Another pause. "Everything fine there, then?"

"Oh yes. They've both got the grades and will be off to uni together. Alice and Sandy are like that." I hold up my crossed fingers. "She's a one-man woman. Sandy's the boy for her." I glance idly at my fingernails. "Of course, that wasn't always the case."

"What do you mean?"

"Oh, come on, George. Stop playing the innocent!"

"What are you on about?"

"Alice fancied you like crazy when she was younger."

"What? Are you taking the piss?" He looks genuinely surprised! I'm amazed.

"Seriously. When she was thirteen, fourteen, fifteen. She thought the sun shone out of your arse."

"You're just winding me up now. You're at it."

"I'm not. Remember those valentine cards with the clues in them?"

"That was just you and your pals taking the piss out of Archie and me. Archie got a card one year as well."

"Archie got a card one year off of Janet McCallum. You got a card three years in a row. Every one of them from Alice."

"You are kidding me."

"I'm not. She was gutted when you never sent her one or ever even acknowledged hers."

"I never knew they were from her. At first, I tried to work out who they were from. I was concentrating on lassies my own age. Then I just thought it was you and your pals having fun at my expense."

"Nope. They were all from Alice. She was heartbroken when you started going out with Margaret Dickie."

"Why didn't you tell me?"

"Tell you what?"

"That Alice fancied me!"

"I thought it was obvious! Anyway, I was fourteen or whatever. I didn't want my pal going out with my big brother."

"For fuck's sake, Eilidh."

"What?"

"You could've told me."

"Anyway, if Alice had wanted me to tell you, she would've said so. But she never. Then she met Sandy, and that was that."

"Aye, I suppose so."

He looks utterly crestfallen. I feel bad. I should've kept my mouth shut. Best change the subject. "So what did Mum want?"

"What do you mean?"

"When you came in, you said Mum wants to know if …"

"Oh, aye. Mum's made some dinner and wanted to know if you're hungry."

I realize I'm hungry. Starving, in fact. "Yes. Dinner would be nice. Tell Mum I'll come down in a minute."

"You don't want something brought up here for you?"

"No. I'm fine to come downstairs."

August 8, 2019

8.

YESTERDAY SEEMS A bit of a blur. I didn't leave the house. I didn't feel like doing anything. If I'm being honest, I was feeling sorry for myself. Mum said that I should just take things easy. That's what I did. I stayed in my room all day binge watching Netflix, only leaving when I wanted something to eat. And I spent half an hour with Gran, pretending to be happy so she'd be happy. I felt too tired to keep it up for longer, and then I felt guilty. I messaged the girls—lots, except Morag. She's probably focused a hundred percent on sorting things out after her results. I wondered about sending her a message, but I don't know what to say. None of the other girls have heard anything from her either, so I don't feel so bad. I think it would be easier to see her face to face.

I slept well last night, right through to half eight this morning. I dreamed about the camp and Kia and Dubya and the others. It was vivid, but it was definitely a dream. Not like the nightmare when I was unconscious. That was real, or at least it felt like it was real. Last night was definitely a dream. Kind of like remembering what happened in the nightmare but not living it the same way. It's right at the front of my mind. The patient, Dubya. And Kia. The camp.

I shower, dress, and go down for breakfast. Gran's in front of the telly, watching it like someone looking out the window of a moving train. I don't go to her. Instead, I go back to my room. I keep thinking about the camp. Especially Kia. And Dubya. What was it he called me? Patti. Yes, Patti. And what about Kia? I take out her button and rub it gently between my forefinger and thumb. I look at it. I remember the mark it made on her cheek. I remember.

This is crazy. I *can't* remember. I'm recalling a nightmare, not reality. Yet somehow, I know that's not right. What can I remember? The camp. The smell. The sea of tents. The people. Mathilde. Lloyd. Marie. The woman at the bed next to Kia's. Louise. Kia. Dubya. Faces, names, and a place with no name. Why can't I get this out of my mind? It's meaningless.

Lloyd! Lloyd told me his name. Hamilton? Hammond? No, more unusual. Like Halibut or something, but obviously not. Think! Lloyd Hambleton? No. Something like that. What did he say to me? Think! He got my name wrong! He called me Haley. That's right. *Hi, Haley. I'm Lloyd. Lloyd Harburton.* Lloyd Harburton! Lloyd Harburton. That's definitely right. A really unusual name. I play it over in my mind. I step over to my desk, sit down, and flip open the laptop. Google. Lloyd Harburton. Enter. *Showing results for Lloyd Harberton. Search instead for Lloyd Harburton.* I click on that.

One article. *Lloyd Harburton—Wyoming Tribune Eagle.* Click. A full page appears. An obituary. Lloyd Harburton, MD, 1960–2009. There's a photograph. A clean-shaven man, wearing rimless spectacles. Bald. Smiling. Is this the same Lloyd as my dream? My nightmare? Older. Hard to tell. Could be. My heart is beating furiously, my palms clammy. I read on, devouring the information.

There's a lot to read. I scan for clues, hoping something leaps out. Survived by his wife, Mary, and twin daughters, Ashleigh and Martha. Died peacefully at his home after a short battle with cancer. He was a doctor in general practice in a place called Cheyenne. Much respected. Long service to the local community. Active Democrat. Champion of various charitable causes. Recognized with a civic medal for his work with disadvantaged youths throughout the district. Lifetime commitment to humanitarian causes, dating back to his days as an undergraduate when he worked as a volunteer in famine-stricken Ethiopia during his 1984 university summer vacation.

Ethiopia! Ethiopia. 1984. I type the name and date into the search bar. Except I don't. *Wthuipis1983.* My fingers are shaking so much that I mis-key horribly. Delete. Retype. Slowly. Carefully. *Ethiopia. 1984. Famine.* Click. Over half a million results. Add *Camp.* Click. Over 375,000 results. Add *Refugee.* Click. Over 588,000 results. I start clicking links. Reading. My desire to find I don't know what overcomes any horror at the information I'm processing. I switch from All to Images and start scrolling. After three pages, I stop, and so does my heart. I'm focused on a picture of a group of people. Very deliberately, I click to enlarge. My throat constricts and my eyes prick. The picture is grainy. There are eleven people. At the centre is the doctor who was briefing people at the camp, complete with stethoscope necklace. Three places to her left is Mathilde. On her extreme right, at the edge of the group, is Lloyd. Lloyd Harburton. Unmistakeable. I don't recognize any of the others. Hesitantly, I click visit. The page takes an age to load. The same picture, smaller. A caption, "Aid workers, Ethiopia, summer 1984. Unattributed." That's it. Nothing else. I hit the back button to return to the larger image. These are real people. *Were* real people. In 1984. What's going on? My head is hurting. The first time I've been conscious of it since I woke up. Is something wrong with me? Am I really recognizing them? How can I recognize these people? Or am I going crazy? Maybe I injured my brain when I fell. None of this makes sense otherwise. But then I reach for Kia's button. I hold it and stare at it. It's real. It was Kia's. She was real. I *was* there.

My phone's ringtone is like an electric shock. I do a double take, like I'm a cartoon character, as I adjust to the interruption. I pick it up. Seonaid. Why is she calling? We hardly ever actually call each other.

"Hello?"

"Eilidh? Are you okay?"

"Yeah. I'm fine."

"You sure?"

"Yes, I'm sure. Why are you going on about it?"

"It's just you sound a bit funny."

"Don't worry. I was just a bit spaced out before you called. I'm fine."

"Only if you're sure."

"Is there something wrong with you? You've called me, and now it's like you'd rather talk to anyone else in the world."

"Sorry."

I can tell from the way she says that one word that something really is wrong. "Seonaid, what is it? What's the matter?"

"Eilidh." A pause. A girding sigh. "I've got something to tell you, and you're not going to like it."

"You're scaring me now. Look, whatever it is, just tell me."

"It's Morag."

"Oh God. What's wrong? Is she all right?"

"She's going out with Findlay."

I'm going to be sick. I can't believe I heard properly, although I know I did. My mind is full of everything and nothing at the same time. All I can manage is a single word: "What?"

"Eilidh, I'm so, so sorry. Alice phoned me this morning. She saw them out together last night. They came into The Tassie after being at the pictures. About ten, or just after. Got drinks and sat in the corner by themselves. Apparently, they were eating each other's faces off." Pause. "Oh, Eilidh. I didn't know what to do. But you had to know."

My head is swimming, like I've been punched in the temple—hard. Dizzy, dizzy, dizzy. Tears blur my vision. I stumble forward onto my bed. Mustn't be sick on the duvet. Mouth closed. Breath in. Out. In. Out. Slower. In. Out. Slower still. In. Out. In. Out. Just concentrate on breathing. In. Out. Slowly. Slowly.

"Eilidh? Eilidh! EILIDH!"

I bring my phone back up to my face. Whisper. "I'm still here."

"Eilidh, I'm so, so sorry. Are you all right?"

"Not really."

"Do you want me to come over? Or me and Alice to come over?"

"No. Thanks, but no. Did Alice say anything else?"

"Not really. She and Sandy were in The Tassie with a couple of Sandy's pals. George Muldoon joined them and said he'd seen Morag and Findlay coming out the pictures together earlier. Next thing they walk in, bold as brass. Alice said she tried to catch Morag's eye, and the bitch winked at her. But they never spoke. Alice is going to see if Lindsey knows any more."

My head is birling again. "I can hardly believe this."

"I know."

"That fucking slut is going out with him the day after I finished with the bastard. *The day after!*"

"She's an absolute cow."

"He's doing it to get back at me."

"You think?"

"Of course he fucking is!"

"What an absolute bastard. Just when you think he can't get any worse."

"And she's as fucking bad, the slag. Fucking slut. She's meant to be my friend. How can she do this?"

"She's not your friend. Or mine. Or anybody's. She's burned her bridges. Big time."

"Seonaid?"

"Yes?"

"Is it okay if I ring off now? My head's spinning. I feel like I might be sick. I can't get my mind round all of this. I just need some time to think. Is that all right?"

"Sure, of course. Are you going to be okay?"

"I'll be fine. I just need some time."

"Okay. Take care, and I'll speak to you later. Bye."

"Thanks. Bye."

I lie back, flat on the bed, the phone still clasped in both hands on my chest. This just can't be real. It just can't. But I know it is. Findlay Calder is an utter, utter bastard. How could I have been so gullible? Why is he being so cruel? And Morag McNulty. How could she do this to me? She's meant to be my pal, my friend. Fucking Judas slag.

I text the snake: *I hear you're shagging Yo-Yo Knickers McNulty. Better wear a condom. She's not clear of her latest dose of the clap. In fact, DON'T wear a condom.*

Text to the slag: *Hear you're shagging Needle Dick. Word to the wise. First time he punches you, he'll say sorry, it'll never happen again. Don't believe him.*

They deserve each other. I hate them both. Him most. And her. I lie on the bed for hours. Crying. Blowing my nose. Imagining all sorts of satisfyingly terrible fates befalling The Snake and The Slag. But mostly crying.

This can't go on. Lying here crying means he's won. I'm better than this. Better than him. I need to get on with things. I look at my phone. Ten to one. I should get some lunch.

9.

I GO DOWNSTAIRS. Gran's still in the living room in front of the telly. She's probably not moved since breakfast. Her glass of water hasn't been touched. What a selfish cow I am. "Gran?"

"Yes?" She looks round and smiles. She knows I'm her grand-daughter because I call her Gran, but she doesn't remember my name. She calls me "the lassie." George and Archie are "the boys," and Scott is "the wee man." We make a joke of it among ourselves. But Mum was heartbroken the first time she realized Gran had forgotten her name too.

"I'm going to make a sandwich for my lunch. Cheese and ham. Would you like me to make you one?"

"A sandwich?"

"Yes. A cheese and ham sandwich. Your favourite. And a nice cup of tea?"

"A nice cup of tea. Yes, dear." She smiles and turns back to the TV.

I go to the kitchen, put on the kettle, and start on the sandwiches. No ham. It'll need to be cheese and tomato. It takes me no time. I cut the sandwiches into quarters because I know Gran likes that. She thinks it's dainty. I put a plated sandwich and a cup of tea on opposite sides of the table so we can face each other.

"Gran! Lunch is ready." I go to her and guide her from her armchair to her seat at the kitchen table.

"Dainty." She nods and smiles approvingly at her sandwich.

"No ham. We'll have to make do with cheese and tomato."

"I like cheese and tomato." She's already almost finished her first quarter.

"Mind and drink your tea before it goes cold." She's not been drinking her water this morning. I need to get fluids into her.

"Still too hot." A frown.

"Let it cool for a bit first, then. After we've finished our lunch, would you like to go for a walk?"

"Go for a walk?"

"Aye. Just a wee walk. It looks a beautiful day out there." I nod toward the window, and her eyes follow. "It would be good for us both to get a bit of fresh air, wouldn't it?"

"Fresh air. That would be good for us both." The second quarter-sandwich is nearly gone. It's good to get her to eat at the kitchen table. The food is right there in front of her. No telly to distract her.

"We could maybe walk down to the Stoorie Burn and back. You can tell me what it was like there when you were a lassie. That would be nice, wouldn't it?"

"That would be nice."

We finish our lunch, and I fetch Gran's walking shoes. Sturdy black lace ups. She still knows how to tie her laces. She sits at the foot of the stairs when she puts her shoes on, like I did when I was wee. Her pixie-like features are a study in concentration below her tightly permed grey hair, as she focuses on knotting her laces into bows. She's in really good condition for her age. Physical condition, that is. In some ways that makes it worse. She used to wander, which was a real worry. But she's not done that for more than six months. She stands up and smiles at me, pleased with herself. There's about three feet between us. She looks right at me and smiles. Her expression changes to concern. "Have you been greetin'?" She steps forward, puts her arms round me, and gently pulls my temple down on to her shoulder.

"Oh, Gran. Gran." I wasn't before, but I'm crying again now.

"Wheesht, lassie. Wheesht. It'll be all right. It'll be all right."

We cuddle together, Gran cooing comfort. Looking after me like she did when I was wee. We hold each other. For minutes. Eventually, my tears stop. I step half a pace back. Gran has tears in her eyes too. I kiss her softly on the cheek and smile. She smiles back. We drink our tea.

"Shall we go for that walk to the Stoorie Burn, then? It'll be lovely in this nice weather."

"That would be lovely."

We walk the three-quarter mile to the burn. Arm in arm. I point to houses and landmarks that I know are familiar to her, and Gran tells me about them, like she does every time. She points to a house and tells me it's where her pal Sandra McDonald used to live. They would eat the strawberries straight from the patch in her garden, and they were the tastiest strawberries in the whole world. At the Stoorie Burn, she points to the place where Daft Jimmy Maguire fell in when he was guddling for sticklebacks. She laughs at the stupidity of guddling for sticklebacks and at the memory of how wet Daft Jimmy got. Then she gets upset when she remembers he was killed in a car accident sometime later, and I have to distract her. On the walk back, she points to a bungalow where a family called Paterson was the first to own two cars in the village. The pampas grass they planted still thrives in a bed in the front lawn. She's happy because she's confident of what she's telling me, and her happiness makes me happy. Walking with her is a welcome diversion.

We get back to the house just over an hour after we left.

"Would you like a nice cup of tea, Gran?"

"A nice cup of tea. Yes, please, dear."

Just as I turn to put the kettle on, Gran takes me by surprise by coming over to me and embracing me. She hugs me tight, pressing the side of her head against mine. We stand like this for over a minute. No words spoken. This isn't something I've seen her do before. Her hold on me eases, and she turns her head so that our eyes lock. There's something in her eyes. A hint. A flicker. Of something. What? Her eyes are searching mine. I know what I see in hers. Awareness.

"You've travelled." A firm statement. Not a question.

"What, Gran?" I have no idea where this is going.

"You've travelled." More firmly. Still a statement. But almost challenging, daring me to question it.

"I don't know what you mean. Gran."

She takes a step back. Turns her head to look toward the window. "Our Suzy travelled."

"Gran, what are you talking about?"

"Our Suzy told me. She travelled. More than once. Told me all about it. Then, the last time, she never came back."

"Gran, who's Suzy?"

She turns back to look at me. Her eyes are brimming. She's upset. Upset and havering. When she gets delusions, it's often a sign that she's got a water infection, although sometimes it can just be dehydration. I step toward her and hug her. I whisper in her ear: "Are you ready for that nice cup of tea?"

"A nice cup of tea. Yes, please, dear."

The diversion's worked. Crisis averted. She seems calm again. I make two cups of tea, and we take them to the living room. I make sure she drinks all of hers before I let her nod off in her armchair. I was thinking about walking out to Dundo Point, just to clear my head. But I can do that tomorrow. It's best that I stay here and keep an eye on Gran.

I watch as her head falls forward. Her breathing is regular. After a couple of minutes, her jaw loosens. Her mouth falls open and issues a low, grumbling snore—like the noise of the faulty extractor fan in the toilet. And stops. Starts and stops. The next thing I'm aware of is a hand gently shaking my shoulder.

"Wakey, wakey, sleeping beauty." Mum is smiling down at me. "Your dinner's out, and George and Scott are champing at the bit to start." She turns away to waken Gran as I shake off the unexpected, dreamless sleep.

The five of us eat together at the kitchen table. Sausages, potatoes, and beans. I feel guilty because I should've made it. Mum's been out working all day, and George was sleeping before his nightshift. Mum doesn't seem to mind. I think she's still feeling protective because of my head knock. The meal is the usual carry-on of George encouraging Scott to wind me up and the pair of them succeeding until Mum plays peacekeeper. Gran always looks particularly bewildered when banter starts flowing. When we finish, Scott says he's off to his room to read his library book, although we all know he'll be on his PlayStation. George takes Gran and two mugs of tea into the living room. He knows she likes her favourite armchair and one-on-one human interaction. He spends at least an hour with her almost every single day. He's brilliant with her. Really patient. I'd never tell him, but he's got a kind heart.

Mum and I stay in the kitchen for our tea. "So what sort of day have you had, love? How are you feeling?"

I don't know whether to tell her. She looks tired. "Gran and I went for a walk today. Just down to the Stoorie Burn and back."

"That's nice. Lovely day for it." She's looking at me that way she does. I can tell she knows I'm building up to something.

"Gran gave me a cuddle today. Twice."

"Oh?"

"She thought I'd been crying, and she tried to hug me better."

"And had you been crying?"

That question breaks the dam, and it all gushes out. Findlay and Morag. Betrayed once. Betrayed twice. He's doing it to get at me. I'm humiliated. Everyone thinks I'm a loser. Can't keep a boy. Can't keep a friend. The two of them talking about me. Laughing at me. Discussing things I've said. I can't go into town in case I see them. I can't go into The Tassie. The thought of them together makes me feel like I'm going to be sick. Everybody knows. Everybody. Why has this happened? I don't know what to do. My words and tears are a deluge I can't control.

Mum is beside my chair, hand on my shoulder. I stand up and fall into her embrace all in one movement. One arm is round my back, and the other presses my head so that our cheeks are resting together. Firm but gentle. We hold this position for ages. And ages. Eventually, the crying stops. She loosens her grip. I take a tiny step back, and she looks at me, chin tilted slightly down, eyes big.

"Better?"

"Uh-huh." I sniff.

She does her magic trick again, conjuring a pack of tissues from nowhere and hands them to me. I blow my nose hard and dab my eyes. I use three tissues.

"If I see Findlay Calder or Morag McNulty anytime soon, they'll be getting told exactly what I think about them." Mum's expression is fierce.

"Mind what you told George!"

We exchange smiles, and the tension eases. Mum makes us both a second cup of tea, and we sit back down at the table. George comes in to make more tea for himself and Gran. He sees the state of me, makes the tea, and shoots off again without saying a word. Mum starts talking. About a boy. Charlie. She knew him before she ever met Dad. They went out for over a year.

"Then one day, he finished it."

"What do you mean?"

"He chucked me."

"Just out of the blue?"

"He came to my house, and we went to my room. He said he was sorry but thought we were getting too serious. We should stop seeing each other."

"No warning before? There weren't any hints?"

"Nothing."

"Was he seeing someone else?"

"I don't think so."

She's never, ever mentioned this before. I hesitate. "Did you love him?"

"I loved him. Or at least I thought I did at the time. He certainly broke my heart. But I didn't love him the way I loved your dad."

She's not making any of this up. But it's a parable told for my benefit, and I'm grateful. She's trying to do whatever she can to help me. Comfort me. And I love her for it. But it's weird to imagine her having a life before Dad. Loving someone else. The conversation moves on. Chit-chat. Humdrum trivialities that matter only to us, to our family. We're still blethering when George sticks his head round the door to say he's off to his work. We realize how much time has passed and set about loading the dishwasher. I take Gran yet another cup of tea and Mum shouts up to Scott that he has to bring any clothes he wants washed downstairs.

Back in the kitchen, wiping the surfaces. Mum stops and turns to me. "Eilidh, you said earlier that Gran gave you a cuddle twice today."

"Oh God, yes! I forgot. Sorry. It was strange. She hadn't been drinking her water during the day, and I think she had a wee hallucination."

Mum has stopped now and is looking right at me. "What do you mean? What happened?"

"It didn't last long, but it was really weird, Mum. I was putting the kettle on, and Gran came over and cuddled me. Then she started talking about travelling. And somebody called Suzy. She got a bit tearful. But I was able to distract her, and she got over it really quickly."

Something's wrong. There's a look on Mum's face that I don't recognize and can't even describe. She's dropped the cloth on the floor, and it's like she's frozen to the spot. "What exactly did Gran say?"

I'm worried now. "Mum, is there something wrong?"

"Eilidh. Tell me what Gran said. About Suzy."

"She said that I'd been travelling. She didn't say where. Then she said Suzy travelled. She called her *our Suzy*. I think she said Suzy travelled lots and told her about it. Then she travelled again and never came back."

Mum picks the cloth up almost absently, goes to the table, and sits. She's holding on to the table with one hand and just staring ahead. I'm really worried now. I go to her and put my hand on top of hers. "Mum. You're really worrying me. What's wrong?'

"Sit down."

I do as she asks. "Mum, what is it? What's the matter?"

"It's ..." She stops. I can see she's confused. Struggling. "There's nothing wrong, as such. It's just such a shock to hear that Gran was talking about Suzy."

"I don't understand. Who's Suzy?"

Mum's looking right at me, talking directly to me, but it's like she's talking to herself. "Suzy is Gran's sister. Was Gran's sister. Her twin." She blinks, probably aware that her answer has spawned a hundred more questions. She waits as I process what she's said and continues. Her voice is low, measured. "When Archie and George were born, your dad's cousin Henry gave us a christening gift. Two copies of a family tree. One each for the boys." I signal encouragement, and she continues. "They were beautiful documents. Huge scrolls. Handwritten copperplate. Very detailed and went back six generations on your dad's side. Only three on mine. Anyway, I was having a proper look at them one day and was astonished to learn that Mum, your gran, had a sister. Suzanne. Jennifer and Suzanne. Born on the same day. But Suzanne died aged just twenty." She pauses. Almost as if she's having to remind herself it's true. "I couldn't believe it. I was at home looking after the babies. Gran was out at work at the time. So I phoned Henry to check that he hadn't made some sort of crazy mistake. Of course, he hadn't. Gran was in the habit of passing by to check everything was okay on her way home from work. When she came, I asked her about Suzanne." Mum sighed deeply.

"What? What is it? What did she say?"

"Nothing. Or next to nothing. She became very tearful. She said Suzy was her sister. She called her Suzy. She said she found it too upsetting to talk about. She left pretty quickly. I felt terrible."

"That was it? That was all?"

"No. Next morning when I got up, there was a hand-delivered letter on the mat. Gran had written it overnight and posted it through the letterbox."

"Go on."

"Not a lot to it, in all honesty. I've still got it upstairs somewhere. She said she was sorry she got upset and sorry that she'd never mentioned Suzy before. She'd been incredibly close to Suzy. Best friends as well as sisters. When Suzy died, she was devastated. She said that she has come to terms with losing Suzy but would never get over it. Her way of coping is to completely avoid thinking or talking about her sister, because it is simply too painful.

"She apologized for never telling me. She said Suzy would've been the best aunt in the world, and it was such a shame I never got the chance to know her. She said that she knows it probably seems strange that she's kept it a secret. But she asked that we didn't talk about Suzy. She said that even having to write her name in the letter was unbearably painful. She'd been up all night upset, thinking about her sister."

"Wow." I immediately regret my inane response.

"Quite. I was desperate to find out more, but I didn't want to cause any more upset. After a while, it seemed less important, and it faded. I've barely thought about Suzy and what it must've been like for your gran. Maybe the odd couple of occasions over the years. Gran has never mentioned her since, and I've never raised it. That's why I was so astonished when you said Gran had been talking about her."

"Poor Gran. I had no idea."

"How could you have?"

"I know. I couldn't. It just seems so … I don't have the words for it."

Mum nods her head. "I understand, love. Really, I do. It's such a shame, but there's nothing we can do about it. What I think is saddest is that, despite everything else that's gone from Gran's mind, she can still remember Suzy."

"I don't know if that's sad. At least she still remembers the sister she loved. And remembers her name."

"I suppose so. Anyway, even though you were asleep when I came home from work, you're still looking a bit tired. Are you feeling all right? How's the head?"

"I do feel a bit tired. It's been a long day. I'll probably look to get an early night. My head's a bit sore if I touch it where I bumped it. But otherwise it's fine. I've not had to take any painkillers."

"Well, that's a good sign. An early night sounds like a good idea too. Have you got anything planned for tomorrow?"

"I was thinking I might take a walk to Dundo Point. Spend some time there. Maybe take a sandwich and a drink. It'll be deserted on a weekday. I can catch some sun, get the fresh air. Clear my head and forget about my troubles for a while."

"Sounds like a good plan. George will be in from the nightshift if Gran needs anything. And I'll pop back in my lunch hour to make sure she's eating and drinking."

"I'll not be out all day. If I head off early, I'll be back in the afternoon. I can take her for another walk then."

I kiss Mum goodnight. Kiss Gran goodnight. Shout "Goodnight, Stumpy" to Scott as I head up the stairs. I get ready for bed and lie down. Maybe because I fell asleep in the afternoon. Maybe because of the revelations of the day. Whatever it is, my mind is spinning, and sleep doesn't come easily. The images on screen of the people in Ethiopia. Morag's betrayal. Mum loving someone else before Dad. Gran having a twin sister. It all plays round in my head. Along with images of Kia. And Dubya. Most of all, how much I hate Findlay. It jumbles together. I pull it apart. Analyze it. Try to make sense of it. Is everything linked, somehow? Of course not! Round and round. Eventually everything fades.

August 9, 2019

10.

THE SKY IS iridescent. Sea campion blooms everywhere in the poor soil among the rocks. It has no perfume now, but I know it'll give off a scent of cloves at dusk. The morning is gorgeous, unlike my mood.

Gulls soar, riding the thermals, then careen away with their distinctive *keow* cry. I'd still be crying now if my insides weren't dust and it didn't hurt so much. I feel my eyes moisten again. I wipe them with the back of my hand and squint at the distant bench behind the bus shelter. I call it Solitude—like Superman's fortress—because nobody goes there except me. My safe place. A place I can heal.

Gran told me that they built the new road nearly sixty years ago, and the bus stopped coming out this way. The shelter's like me. Abandoned. Its cracked paintwork is peeling away to reveal rot setting in at numerous points—a structure betrayed by those who were meant to care for it. The bench behind it's in good nick though—moss green paint on the wooden parts, sturdy concrete legs.

I've got sandwiches and a bottle of water in my rucksack, plus a sun hat and lotion if I think my face might burn. The patch of grass between the bench and the cliff edge overlooking the sea is a place I can stay for hours undisturbed. My phone is off. Proper off. I just want to be alone. Solo. When I woke up this morning, everything was still racing round in my mind, and I became overwhelmed and started crying again. That's not me! I don't want to be that girl—confused, weak, a victim. I want the time to clear my head. To forget about The Snake and all the shit that's happened to me since the Great Betrayal. I need to convince myself that I'm not going mad.

Movement. By the shelter. I screw my eyes even tighter, my right hand over my brow for shade. There's somebody there! I can't make them out properly, but there's definitely somebody. Low down, behind the shelter.

Who? Who in the name of shite is it? Nobody else comes here. Nobody. And nobody knows that I come here. Not even *him*. I shared everything with him—everything. But I never told him about here. My only secret. Not like *him*. The thought pricks more tears, making it even harder to see. I brush my eyes with my knuckle and blink them clear. I can see now. Someone's on the other side of the shelter, on the ground leaning back against it.

I'm cross and curious, both at the same time. The combination increases my pace, and I speed walk the hundred-odd yards almost to the shelter before slowing right down. I'm suddenly overcome by caution. Who is it? Why are they here? What do they want? You hear all sorts of horror stories. This place is pretty remote—it's a good twenty minutes since I passed the last house on the outskirts of the village, and Dundo Point is well off the beaten track. Best be careful.

Curiosity overcomes caution, and I edge forward slowly and to the right, positioning myself for a better angle, but still with a bit of distance between the invader and me. I take my rucksack from my back and hold it in both hands as if it's a shield or a weapon or both. I'm moving slowly, like a big cat stalking an antelope or something on a telly documentary. Only I'm scared that it might be me who ends up as the prey.

I can see him now. Definitely a him, a man. He's sitting on the grass, leaning on a backpack propped against the shelter. His eyes are shut, and he's old. Like really, really old. I'm wondering if he's a gipsy. A tramp maybe. But his clothes look clean and in okay condition. He's wearing decent walking boots. And the backpack looks like a proper, expensive bit of gear. He's got wispy grey hair and five o' clock shadow, but seems otherwise well groomed. He's definitely not a tramp.

I feel bolder, less at risk, and I inch toward him. A gull squawks a piercing *ha-ha-ha* alert overhead, and not-a-tramp's eyes open. In half a blink, he clocks me, throws his arms defensively in front of his face, and falls over sideways.

"Oh my God! Are you all right?"

"Jesus Christ Almighty!"

"Are you all right?" I take a step toward him. "Can I help you? Do you need a hand up?"

"What's your game? Are you trying to mug me? If that's what you're up to, you better think again. I can handle myself."

He doesn't look like he could handle a gust of wind, never mind a mugger. "No, no, no. I'm sorry. I didn't mean to startle you. Can I help you up?"

"A lassie! Jesus Christ! A lassie!"

"Aye, a lassie that's offering to help you get back up." I drop my rucksack, lean forward, and offer my hand.

"I'm fine." His tone is dismissive, which I find irritating. He pushes back up into a sitting position and shakes himself slightly, I suspect more to recover his dishevelled dignity than dust himself off.

I can't help myself correcting him. "I'm fine, thank you."

"What?"

"I'm fine, *thank you.*"

"You cheeky besom!"

"Less of the besom, you!" The anger, hurt, and frustration of the past few days resurface as I snap back at this old fool.

"Aye well, what do you expect, sneaking up on folk? And what were you going to do with that rucksack? Smother me?"

"I wasn't sneaking up on you. Well, maybe I was a bit, but not the way you're thinking. I was more worried that you might be waiting to jump on me."

"Jump on you? I'm sitting here on my arse. How am I going to jump on you?"

"Och, whatever. Look, I'm sorry. I didn't mean to scare you."

"Who says I was scared? Startled maybe, but not scared."

"Aye, okay. I didn't mean to startle you."

"Fair enough." His glower doesn't match his words.

"I've said I'm sorry."

"Aye, all right, then." His tone is softer now. He tilts his head and shields his eyes with his hand, looking right at me. "Have you been greetin'?"

I feel my neck and face catch fire, my blood lava. "No," I lie.

11.

She's obviously lying. Her pink, puffy eyes make her look like she's been crying forever, although there aren't any actual tears right now. I wonder if she's going to say anything else, but I don't think so. She's avoiding eye contact and seems awkward. I'd guess she's in her late teens, the age when embarrassment feels most acute. She obviously doesn't want to talk about whatever's upset her.

She takes a couple of paces nearer the cliff edge, where there's a level grassy patch, and kneels down with her back to me. She pulls one of those microfibre towels from her rucksack, plain canary yellow with no pattern, and spreads it over the grass. Her right hand squeezes a bottle of sunscreen, squirting its contents into her left. She places the bottle gently by the towel and applies the lotion to her face and neck with both hands. She turns ninety degrees and lies down on the towel, her legs half on it and half on the grass.

The entire performance is played out in complete silence, but the message is deafening. She resents my presence and is determined to ignore me. Good! I bloody well begrudge her being here too. If we just ignore each other and I can imagine I'm here alone, that suits me perfectly.

I try to get comfortable against my backpack again, fold my arms across my chest, and close my eyes huffily. But getting comfy is easier said than done. I'm tense and angry and a bit embarrassed myself. I know from experience that I'm not going to nod off in this mood, so I shoogle myself up into a sitting position and open my eyes.

It's barely mid-morning, so the sun's some way off its peak and rising behind me. The sky has just the odd dash of cirrus, high and thin and streaky. But there's loads of gulls, maybe thirty or forty. They're bunched tightly, moving as one mass like a mini murmuration. I scan for a predator—nothing, just gulls. Must be insects hatching—flying ants maybe—taking to the wing, and rising up in the heat. An all-you-can-eat feast for the gulls brought right to them by a thermal Deliveroo. I remember seeing this before, but only very rarely, on the hottest of days long ago. I can't quite remember when.

I've succeeded in not looking at the lassie. I want to pretend she's not here. I also don't want her to catch me looking at her in case she thinks I'm some kind of creep. My eyes dart involuntarily and pilfer a glance in her direction. She's flat on her back, hands behind her head, eyes shut. She's not very tall, maybe five-three or four, at a guess. Wearing those jeans with the ripped knees like Molly wears.

It's hot. I loosen the top two buttons on my shirt and roll my sleeves up above my elbows. My boots are fine for walking, but I needed to put on thick socks to make them fit properly, and I can feel my feet sweating already. I'll probably take my boots off and let the air in about my feet. But I've come out without a hat—or even a hankie—and this sun is going to burn my bald napper before long.

I look across in her direction again, letting my eyes linger a few seconds. The sun lotion is this side of her, resting on a tight bed of pink devil's hatties. I look at her. She's not moved, and her breathing is slow and regular. She can't be asleep, surely? Not so quickly? I bet she's just faking sleep so she doesn't have to talk to me. I'm fine with that.

But that sun's hot. And it's just going to get hotter. The occasional gust of wind isn't going to bring much relief. I'm going to have to swallow my pride and ask if she'll spare some lotion. I clear my throat to catch her attention, but to no effect. She's still as the dead, bar the shallow rise and fall that shows she's breathing. I wonder if the sound of the waves maybe drowned out my attempt. I cough again, but much louder and longer. Still no reaction.

Maybe she really *is* asleep. I raise my right hand high above my head, in front of where a glass panel would once have protected folk in the bus shelter from wind and rain. It casts a shadow just beside her head. I move my hand slowly, and the shadow obediently crosses her face. Nothing. Slowly back across. Still nothing. I wave rapidly so the sun flashes like a strobe, but her eyes don't even twitch. She really is asleep. I ease myself forward onto my knees and haltingly crawl two of the three yards toward the sunscreen bottle. A pause to check she's still motionless, then ease my arm forward.

The scream causes my whole body to jerk. She rolls away, grabs a large stone, and springs to her feet—all in one movement, like some kind of commando. She's standing about two yards away, stone in hand, primed and aimed right at my head. "What the fuck are you up to?"

"Nothing. Nothing at all. Please don't throw that."

"Crap! You were creeping up on me, you dirty old pervert."

"No! Honestly, no. I really wasn't."

"Don't talk shite. Look how close you got to me." She draws her arm back as if preparing to throw.

"No. Don't! I was just trying to borrow some of your sun lotion."

The tension in her arm eases a notch, and her head tilts, eyes quizzical. "Do you think I'm that stupid?"

"I haven't got a hat. Not even a hankie. The sun's hot and going to get even hotter." I'm babbling, but I can't help myself. "I just thought that if I could borrow some of your sun cream, I'd be okay. It's the truth. Honest to God."

She's quiet for a second. "Why didn't you ask, then, instead of trying to steal it?"

"You were asleep. I didn't want to wake you."

"I wasn't sleeping. I'd barely just lain down."

"Well, I tried to see if you were awake. I coughed to try to get a reaction."

"I just thought you were being a disgusting phlegmy old man."

"I used my hand to cast shadows on your eyelids to see if you were awake."

She lowers her hand with the stone. I think she believes me. "I thought you were just trying to annoy me. Then, when it went all quiet, I opened my eye and you were right over reaching out for me."

"Not for you. For the sun lotion. I only wanted to borrow some."

"What? Were you going to give it back after you'd rubbed it into your baldy head? I don't think you mean *borrow* at all. The word you're looking for is *steal*."

I can tell from her tone and the glint in her eye that she's teasing me now. I'm happy to play along. "No. Well, not really stealing. Not like proper stealing."

She passes the stone from one hand to the other and back. Her eyes are studying mine. "M'Lud, the defendant denies being a pervert and claims to be a mere thief. A most novel defence indeed." I'm the butt of her joke, but there's no cruelty in it. I look hard into her red-rimmed eyes and recognize something. I *know* this lassie.

12.

I THINK HE's telling the truth. The situation's so ridiculous that he couldn't be making it up. The other thing I realize is that he's not frightening. Not at all. He's a big enough guy, maybe six-two. And despite his age, he's neither carrying too much weight nor looking as if he's shrinking the way so many old folks do. If he wanted to overpower me, he probably could, contrary to my initial impression of him. Easily, in fact. But there's something about his demeanour that makes me know that's not the case. He's got that stance and expression you see on a deer when you stumble across one in the early morning, when it's eyeing you and preparing to bolt. There's a vulnerability about him that's vaguely familiar.

"I know you."

"What?" He's wrong-footed me.

"I know you."

"What do you mean you know me?"

"I *know* you."

"How do you know me?"

"I don't know. I can't place you. But I do know you."

I can see the frustration in his face. He believes what he's saying, even if he's mistaken. "I'm pretty sure we've never met."

"What's your name?"

"What's *your* name?"

"I asked you first."

"Aye, and I asked you second." I look him in the eye and see a glint there.

He smiles gently. A pause. "Wattie … Walter. Walter Buchanan." He leans forward and extends his right hand. Mine responds automatically. "How do you do? I'm Walter Buchanan. Wattie to my friends." His left hand closes on the back of my right, pressing softly. I glance down and register prominent veins, long fingers, and a wedding band. The handclasp is firm without being oppressive and is over in a couple of heartbeats.

He leans back and looks at me expectantly. His sudden formality has thrown me, and I hesitate. "Eilidh. Eilidh McVicar. Pleased to meet you."

There's something gnawing at the back of my mind, a feeling that there's something familiar about this guy. There's something that I know I should recognize.

"Pleased to meet you too, Eilidh McVicar. I'm sorry we kind of got off on the wrong foot."

"Aye, well, these things happen." I'm surprised at myself—and at how quickly the mood is changing. From war footing to detente in moments, I fire him a half-smile.

"Aye, they do." Beaming. The thaw is virtually complete. "So come on then. How is it I know you?"

"I've already said: I don't think you do." His persistence should be making me cross—*back of the queue when patience was being given out*, Mum always says—but I'm keen to set him right without being confrontational.

He's looking straight into my eyes. You know when you're looking for something for so long that you half forget what it is? Well, he's looking at me a bit like that. And long enough for it to just start feeling uncomfortable, although he seems oblivious. The piercing alarm chuckle of a gull swooping aggressively overhead causes us both to look up instinctively. When I look back at him, he's turning away from me. "I'm going to sit over here."

"What?"

"I'm going to sit over here. There's a wee bit of shade from the shelter."

"Oh, right." He picks up his backpack and adjusts its position. I pick up my towel, sunscreen, and rucksack, then move toward the shelter.

He looks over his shoulder and smiles. "The shade will be gone in a couple of hours. Might as well make the most of it now."

I spread my towel out again, prop my rucksack against the back of the shelter, and sit down to lean back on it. We're facing the sea side by side, a metre apart, upright with our backs to the shelter. Both of us have our legs in the sun and bodies in shade. There's a sail away out to the left and beyond that a tanker, red oxide squashed low against the horizon. The wind, waves, and gulls provide a soundtrack that makes the absence of conversation not at all awkward.

"So what brings you here then?" I'm surprised to hear my own words.

"I used to come here."

"When?"

"Long time ago. When I was a boy."

"How long ago was that?"

"Long enough. There were still bears and sabre-toothed tigers about."

"And dinosaurs?" I look at him.

"Cheeky!" He grins a big wide cheeser, and I smile back. I like him. But there's still something at the back of my mind. That thing I can't put my finger on that's somehow familiar. Maybe I do know him somehow?

"So you don't live around here now?"

"Sorry?"

"You said you *used* to come here. Long time ago, you said."

"Oh, aye. Aye, that's right. I don't live about here now."

"So what brings you back? Are you visiting someone?"

"Aye, visiting. That's right."

"That's nice." It's a nothing answer, filling the gap on my side, buying me time as realization dawns and I start to marshal my thoughts. Now I know what's familiar. He confirms it.

"What's your name?"

"What's *your* name?"

"I asked you first."

"Fair enough. My name's Eilidh."

"Eilidh. That's a nice name."

"Thank you."

13.

EILIDH. DOES THAT ring a bell? It should because I know that I know her. She's reached over and taken my hand, so she must know me.

"Walter, do you ever get a wee bit confused sometimes?"

She knows my name, so she definitely knows me. I just wish I could place her. "Sometimes."

"And are you a bit confused now?"

"Aye, maybe a bit." More than a bit really. I know this lassie, this Eilidh. And she knows me. But I can't remember how I know her. Think, man. How do I know this Eilidh lassie? I know her *really* well. "Are you my wife?"

"Walter! Do you not think I'm a bit young to be your wife?"

She's smiling, and her eyes are kind. But I've offended her. She's only a young thing. Far too young to be my wife. How could I be so stupid as to think that? "I'm sorry."

"No need to be sorry." She's beaming at me now. "I'm flattered that such a handsome man might mistake me for his wife. But I think somebody beat me to you." She nods at the ring on my finger. My wedding ring.

She's being nice to me. She's a nice lassie. I think she's trying to flatter me. She's kind and I like her. I wish I could remember how I know her.

14.

I'M BEING NICE to him. I even called him handsome—and he kind of is, or at least he would've been a long time ago. It's important for him to feel reassured, I think. He seems like Gran was a couple years ago, before her decline. He appears fine on the surface, and he's developed coping mechanisms to disguise it. But he's definitely starting to lose it. Maybe only early stages, but I recognize the signs. "Walter, do you have a water bottle in your backpack?"

"What?"

"A water bottle?" I see confusion in his eyes and a hint of fear. "Would you like me to have a look for you?" Easy questions. Ask easy questions. Yes-or-no questions. Talk about the weather. Make it easy for him.

"Aye. You look."

I open the straps and look inside. "Yes, there's a water bottle." I hand him the unopened litre bottle. "And there's a hat too. I thought you said—" I stop myself just in time. "I remember you said you'd probably need it."

"Aye. That's right. Thank you." He takes the baseball cap and puts it on.

I reach into my own backpack and get my water out, take a quick swig, and nod to him. "Aren't you having some?"

"Eh? Oh, yes. Yes." He takes a long draw from the bottle, sucking so that the plastic contracts around the vacuum before cracking back into shape.

"Did you enjoy that?"

"Yes. Hits the spot."

"Have some more. I am." I take another pull and nod again encouragingly. I know from experience with Gran that it's really important to make sure he's properly hydrated. I glance at him sidelong as he chugs at the bottle 'til it's three-quarters empty.

We sit in silence for almost half an hour, the shadow of the bus stop creeping along our legs toward our upright bodies as the sun continues its ascent. Walter takes occasional sips of water. Out of the blue, he asks, "What time is it?"

I glance at my phone. "Twenty to eleven."

"Thanks."

"In the morning."

"Obviously. Do you think I'm a complete tube?"

I turn to face him. He's smiling, and his eyes are alive. He's back in the room, lucid. And he's bantering again. He's like Gran was when we first realized she'd got dementia. Fine, then not fine, then fine again. Later, it became not fine, fine, and not fine. Now it's just not fine all the time. I realize he sees I'm distracted and is about to say something else. I cut him off quickly: "Aye, a *complete* tube."

He grins. "Just so long as we know where we stand. So what brings you out here?"

"None of your business. Why are *you* here?"

"I'm here because I have to be here."

"What do you mean, you have to be here?"

He tilts his head as he looks at me. "Honestly, I don't know why. But I do have to be here. I have to be here on the eighth of August 2019."

"Well, you've made an arse of that, then."

"What?"

"It's the ninth of August."

"What?" This time there's a note of anxiety.

I take out my phone and show him the date. "See? Friday, August the ninth."

His head dips and he whisper-moans into his chest.

"Are you all right?"

"It was late."

"Sorry, what was late?"

"Yesterday. When I got here. It was late."

"And?"

"And when I got here, I settled against this old bus shelter. I must've fallen asleep."

"You slept out here last night?"

"Aye. And now I've missed it."

"Missed what?"

"I don't know. Whatever it was that I was meant to come here for."

I can tell he's genuinely put out. More than that, he's getting emotional, maybe losing control. "Why did you think you had to be here?"

His eyes are moist as he looks at me. He undoes his watch strap, removes it, and pushes his wrist toward me. The tattoo is tiny and faded, but perfectly legible: *Dundo Point 8.8.19.* "See?" He looks at me with bereaved eyes.

"Walter, when did you have that tattoo done, and why?"

The tiniest of shrugs. "I don't ..." Slow, gentle shake of the head. "I don't know." The dam breaks, and a sob convulses his torso. He looks into my face—hopeless and helpless.

Distraction isn't going to work, so I opt to reassure. Physical contact can help. I lean toward him and pull his head softly on to my shoulder. I place my free hand on the back of his. "Do you think that maybe I'm the reason, Walter?"

"What?"

Good. I've got his attention. "Do you think I'm the reason you're here? The reason you have that tattoo on your wrist?" Repetition is good. It gives them time, helps them understand and feel less vulnerable. "Maybe the reason for that tattoo is that you were meant to meet me here. Do you think that's possible?"

The pause is almost too long, and for a second, I think I've lost him. "You think I was meant to meet *you*?"

"I don't know. Maybe."

"Why? Why am I meant to meet you?"

"I'm not saying that you definitely are meant to meet me. I'm just saying maybe you are."

"Are you my wife? You look like my wife. What's your name?"

I'm pretty sure the slight irritation in his voice isn't anything more than that. I sense he's a gentle soul. "I'm not your wife, Walter. I'm too young for you—you don't look like a baby snatcher. Anyway, I don't think I'm good looking enough to land a handsome devil like you. And my name's Eilidh, by the way."

"Eilidh, aye? Did you not tell me that before?"

"Did I? I don't remember. Probably. I like talking about myself."

He's sitting back up, smiling at me like I imagine a kindly grandpa would. "I think maybe you are just a wee bit too young for me. And you're right, of course, I'm a fine-looking man."

Jesus! All those clichés about old men with twinkly eyes are true. His smile is kind and cheeky at the same time, and there's a sparkle to him. He's old and crumbly, but he's lovely. I can't help but like him. "Not *that* fine looking, with your baldy heid and your big nose."

"You cheeky wee … it's a good job I'm a gentleman."

"A gentleman! A sun lotion thief more like!"

His eyes flick to the bottle, and I see that he remembers. He's in his element. "Pots and kettles, young lady. I hardly think a mugger of old age pensioners is in any position to be casting aspersions."

He remembers all that, so his short-term memory is actually in pretty good nick. Maybe he's only in the very early stages. He seemed worse earlier, maybe because he was dehydrated. "Shall we call it quits?"

"Scared?"

I feel my hackles rise. "Do you think so?"

"I'm only kidding, lassie. Eilidh. You're right. We'll call it honours even."

We resume our positions against the shelter, and I note the sun has chased the shade almost to the tops of our thighs. I close my eyes and listen to the waves below and the gulls above. By rights, they should clash, but they sound good together, knitted into the wind. I could maybe fall asleep, but I'm conscious of movement to my left and open one eye. Walter is leaning forward, rolling up his trouser legs. He struggles to manoeuvre the thickening material over his very large calves, then continues pushing up the trouser legs to his knees. Both shins are heavily scarred their full length, and his left knee obviously underwent a major operation at some point.

"Wow."

"I thought you were nodding off. So what's so amazing—my magnificent legs? Well, if you can contain your excitement, I'll take off my shoes and socks. That will really blow you away. I've got ankles like a Greek god."

That should sound weird, but it doesn't, coming from him. He's funny. Not like old-man funny. Just funny. "That's some set of scarring you've got on your legs. What happened to you?"

"I'll tell you about my legs if you tell me why you've been crying."

My whole body tenses like I'm anticipating a punch. "None of your business."

"Fair enough. Just sometimes it can help to unburden your troubles to a stranger."

I don't know if he's just being nosy or if he really is simply offering a listening ear. "So what did happen to your legs?"

"Nothing sinister, just football. The way I played meant I took a lot of punishment. I wasn't a particular fan of shin pads, so I ended up with legs that look like this." He taps his left knee gently. "This was the bad one though. The one that effectively finished me. Never the same after it." His eyes are empty mirrors. His mind is elsewhere, the past probably, and he's fallen silent.

I jerk him back. "Were you any good?"

He pauses sufficiently for me to think I haven't hooked him, then says, "Aye. I was good. Not great. But I was good." He's smiling.

"You used to stay around here. Did you ever play for the Primrose?"

"Aye. Aye, I did. Signed when I was still at school and stayed with them while I did my apprenticeship. Do you follow them?"

"I used to."

He's really engaged, animated. Football talk sparks a fire in him. "Used to?"

"I used to go with my dad, until he died."

The flame is extinguished immediately, unintentionally, and we both fall into silence. Some seconds pass.

"I'm very sorry." Another pause. "Is that why you've been greetin'?"

I shake my head. Hard and fast. I can't make words. I turn sideways so that my back is toward him. My eyes are full of tears again. The nosy old bastard. It's none of his business. I'm angry. Angry at him. At myself. At Findlay. At the whole fucking world. I'm trying to breathe slowly. To keep control. My body trembles as I inhale, exhale, inhale, exhale. It subsides. I'm in control now. I don't need any of this shite. I don't need this stupid old man with his fucked up legs and fucked up brain. I'm going to stand up, pick up my stuff, and fuck off home. But I hear a voice. The voice is low, female. It's explaining. It's talking about Tuesday. About getting results. About arranging to meet Findlay.

I hear the voice, like I'm in a trance or something. I can't hear anything else. No waves, gulls, or wind. Just the voice. A bee meanders close in front of my face, like a silent movie, no buzz. Just the voice. Telling it all. Everything. It doesn't matter. He won't remember. In one ear. Out the other. It feels strange to listen to the voice. It's talking about excitement. Meg's tea shop. Hugging the life out of Findlay. Realizing something was wrong. The betrayal.

A tear escapes down my cheek.

15.

"I'm sorry to hear that."

He's sincere. I know it. Maybe even actually concerned for me? I can hardly believe I've spilled my guts to a complete stranger. But it didn't feel awkward. Because he's so unthreatening? Because he's losing it and vulnerable himself? I don't know. I do know that I'm comfortable in his presence. I dry my eyes with the backs of my hands and switch on a smile for him. I like him. I'm grateful. And I'm worried for him. "Thanks, Walter."

"Not at all."

"I'm sorry for going on like that."

"No need. Sometimes it's good just to let everything all out.'

"Maybe. Thanks for listening anyway."

"You'll be fine. People like that Findlay lad always get their comeuppance in the end. You're better off without him." He tilts his head slightly to the side and smiles softly to me.

He's genuinely kind, this old man. But he's vulnerable too. I shouldn't be so self-centred. "Walter?"

"Yes?"

"Are you hungry?"

"Famished, now that you mention it." Straight back at me. No hesitation.

"Do you want to share my sandwiches?"

"That's kind, but no. I'm sure I'll be able to find somewhere nearby to …" He breaks off as he looks around our remote location.

"Aye, fine, then. If you want to eat grass and wildflowers." I'm grinning.

His return beam acknowledges defeat. "So what's on them?"

"Cheese and pickle."

"What kind of cheese?"

"The kind of cheese that you can either like or lump, you fussy get. Beggars and choosers."

He turns away from me, raises his head haughtily, puts his arm up, and snaps his fingers. "Can I see the manager please? I want to complain about the attitude of this waitress."

I smile despite myself. "Do you want some or not, you cheeky sod?"

"How can I refuse such a gracious offer?" He leans over, helps himself to the proffered half-sandwich, and bites a third of it in one go. Ten seconds later, there's only the final third left. Walter's appetite is voracious.

"Do you want my half too?"

He looks at my outstretched hand. Then at me. "Thanks, but no. You're very kind. You have it."

"Walter, I'm not that hungry. If you've been here overnight, you'll have had no breakfast. And God knows when you last had something yesterday."

"Are you sure?" He's looking at the other half sandwich the way a kid looks at a chocolate bar.

"Honestly."

"Thanks." He pops his last piece in his mouth then takes the second offering.

"Better have some water to wash that down." I nod at his water bottle, nearly three-quarters empty.

"You're right." He takes a swig and then a surprisingly modest nibble of the next sandwich.

There's a lull as he eats. I use the time to rub some sun lotion on my arms and face. When he's finished the sandwich, he drains the last of his water. I offer him some of mine, but he signals no with a hand gesture. We're still sitting alongside each other, against the shelter. Both looking out at the living seascape.

"Walter, *how did you get here?*"

"What do you mean?"

"Do you have a problem understanding English? How did you get here?"

"I walked."

"You walked? From where?"

"The station."

"The station? What station? Ardnahuish is the nearest station. But that's got to be six miles away.

"Aye, Ardnahuish. That's right. And it *was* a hell of a walk. I didn't realize how long it would take, but there were no taxis or buses."

"So you came by train to Ardnahuish and then walked all the way to Dundo Point? Did you not get lost?"

"Obviously not."

"Fair enough. I walked into that. But where did you get the train from in the first place?" He makes as if to answer, then stops. I can see the struggle on his face. He's forgotten. Distraction time! "No! Don't tell me. Let me guess. I'm brilliant at this. Ninety-nine times out of a hundred, I can guess where someone has come from. It's a gift."

He gives me a *you're at it* look. "What are you havering at?"

"No. I'm serious. I'll tell you where you come from. Then you show me your ticket to prove I'm right. You have to show your ticket. Otherwise you could cheat and pretend I got it wrong. You have kept your ticket, haven't you? You'll have got a return?"

He's been focused on what I was saying, but now the confused expression is returning. I've completely messed this up. Tried to distract him and just made it worse.

He's got his arm deep into his backpack. Rummaging. A smile of triumph as he locates whatever it is he's after. He brings out a grubby cloth bag with a drawstring pulled tight. It looks like it's got something the shape of an envelope in it. What in God's name is he up to? He loosens the string and pulls out a battered brown leather wallet. He holds it close to his face as he searches through its contents with his free hand. "Aha!"

"What is it?"

"My ticket. What else? Now then, Miss Second Sight, let's see you do your party piece." He's all smiles, confidence returned, teasing.

"Okay then. Prepare to be amazed." I make a production of touching both temples with my fingers, tilting my head forward, and closing my eyes. It took him at least three hours to walk here from Ardnahuish. Forty-five minutes from Glasgow on the train. Suppose he got here at around eight last night—that means he was in Glasgow around four. If he set out at the start of the day, say nine o' clock, and used trains all the way, he must have travelled hundreds of miles. "It's clear to me that you have come from …" Pause for dramatic effect, then with a flourish of both hands, "London!"

Walter looks at me, joyful eyes under grey brows. Looks to his ticket, then back straight at me. "Oh! *Quite* close Mystic Meg, but no cigar I'm afraid."

"Nonsense! I'm never wrong. Tell the truth!" I grab for the ticket in his hand, but he's too quick for me. As he draws it away, he loses his grip and the ticket falls to the grass. Another burst of wind gusts round the shelter, and the ticket tumbles over and over toward the cliff edge. We both chase it on hands and knees. I get there first. Just. I stand up and wheel away, arm upstretched like a footballer celebrating a goal, the ticket clutched in my hand.

Walter follows me back, smiling. "Well?"

I squint at the ticket. "Cobham. Cob-ham. Is that how you say it? Or is it Cobbam, with the 'H' silent? Or, as I strongly suspect, is it actually pronounced *London*?"

He laughs instinctively. Warm and genuine. "You don't like to be beaten, do you?"

"Not by the likes of you." I'm laughing back. This old guy makes me laugh. "So where exactly in London is this Cob-ham?"

"It is pronounced Cobbam. And it's in Surrey. Not London."

"We'll see about that. Wait." I consult my phone. Scrolling. Reading. "Aha!"

"Aha what?"

"It says here that the fastest time from Cobham station to Waterloo is thirty-four minutes. It's just a suburb of London. I was right!"

"Let me see." I hand him my phone, and he squints at the screen. "Hang on. It says Cobham, Surrey."

"And?"

"Not Cobham, London. Cobham, *Surrey*."

"You're splitting hairs now. We both know fine well it's London. I'm right—yet again."

"Shall we call it a draw?"

"Only if you agree you came from London."

"Well, obviously I must have come *through* London. The train to Glasgow would've left from Euston."

I can see he's concentrating as he says it. He's trying to remember something. He obviously knows the mainline west coast route. Is he trying to remember actually making the journey? There's a danger the fog will come in again. Best be gentle with him. "All right, Walter. We'll call it a draw."

"Good." Happy eyes. Kind. Trusting.

We both make our way back to the bus shelter, neither of us leading nor following, and resume our previous positions. I hand him the bottle of sun lotion, and he applies some to his nose and shins. Communication is by gesture, nods, and facial expression. No words. It really should feel weird. But it's comfortable. I feel at peace with myself for the first time since The Snake showed his true colours at the cafe. But I know this can't last. I can't sit here with this old guy forever. He needs help. It's just that I don't know how to help him. But I have to try. I need to be careful with him. Careful with my words.

"Walter?"

"Yes? What?"

"You know when we were speaking earlier on? You know, before we played the game about you coming from London?"

"Uh-huh."

I'm not sure if he actually does remember. "When we discussed why you were here? How you sometimes get confused?"

"Uh-huh." Quieter this time.

I shuffle round a hundred and eighty degrees on my bum so that I'm beside him and we're looking at each other's faces. "Is it okay if we talk a little bit more about that?"

"If you like." Pensive, but still with me.

"You said that you had to be here. You showed me your tattoo."

"I did." He's eyeing me. Maybe wondering where I'm going with this. I'm not sure myself.

"I'm not sure that I really understand."

"Understand what?"

"You can't remember when you got the tattoo. And you don't really know what it meant, except that you should be here on that date."

"That's right."

"Is there anything else at all you can tell me about it? Don't worry if you can't."

Walter's face screws in concentration. He holds the expression long enough for me to think he's even forgotten my question. "Important. It's important that I'm here."

"Good. That's good, Walter. Can you remember why it's important?"

He leans forward. Places his hand on the back of mine and looks at me with an expression that signals something momentous. "Something good. It's important I'm here because of something *good*." He smiles, pleased with what he's managed to dredge up. As his face relaxes, I know instinctively that there's nothing more to come.

"I can understand that, Walter. I'm pleased you're here for something good." There's no point in pursuing this. He's calm. Content. Looking out at the ocean. I leave him be briefly, enjoying the moment. Try a different tack. "Walter?"

"Yes?"

"You know how you told me you come from Cobham?"

"Aye."

"Do you have a nice house there? Or maybe a flat?"

"A nice house. Lovely big garden. Lots of fruit trees." He's picturing it in his mind's eye. Responding to my prompts rather than to me.

"And does anybody else live with you in your nice big house in Cobham?"

"Molly. She lives there with me." He's reengaged eye contact, focused back on me again.

"And does Molly know that you're here?"

I see bewilderment return in an instant. Shit! He's going to get upset if I don't rescue this. "Tell you what, Walter. How about we give Molly a call on your mobile, just to let her know that you got here safely?"

"Aye. That would be good." He's still adrift in his sea of confusion. I need to throw him a better lifeline.

"Shall I get your phone from your bag?"

"Yes. Yes, please." Relief all over his face. And gratitude.

I hope to God that he's got a phone! I lean over for his bag and plunge my hand in, right to the bottom, and feel it straight away. I produce it with a small flourish and hand it over. "Here you are, Walter. Let's give Molly a ring."

He holds the phone in his left hand and stabs at it with his right index finger, becoming increasingly befuddled and mildly agitated. "Not working."

"Do you want me to take a look?" He hands it to me without hesitation. I take a few seconds to familiarize myself with it and then press the on button. A feeble brief flash of the screen. Battery's flat! "Your battery's out of charge."

"Ah." I hand the phone and his rucksack back. He looks at the phone briefly, then pushes it back into the bag. He looks up to me, smiles and shrugs.

"Walter, would you like to come back to my house?" Pause. Let that sink in. Now explain why. "We can get your phone charged there so you can call Molly." Another pause. I can see he's considering it but isn't sure. "And you can have a nice cup of tea." His grin and nod confirm the deal is clinched.

The walk home is leisurely, filled with easy chit-chat, and we're back at the house in forty minutes. We go around to the back door and enter directly into the kitchen. "Please take a seat at the table, Walter. I'm just going to tell Gran that I'm back."

Gran's asleep in front of the telly, so I pull the living room door closed and return to the kitchen.

"Walter, do you mind if I get your phone from your bag so that I can charge it for you?"

"Please, go ahead."

He seems calm enough, if somewhat slightly subdued. It's probably because he's somewhere unfamiliar. I root through his bag and locate the phone. There's a charger lead plugged into a socket by the kettle. I insert the USB into the phone. It beeps and the red outline of an empty battery shows in the corner of the screen.

"There! It's charging now, Walter. Shall I make us that nice cup of tea we discussed? And then you can give Molly a call."

"Yes, please. Tea would be nice. Do I have to wait long for the phone to charge up?"

"No, not at all. You can use the phone while it's still charging. How do you take your tea?"

"White, please. No sugar."

I make the tea and take his mug to him at the table. "Try that. Is it strong enough? Do you want a splash more milk?"

He sips and winces slightly. It's too hot to drink yet. "That's perfect, thank you."

"Good. Do you want to put it down on that coaster and let it cool for a few minutes? That'll give you a chance to ring Molly." I nod first toward the coaster and then in the direction of his phone.

Walter puts his mug down, rises, and steps over to the work surface where his phone is charging. He picks it up and uses his thumb to activate the fingerprint recognition. So he hasn't forgotten how to use it. Except now he pauses and looks blankly at the screen. He turns to me. "Molly?"

"That's right. You're going to ring Molly."

"Knew it. Just testing." He winks. Smiles. I don't know whether he's kidding or if it's another well-rehearsed coping technique. He presses the screen a few times and then holds the phone to his head, the charging wire pulled taut. A few seconds elapse. "Molly?"

A long pause. I can hear someone talking back to him, but I can't make out anything that's being said.

Eventually, Walter says, "I'm in a kitchen."

A much shorter pause.

"Waiting for my mug of tea to cool down."

Another very short pause.

He turns his head to look at me. "Eilidh's kitchen. She made me the tea."

Another, slightly longer interlude.

Walter's still looking straight at me. "Yes. Yes, she's here right now. Do you want to talk to her?"

She obviously says yes, as Walter beckons me over with a nod of his head. I move toward him and take the phone, careful to avoid dislodging the charging cable. "Molly would like a word with you." Talk about a statement of the obvious!

"Hello, Molly?"

"Haley? Hello."

"Hello. It's actually Eilidh. No H."

"Oh! I'm so sorry, Eilidh." The briefest of pauses. "Obviously, Walter's with you. Is he all right? Is there anything wrong?" English accent. Southern English. Quite posh. But nice. Trying to sound composed, but not doing a great job of it.

"Walter's fine." I look over to see he's sat back down at the table and is gingerly taking another sip of tea. "He's just sitting down at my kitchen table and having a mug of tea."

"And where are you?" Polite, but with real tension. I know she's dying to scream at me: *Who are you? Where are you? What are you doing with Walter?* But she remains controlled. "Are you in Scotland? I'm guessing from your accent."

"Yes. We're in Scotland."

"I knew it! How did he get there?"

"He caught a train. From Cobham to Ardnahuish."

"Where?"

"Ardnahuish. It's about three-quarters of an hour from Glasgow on the train. We're in a village called Kilmadden, about seven miles from there, on the coast."

"Right." Confusion. Hesitation. "It crossed my mind that might be one of the places he could have gone. It's the area he's from originally. But it just seemed so far. He's never gone off like this before. I didn't know what to think."

"Molly, can you excuse me just for a minute?" I lower the phone and turn to Walter. I gesture him toward a cupboard with my eyes. "Walter, if you go into that cupboard, you'll see a round tin with a red and white flower pattern on it. It's got biscuits in it. If you take it to the table, you can help yourself to a biscuit to have with your tea. I'll join you when I've finished talking to Molly. Is that okay?" I watch long enough to confirm he's following my suggestion, then turn away from him and lower my voice. "Sorry, Molly, I was just making sure Walter was all right."

"I heard."

"Look, he's all right. I met him this morning at a remote beauty spot. I soon realized he's got a touch of dementia. He explained that he'd slept rough last night—"

"Oh my God!"

"Don't worry. Like I said, he's fine. Anyway, we tried to ring you on his mobile to let you know where he was, but it was out of charge."

"He never remembers to charge it." Still anxious, but a note that suggests she trusts me.

"That figures. So I suggested he come here, to my house, so we could get it charged and he could call you."

"That's really kind of you. And you're sure he's all right? I've been going out of my mind with worry. I got home from work last night and there was no sign of him. I searched everywhere I could think of. I phoned the police, and he's been reported as missing and vulnerable. I haven't left the house in case he came back. I've been frantic. Thank you so much."

"No need for thanks. He's a lovely old man. My Gran's got dementia. Much worse than Walter, but I remember when she used to be like he is now. That's how I knew what was wrong."

"I didn't really know for sure what was wrong until just six weeks ago, when he was diagnosed. But in the last two weeks, he seems to have got so much worse. The episodes are much more frequent. And they last longer. When he wasn't here last night, my imagination ran riot." Her voice is speeding up. Not cracking but hinting that it might.

"I understand, Molly. It must've been horrible for you, but the important thing is that he's safe."

"Yes. Yes, of course. You're right. Thank you."

"No need for any thanks, honestly. I'm only doing what anyone else would in the circumstances. He's fine here. You really don't need to worry."

"Thank you. You're very kind. And modest." Quite a long pause.

"Hello? Are you still there?"

"Yes, sorry. Yes. I was just checking the time and working out how long it will take me to get up there."

"It's nearly two o' clock now. Are you planning to come up this evening?"

"Yes. I'll need to check on arrangements. My car is in for repairs, and they said it won't be ready until six. I'll need to look into trains or flights."

"Of course. Look, why don't you do that? Then you can call back when you've had a chance to work things out."

"Are you sure? I really feel like I'm imposing Walter on you."

"Honestly, it's fine. I'll text you my number so that you have it as well. You can ring back on that number or on Walter's if you prefer."

"That is so kind of you. Thank you."

"Not at all. I'll text now and wait to hear back from you."

"Okay. Thank you. I'll call back soon. Bye."

"Bye."

16.

I text Molly from my phone so that she has my number, then join Walter at the table. His tea is barely a quarter drunk, and he's doing a poor job of not looking at the biscuit tin.

"Have another biscuit, if you'd like."

"Are you sure?"

"Of course, there's plenty. And if anybody complains, I'll just blame Scott."

"Scott?"

"My wee brother. He's forever nicking biscuits when Mum's not around."

"I see. He's the fall guy." He smiles. "What age is he?"

"Ten." I could ask how old Molly is, but I don't know if he'll remember. "Molly sounds nice."

He looks at me. "She is nice."

"Sometimes you can just tell by someone's voice." He's nodding *go on* at me. "Anyway, she's pleased you're all right. And she says she'll come up to collect you and take you back."

"All right."

"Her car's in the garage for repairs, so she's looking at maybe catching a train or a plane. She says she'll ring back to let us know once she's made the arrangements."

"That's good."

He's responding but not engaging. Maybe he's tired. God knows what time he was awake this morning, and how much sleep he got last night. "Walter, would you like a wee rest?"

"Can I finish my biscuit and my tea?"

"Of course you can." I can't put him in the living room with Gran. No telling what might happen. "Shall we take our tea and biscuits out into the garden? It seems a shame to be inside on such a lovely day." I get up and make toward the door. Walter follows me, then pauses. He's looking at the biscuit tin. "Let's sit out at the patio table. I'll fetch the biscuits out with us." I smile and get a wink in return.

We sit under the umbrella. Walter helps himself to another biscuit, after a silent check that it's okay. I watch him eat. Slow, small bites followed by mouthfuls of tea. There's no conversation at all. I realize that's not a problem for him. I'm used to it with Gran. I notice again that he has proper five o' clock shadow. It looks quite cool on young guys, but Walter just looks like what he is: an old guy who has spent the night outside. There were fresh clothes in his bag, but he's probably been wearing what he's in now since yesterday morning. Aside from the stubble, he's pretty well turned out. He, or maybe Molly, makes an effort with his appearance. There's something about him, beyond the vulnerability. Beyond his ability to make me laugh when his mind is all there. More than just the kindness and compassion. But I can't think of the word. Walter puts his mug on the table. His eyes are heavy lidded. I watch for a couple of minutes as he succumbs to sleep. It's funny and endearing at the same time.

The shaking of my shoulder is persistent. I open my eyes and squint to adjust to the light. George's features come into focus. He turns his head and nods in Walter's direction. Head back, mouth open, snoring softly. "Who the hell is this?"

George's whisper-hiss snaps me back to the here and now. I gesture to him with a nod of my head, and he follows me as I rise and make my way back indoors. He pulls the door closed behind him. Scott is in the kitchen too. He's relishing the coming exchange between George and me.

"I said who the hell is that?" He tilts his head toward the garden.

"His name is Walter. He has dementia and he's lost."

I can tell George is ambivalent. "And?" Processing. "So what's he doing here?"

"I met him this morning. At Dundo Point. He's vulnerable, George. He needs help."

"And that falls to you why?"

"Don't be such an arse, George. If it was Gran, you'd want whoever found her to look after her."

George's face softens, although he finds time to glance a dagger at Scott, who's sniggering because I said *arse*. "I suppose you're right. It's just that smart Alec here—" he nods at Scott "—woke me up to say you were in the garden with a strange man."

"For Christ's sake, Scott. You didn't have to wake George. Why didn't you just wake me and ask what was going on?"

"Might've woken the old guy at the same time. Could be a murderer or a child molester for all I knew." There's defiance all over the little toe rag's face.

"Well, he's not a murderer or a child molester, you horrible little turd. He's an old man who needs a bit of help. So why don't you piss off up to your room and leave me to sort it?"

"I'm going to tell Mum that you told me to piss off." Scott pisses off upstairs.

George walks back over to the kitchen door and looks at Walter through the window. "So what's the story with the old guy?"

I rattle off what's happened. George listens attentively, nodding occasionally. When I get to the bit about calling Molly, I have that awful moment of realization. "Shit!"

"What is it?"

"Molly! She was going to ring me back. I reach and pull out my phone. It's quarter to four. Phone on silent. Two missed calls from the same number. I go across to Walter's phone. I press on. It doesn't recognize my finger print, but the screen flashes to life briefly. Sufficient for me to see three missed calls from Molly. "Shit, shit, shit!"

"I take it you missed her call?"

"Brilliant, Sherlock. You're wasted in that crap job." I regret saying it immediately, as I see George's face fall. "Sorry. Just stressed. Didn't mean that." I hit reply to Molly's last call. It rings for barely a fraction of a second.

"Eilidh?"

"Yes, Molly. I'm so sorry I missed your calls."

"Is something wrong? Is Walter all right?" Almost panic in her voice.

"Walter's fine. Absolutely fine. He's just dozing in a chair out on the patio. I'm so sorry, Molly. Walter and I went outside for a seat in the fresh air, and we both fell asleep."

There's a pause long enough for me to think about checking she's still there. "Is he still sleeping just now?" she finally asks.

I look out the window. "Yes. I'm looking right at him. Sleeping like a baby. I'm really sorry."

"No, don't apologize." Much calmer now. Controlled. "Eilidh, I'm not sure how to ask this."

"Go on. What is it?"

"You've already been so kind. But I wonder if I can ask you another favour." The calm didn't last long. Anxiety is back in her voice.

"Of course. Anything. Just ask away."

"I can get my car back at six. Google says that I can drive to Kilmadden in seven hours and three minutes. That will be just after one tomorrow morning. If I catch the next train, I can get to Ardnahuish at quarter past midnight. There are no seats left on flights to Glasgow tonight. The best I can do is fly to Edinburgh and hire a car. That flight lands at quarter past eleven. By the time I get the car and drive through it will be after one." The more she speaks, the faster the words gush. The poor thing is stressed beyond belief.

"It's okay. Don't worry."

"I was just wondering if there's anywhere local to you that Walter could stay. A hotel or something?" She waits. I spend too long thinking about it. "Of course, I'll pay."

"No, it's not that. I'm just struggling to think of anywhere. The local pub, The Tassie, has a couple of rooms. But it's really not suitable."

"Eilidh." George steps into my line of vision.

"Excuse me just a minute, Molly." I glare at him. "What?"

"The old guy can stay in my room."

"Eh?"

"Archie's bed is made up. And I'll be out at work. If the old boy needs a bed for the night, he can sleep here."

"What will Mum say?" I screw my face into an are you sure look.

"It's my room. She'll be fine with it."

"It's Archie's bed, not yours."

"He's not exactly using it, is he?" He's looking at me like I'm a daftie. I swear, if he says *duh*, I'll slap him.

"Is something wrong?"

"Oh sorry, Molly. I was just talking to my brother. He's saying that Walter can stay in his room overnight."

"Oh." Hesitation. "That's really kind of him. But I couldn't possibly ask that. I've put you out enough already."

She's ambivalent. I can hear the worry. The desperation. The hope. "Look, honestly, Molly, it's no big deal. I've got older twin brothers. One's away travelling, and the other works night shift. They share a room that's empty tonight. There's a fresh bed made up. Walter can sleep there. He'll have a room to himself."

Still hesitant. "Are you sure it's not too much trouble? I thought I overheard you wondering if it would be okay with your mother."

Shit. Should've muted when I was speaking to George. "Look, honestly. It's really no bother at all."

"I just feel I'm asking too much."

She's wavering. "Really, Molly. It's fine. I told you my Gran's got dementia. We're only doing what we'd hope somebody would do for her."

"Are you sure?"

"Definitely. Look, you've already said there's no way you could get here until the early hours tomorrow. This way, you can get a good night's sleep, set off in the morning, and get up here tomorrow afternoon."

"I'd probably set off really early." Good. She's accepted it!

"Whatever works best for you. I can text you our address and postcode for your satnav."

"This is unbelievably kind of you, Eilidh. You've no idea how grateful I am. I simply can't thank you and your family enough. I look forward to meeting you tomorrow. Thank you." Her voice is in danger of cracking.

"No problem. Walter will be absolutely fine. See you tomorrow."

I finish the call and signal George to shush as I text the promised details. "I take it you heard all of that?"

"Yup." He nods toward the garden. "Are you going to introduce me?"

I glance outside. Walter is on his feet. Looking around. "Shit! Follow me and ask that again, but use my name." I look at George meaningfully. He gets it. He follows me out.

"Eilidh, are you going to introduce me?"

Walter turns. Looks at George. Then at me.

"Walter, this is George. My brother." Pause. Walter smiles. Good. "George, this is my friend Walter. Molly is coming up from Cobham to take Walter home. But her car is in for repairs, and she can't get here until tomorrow. So Walter is staying with us tonight." Walter's eyes are bright. He's all there. And he's bought my story.

George steps forward and offers his hand. "Very pleased to meet you, Walter."

"Likewise, George." He's embracing the handshake heartily.

"It's only an hour until Mum will be back from work. I'd best get on and make something for tonight's tea. Are you two okay sitting out here while I knock something up?"

"Aye, no bother." George turns to Walter. "Eilidh tells me you used to be a bit of a footballer." He guides them back to sit at the patio table, and I return inside. I go upstairs and tell Scott he'll need to sit with Gran 'til tea time because George is looking after Walter. He's not best pleased, particularly when I tell him he's got to talk to her and to leave his PlayStation upstairs.

Back to the kitchen, where I stick on a big pot of new potatoes. Ayrshires. Once they're done, I'll leave them to cool. Nothing nicer than just-warm Ayrshires. I rattle up some salad. Two big bowls full. Plenty for six. Nothing fancy—lettuce, cucumber, radish, cybies, and tomatoes. Clingfilm over the bowls. There's a couple of bottles of dressing in the fridge. I'll put them out later, along with cold meat and cheese. There's a fresh loaf as well. I'll set the table for six, and everyone can help themselves to whatever they fancy.

Just as I go to put the chopping knife in the dishwasher, there's this pain. Inside my head. Sudden. Fierce. Bad enough for me to drop the knife. The point pierces the skin just above my left ankle. Ow! I drop to one knee. My head's woozy. Blood is trickling down to my ankle. I stand up to get a cloth, but I'm still dizzy. I hold the edge of the worktop for balance. My head's still sore, but it's less sharp—more of a dull thumping. I head to the downstairs loo for toilet paper to wipe the blood and then apply an Elastoplast. I take two paracetamol for the pain.

I head back to the kitchen, pick up the knife, and put it in the dishwasher. Then I pour a big glass of water and sit at the table. I'm starting to feel better, slowly. I get back up and look outside. George and Walter are blethering away to each other. I start to set the table. Mats. Cutlery. Condiments. Plates. Best get the big jug and fill it from the tap.

"Who's that George is talking to?"

"Jesus, Mum! Where did you come from?"

"I came in quietly. Didn't want to disturb George and that old man he's with." Her head tilts, and her quizzical expression morphs into concern. "Are you all right, Eilidh?"

"Bit of a headache. I've taken some paracetamol. It's starting to ease."

"You're gey peely-wally looking. Sit down and I'll finish setting the table. And how have you cut your leg?"

I explain to Mum what happened, playing it down to avoid alarming her. Once she's reassured on that score, she asks again about Walter. As I explain, it becomes more like an interrogation. Then she stops and looks at me. "Are you all right?" I nod gently, so as not to hurt my head. "You did the right thing, Eilidh. Bringing him here, I mean. That was the right thing to do. And this Molly person, did she say when she'd be here tomorrow?"

"We never agreed a time. She said she'd probably set off really early. Said it's about a seven-hour drive. Although it might be longer if it takes in rush hour. I'd guess at early to mid- afternoon."

"I see. And how does Walter feel about all this?"

"I explained the arrangements to George for Walter's benefit. He seemed to take it on board. I was hoping he'd believe that he'd agreed to it before and had forgotten. I think it's worked."

"Okay." Mum's nod confirms she'll support the conspiracy. She understands. "I'll put the last of the stuff on the table. You go and round everyone up."

The meal passes off fine. Gran seems a wee bit wary of Walter, but she doesn't say anything and eats well. Walter is in fine form and is happy bantering with George and Scott, the latter loving the attention. Mum shoots me a quizzical look that I know means she's questioning whether he's actually got dementia. Later, she catches my eye after Walter repeats something he'd said not long before.

After we've eaten, we all take cups of tea into the living room and park in front of the TV. It's cramped. Even Scott is with us. Conversation flows easily between Mum, George, Walter, and Scott. I realize I'm not saying much. But my head still aches. And I feel knackered.

"Eilidh, love, are you needing an early night?" Mum's slightly raised voice makes me realize I've nodded off. Scott is smirking at me. Little sod.

"No. I'm fine."

"You don't look fine. And you can hardly keep your eyes open." She turns to Walter. "Eilidh had a very nasty bang to the head the other day."

"Oh dear." Walter looks concerned for me. I think he's probably forgotten I told him about it earlier.

"You know how it is, Walter." Mum's got her *I know you're meant to be an adult* voice on. "Sometimes they just won't acknowledge what's best for them." Looking back pointedly at me now. "I'm not *telling* you to go to bed, but I think you'd be better off there. George will show Walter to his bedroom before he goes out to work." She looks to the pair of them, and they both nod their support.

I know she's right, so I'm not going to argue. Not even to make a point. "Okay." I say my goodnights, give Gran a kiss, then make my way upstairs and close the bedroom door behind me. My head is still thumping. I'll have a quick lie down on the bed before I brush my teeth and get changed.

September 2, 1993

17.

"I'm worried about Mikey. It's been a week now."

Donny's a straight-talking guy, and his face betrays frustration at his suspicion that I'm not saying what's really on my mind. His brow is furrowed, and the little scar over his left eye is reddening up the way it always does when he's pissed off. "Get to the point, Walt."

"The kid loves the game. He's more talented than anyone else we've ever coached. He's thirteen years old, but he's playing for the under-sixteen team."

"We know all this already. For Chrissake, make your point."

"I spoke to some of the other kids. The ones Mikey is most friendly with. Like Marty and Jesus and Jo-Jo."

"And?"

"The usual. Shoulders shrugged. 'How should I know?' 'Why doncha ask him yourself?'"

"And you expected something different?"

"No. But there was just something about their attitude. It's like they've written him off. Like they know he's not coming back."

"So he's not coming back. So what?"

"Come on, Donny. He's a good kid. A kid with a talent. He's got a real chance to make it in the game."

"Walt, I get that you think the kid is an outstanding talent. And I know that you like him. Me too. We all do. But we're not his keepers. We can't force him to come to training. Sometimes we gotta accept that's just the way it is."

The conversation is going nowhere. "Guess so." I shrug.

Donny's eyes narrow. He's suspicious. "You're not going to do anything stupid?"

"No. Now come on. Let's check the boys have tidied and locked everything away. Then we can get home."

We're done in ten minutes and head for the front entrance. "Shit!"

Donny looks at me. "What?"

"Left my wallet in the office." I pull a dumb schmuck face. "I need to go back and get it."

"Do you want me to wait?"

"No need, man. You get home to that family of yours. I'll catch you in the morning."

"Okay. See ya, then."

We fist bump goodbye like we always do, and Donny heads off.

I head back to the office and go straight toward the filing cabinet to pull Mikey's file. I know he lives in one of the projects, just not which one. The address is right at the top of the first insert—Southside. Wow! That's gonna take me forty-five minutes in traffic at this time of day. Mikey travels by bus. It must take him an hour and a half at least each way to get to the stadium. I copy the address onto a piece of paper and leave the office.

I'm last man out of the building, so I lock the door as I leave and head to the lot. This is one of those rare occasions I'm glad I drive a beat-up old Pontiac. I don't really want to be seen driving around the Southside in a fancy car.

I've miscalculated, and it takes me nearly an hour to get to the Southside. The radio is up full, but it's not that loud and struggles to compete with the traffic noise. I've got the windows wound down because of the heat, and when I'm stopped at lights, the fumes make me cough. The transmission is real clunky at low speeds, and the whole journey just seems like a bad idea now. Especially as I'm cruising the area where I thought Mikey's home was and can't find the street. There seems to be a different gang of kids on every other corner. I deliberately accelerate whenever I approach one. There's no point drawing unwanted attention.

I'm on the point of giving up when I find the place. The street's deserted. I park right outside the house and get out the car. Thank God it's so quiet. The door is blue but probably hasn't seen fresh paint in ten or twenty years. I rap it with my knuckle three times and trigger frantic dog yapping from inside. I hear a female voice hushing the mutt. The door opens just enough for me to be face to face with a woman of about five-eight. She looks straight up at me with tired, suspicious eyes that dominate a pretty face. I wait in vain for her to say something.

"Hello. I'm sorry to bother you. I'm Walt Buchanan, Mikey's soccer coach. I was just wondering if I could have a quick word with Mikey."

The door opens slightly more. She looks me up and down quickly, sizing me up. And I do the same automatically. Mid-late twenties. Slim going on skinny. Pink dress, frayed at the collar. Bare feet.

"Mikey ain't in."

"Oh, I see. Could I leave a message for him? Or maybe speak to his mom or his dad?"

"I *am* his mom!" There's real fire in her eyes. She steps forward and looks quickly in both directions along the street. "Step inside now!" She commands before closing the door behind us. I think I'm as confused as she seems angry. "You got any idea how crazy this is? You comin' here? A white man?"

"I'm sorry. I didn't realize." Of course I did, but I just didn't think it would be *this* big a deal. "I only wanted a quick talk with Mikey. To understand why he hasn't come to training this last week."

Her face softens. "Go in there." She nods toward a door. I go through. She follows. Two girls, maybe nine and eleven, are playing on the floor. A baby starts crying upstairs. "Ella, May, go to the kitchen and warm a bottle for Edward, then take it up and give it to him. Be careful not to let Rex get out the kitchen when you go in there. Don't want him biting Mr. Buchanan." The girls are gone in a flash, without even looking at me.

"Mrs. Wilson, you clearly have your hands full here. I'm sorry for barging in unannounced. I'd best be on my way and let you be."

She's having none of it and fixes me with her eyes. "Tell me about Michael. About how good he is at soccer."

I can see now that she's older than I first thought, although not much—maybe early thirties. And there's a strength to her—a fierce determination. I recognize the same determination that helps Mikey stand out on the soccer pitch.

"Mrs. Wilson, lots of parents ask me about how good their sons are. And while I try to be diplomatic, I'm always honest with them. Sometimes that means I have to tell them things they don't like to hear." I pause to asses her reaction.

"Get to it, Mr. Buchanan."

"I'm forty-three years old, Mrs. Wilson. I've been kicking a ball around for as long as I can remember. I played soccer for over thirty years, first as a child and then as a professional. I've been coaching kids for almost eight years." I pause. Her eyes are eager and fierce. "Mikey has a real talent for soccer. He has the potential to do really well in the game. He's the most exciting prospect that I've ever coached."

Her eyes filled as I spoke, but they're still boring into mine. Her lips are pursed, and she inhales deeply, powerfully through flared nostrils. "You really mean that?"

"Yes. I really mean that."

The façade cracks as she releases a mighty sigh and seems to shrink before my eyes. "I don't know what to do."

"Do you know why he's stopped coming to training?"

She gestures for me to sit on the worn sofa, then places herself beside me. There's sufficient of a gap for us to look at each other without invasion of personal space. "Just this last week, he's changed. Stopped goin' to his soccer. Started goin' out and not sayin' where he's goin'. Not talkin' nice to his sisters or me. And last Sunday he—" she breaks off, and I can see she's steeling herself "—he says he's not comin' with us to visit Thomas. Says no way he's wastin' time to go see that spastic." A tear rolls down her cheek as she chokes on the last word. She can see my confusion and manages to compose herself. "Thomas is his brother. Seven years old. There was problems with his birth. He got brain damage. Bad. He lives in a special hospital. Every Sunday, I take the other four to visit him. Every Sunday. 'Cept last Sunday."

She's maintaining remarkable self-control, although I can see it's a monumental effort for her. "Has Mikey started to see any new friends?"

She looks at me with disdain. "He's not goin' tell me, is he? What do you think?"

"Sorry. Stupid question."

"It's okay. It's obvious. Been waitin' for it and dreadin' it at the same time. You know Michael. Big—near as big as you, Mr. Buchanan. And strong. Looks like a man. Always a risk the gangs would want him. This whole project runs on crack. Gangs always lookin' to recruit. That's why I was so keen for him to keep doin' his soccer."

"And the change really was this sudden? No warning?"

She pauses, her face a picture of concentration. "Three, maybe four weeks ago. I was giving him his allowance for fares to his soccer. He says to me that it's crazy me havin' to give him money like he's a kid. Didn't think any more about it then. But he's that age now. Thinks that he's a man. Needs to act like a man. Even though he's just a boy." She puts her hand on top of mine and tilts her head for emphasis. "He's a good boy, Mr. Buchanan. A good, good boy."

"I know that, Mrs. Wilson. If I didn't believe that, I wouldn't be here."

"My momma's upstairs. Can't get outta bed, 'cept to go to the toilet. But 'cause she's here, I can go out to work. Nights. Six nights a week. Just about pays the bills. Buys food. Pays for some extras. Like Michael's fares to soccer. He can see it all. He knows that he can make more money in a week with a crack gang than I bring home in a month. Always knew they'd come for him. Worried for him. And now it's happened. And my girls, Mr. Buchanan. They're just twelve and ten. But they're pretty. I already see men lookin'. I do my honest-to-God best. I really do. But I'm fearful. There comes a age when you can't protect your babies anymore."

My heart goes out to her combination of dignity and vulnerability. I put my other hand on top of hers so that I'm clasping it. "Mrs. Wilson, please tell Mikey to get in touch with me. Tell him that I'll keep coming here unless he gets in touch with me."

"I'll tell him."

I know she means it, and she knows I mean it too. "Thank you. And now I really had best be going."

I get up, and she leads me to the front door, opens it, and checks outside. "All clear. Thank you for calling. Now you best be goin' while you can."

18.

I GET INTO the car and turn the engine on. UB40's "Can't Help Falling in Love" reggaes from the radio. I accelerate off, driving on autopilot, my mind full of rage at the injustice. I turn right at the junction, toward the city centre. After two blocks, I see a bunch of kids on another corner. Mikey is one of them.

I slam the brakes, which shriek in protest, catching the gang's attention. There are eight of them, or maybe nine, including Mikey. Three are girls and the rest boys—or men, pretend men. I switch off the engine, pull the keys from the ignition, and get out the car toward them. They spread into a fan, and three of them step toward me. Mikey stays back with the girls and two other males.

"Mikey! Mikey, I want to have a word with you." I'm half-shouting as I stride in his direction. He's looking at me. His face is motionless, but his eyes are aghast. "Mikey. I'd like a word. Please." My voice is deliberately still loud, but quieter as I get closer, slaloming between two of the boys who stepped forward.

"Hey, Mikey, this dude wants you." I'm three paces from Mikey when I stop and look back over my shoulder. The kid who's spoken is about eighteen. He's nearly my height, scar on his forehead, with arms as much ink as skin. He's looking right at me now. "So whatcha want with my boy Mikey?"

"I just want to speak to him."

"Speak to him 'bout what?"

"Look, I don't want any trouble. I'd just like to talk to him."

I half-turn as he steps toward me. "Nobody said nothin' 'bout any trouble. Just wanna know what you want with Mikey." His manner is much more menacing than his words.

"I'm Mikey's soccer coach." I look toward Mikey, who immediately looks to the ground. "He's missed a few training sessions, and I just wanted to ask him why."

"Soccer coach?" He's circling me, sneering. "Soccer. Game for girls and spics. And faggots. Is that what you want with Mikey? Are you a faggot? You into boys? With your funny sounding voice and coaching a girl's sport? You're just a faggot, man."

"Leave him, Tyler." Mikey has found his voice and stepped forward. "He just sounds funny 'cause he's British. He ain't no faggot. He's okay."

"British?" Directed at me.

"Scottish, to be precise."

"Scottish? Wow! Why didn't you say? Dude, I love Scotsmen. You an Immortal?'

"What?" I have no idea what this Tyler is talking about. I look into his eyes. I'm convinced he's on something.

"An Immortal. Like *Highlander*, dude. Are you a MacLeod?"

He's talking about that TV series that Donny keeps harping on about. "No. No, I'm not a Macleod. My name is Buchanan."

"Bew-can-ann. Bew-can-ann? And tell me, are the Bew-can-anns friend or foe to the Macleods?" He's absolutely hyper. Definitely on something. There's a rasp to his voice and spittle in the corners of his lips. He's stopped moving and positioned himself between Mikey and me, glaring his challenge. "Friend or foe? FRIEND OR FOE?"

"Tyler, please leave him. Let him go." Mikey steps forward and places his fingers on Tyler's shoulder. Tyler spins round wildly, throwing Mikey backward, and I step forward to intervene. The gun appears from nowhere. The flash, the bang, the gunpowder smell, the pain, and the powerful blow that knocks me back all happen in the same bewildering instant. Then everything goes into slow motion.

I'm falling, but slowly, like I'm drifting down underwater. I'm deaf. I see the look of horror on Mikey's face. I see the gun in Tyler's hand and the madness in his eyes. I see other faces yelling, screaming—but all like a slow-mo movie. My head hits the sidewalk with a bump and bounces. I see a red whorl on my white T-shirt. On my left breast, like the poppies I used to wear as a wee boy back in Scotland. Then everything goes dark.

September 3, 1993; 12:40 a.m.

19.

EVERYTHING HURTS. EVERY breath spikes me in the chest. I try opening my eyes, and the brilliant white light stabs my pupils. My head is just a constant, thrumming drumbeat of ache, ache, ache.

"Dubya? Walt, are you awake?"

I try to respond to Donny's voice, but my tongue is too big in my mouth, and my lips are zippered together.

"Nurse! I think he's waking up."

There are other voices, indistinct noises that I'm struggling to recognize. I feel fingers butterfly kissing my shoulder. There's a clear, calm, reassuring female voice in my ear. "Walt, my name is Doctor Walshaw. You're in County General. And you're recovering really well after an operation. I'm sure that you'll be feeling pain or discomfort. Don't worry. That's normal after what you've been through. And we can give you something to help. Now, I have my hand shading your eyes. If you want to open one or both, I'll shade you until your eyes adjust. It's very bright in here."

I open both eyes again and screw them up instinctively. There's shadow just like she said. I can see it's her left hand, black, wearing a wedding ring. I try to say thank you but my mouth is still not working.

"Well done, Walt. Just take your time to adjust to the light. Don't try to speak yet. We'll get you a glass of water and a straw. That will help the dryness in your mouth and make it easier to speak." There's a brief pause. "Mr. and Mrs. Handleson—" she hesitates before identifying them less formally "—Donny and Martha are here." Another pause. "Now the water is here. Am I okay to move my hand away from shading your eyes? Blink twice for yes."

I blink twice then screw my eyes up again as the brightness turns up and I try to focus. A bespectacled black face is smiling at me. She seems much younger that I expected. Maybe this isn't Doctor Walshaw. "Well done, Walt. Now, are you ready for some water? Two blinks again for yes."

The voice confirms that she is Doctor Walshaw, and I blink twice. She manoeuvres a straw carefully between my lips, and I suck greedily. The water is tepid, but still welcome. "Easy! Small sips. Nice and slow. Roll the water around inside your mouth slowly. *Then* swallow." I do exactly as she says. It feels almost like she's hypnotized me.

I push the straw back with my tongue, and she moves the glass away "Thank you."

"You're very welcome. Are you feeling well enough to answer a couple of questions?"

"Sure."

"Do you know where you are?"

"County General." I try to crack a smile, but my lips hurt too much.

"That's right. Good. Do you know why you're here?"

"I got shot. You operated."

"Yes. Right again. Looks like your memory is fine. Now listen, Walt. Your friends are here. Been here for hours. So I'll let you talk with them. But just for a short time. The police also want to talk to you. They asked to be informed when you became conscious. I'll tell them you're awake but not strong enough yet to be interviewed. I'll suggest they come to see you tomorrow."

"Thank you."

"You're welcome. Nurse Jackson will be along shortly with some meds that should help you feel more comfortable. I'll check back in on you tomorrow morning." Doctor Walshaw turns away toward Donny and Martha. "Okay, folks. He's doing fine, and I'm confident that he'll make a full recovery. But he's very tired and weak from the operation. Ten minutes maximum. Understood?" She turns back to me, smiles, and is gone.

"Would you like some more water?" Donny's leaning forward with an anxious expression.

"Uh-huh."

He brings the glass alongside my cheek and guides the straw to the side of my mouth. I sip nice and slowly, rolling the water around just like the doctor ordered before pushing the straw away with my tongue.

"Is that better?"

"Yes. Thanks."

"Christ, Dubya. You had us worried. Scared the shit outta me. We got the call. Said you were shot in the chest. In County General here. We came right away. They said it was serious. Wouldn't know anything until the operation was done."

Martha leans forward and puts her hand on his shoulder to quiet him. As always, her blond hair and subtle makeup are immaculate, and also as always, she's the voice of reason and calm in their partnership. "Walt, we're so relieved it's all gone well. You just need to take it easy now and do what the doctors say. This is the best place for you in the city, and you've got good insurance. So you just need to stay here and do as they say until you're better. Donny can cover the coaching drills and take the team on Saturday. You should only focus on getting yourself better. We're here for you. Anything you need, you just say." Her voice is soft, sincere, and reassuring as she smiles down at me. Then she turns to Donny and glare-dares him not to say anything to upset me.

He can't help himself. "What were you doing on the Southside, for Chrissake? Did you go there looking for Mikey?"

"I just wanted to ask him why he'd stopped coming to training."

"And you thought going to find him on the Southside was a good idea? Alone? How long you lived in this city? Asshole!" He stops as Martha's hand again presses down on his shoulder.

"You know how much I like to get shot."

He smiles despite his outrage. "Asshole."

"Jealous."

"I'm not the attention seeker."

"Touché!"

So far, we've been whispering to each other, the way folks in hospitals do. But now Donny leans in and drops his voice even further. "Did you see Mikey?"

"No. Couldn't even find the address."

"So Mikey had nothing to do with this?"

"I just said, didn't I?"

He believes me, and I can see he's pleased. It's what he wanted to hear, so he doesn't push it any further. The police will be more probing.

They'll want to know why I got out of the car. I need to think of a credible reason. But that can wait 'til morning.

"Donny, you can see he's exhausted." Martha leans in and gives me a feather duster kiss to the temple. "Take care, you. We'll be back in the morning." Her whisper tickles my ear.

Donny touches the back of my hand. "Yes, we'll see you in the morning. You take care, buddy."

I smile my gratitude and mouth goodbye at them as they disappear from view.

July 17, 2000

20.

THE VOICE IS gentle, fuzzy, but persistent. Intrusive. It banishes the distinct and familiar sense I have of being chased. I sense that whatever it is, it seemed closer to catching me than before. My head feels woolly, and I can taste vinegar. Voice slightly louder, clearer, more urgent.

"I said, can you hear me, young lady?"

"I can hear you." I start to open my eyes and have to raise my hand to shield them from the fluorescent light. As my vision adjusts, a black woman materializes. Middle aged. Wearing scrubs?

"Good. Good. Now, how are you feeling?" American accent. Compassionate.

"My head feels a bit woolly."

"No surprise. Do you feel well enough to sit up? I'd like you to drink some water, and you can't do that lying on your back."

"I think so." I sit up slowly. That's difficult because my legs are still flat on the trolley I've been lying on. "Where am I?"

"In the First Aid Station." She reads the bewilderment on my face. "Security guards brought you in. They found you passed out on a bench in the far corner of the mall. You were lucky. Hardly anyone goes to that part since the Edison Brothers store closed. You're the third person brought in this afternoon. A/C in the mall is busted. It's reading ninety-five in there. That's why we need to get some water into you." She hands me a small paper cone full of water. "Now drink this while I fill up a big glass for you from the cooler."

"Thank you."

"You're welcome. Now, can I ask your name?"

"Eilidh. My name is Eilidh."

"Eilidh. How do you do? I'm Margaret. That's an unusual name you have. And so is that accent. You're not from around here, are you?"

I hesitate. Partly because I don't know where around here is. And partly because my mind is racing nineteen to the dozen. It's like all of my senses are supercharged. I *know* I'm in another not-dream, like the one in Ethiopia. I just *know* it. The fading fuzziness in my head, the disappearing taste of vinegar in my mouth. Like before.

"Are you okay?" A pause as she looks at me meaningfully and gets a nod. "I said, you're not from around here, are you?"

"Sorry. No, I'm not. I'm Scottish. And so is my name."

She takes a half-step back, like she wants to take in everything about me. She's sporting a huge grin. Positively beaming. "Scottish! You must be here for Walt's thing!"

I'm baffled. "Waltzing? I'm sorry. You've lost me."

"Walt! Walt Buchanan. You must be here for him, right?"

Maybe it's the look of expectation. Or maybe it's because I recognize the name. Whichever, I find myself agreeing. "Yes, that's right."

"Wonderful. Wonderful. My oldest boy's a junior at the club. Loves that man. Everyone loves that man. You've come all the way from Scotland? Wow. Are you the surprise guest? Are you his niece, or something?"

What on Earth do I say? "I can't possibly answer that." I try a smile and she returns a conspiratorial wink. "And I only just got here today."

"That probably helps explain why you passed out. All that travelling and then exposed to this heat." She pauses, quizzical again. "Do you mind if I ask you something, Eilidh?"

Oh God! What now? "Of course not. Ask away."

"Did you have some kind of trouble? Did something happen to you?"

"Sorry. I don't know what you mean."

"Well, you've got that Band-Aid on your ankle with the blood all showing through. And your jeans are so badly ripped at the knees. What happened?"

"My jeans? Oh, that's just the fashion. Back home." There's scepticism all over her face. "And my ankle is where I dropped a knife and cut myself."

"Hmm. If you say so. Do you mind if I clean up that ankle for you?"

"Not at all. That's very kind of you. Do you want me to take the old Elastoplast off?"

"Say what?"

"I asked if you want me to take the old Elastoplast off."

"Your accent *is sooo* cute! Ee-last-oh-plast! I guess that's what you call a Band-Aid. Don't you fuss, sweetie. I'll get it." Margaret pulls the plaster off in one swift movement and peers at the wound. "Hmm. Not dried out. When did you say this happened?"

Not only don't I know where I am, I don't know *when* I am. "Just yesterday."

"Figures. Now don't you worry. I'm going to fix you up real good."

"You really are very kind."

She goes to a cupboard and returns with a small white tray bearing a tube of ointment, a box marked *Band-Aid*, cotton wool balls, a crepe bandage wrapped in a paper cuff, a foil marked *Wet Wipe*, and a couple of small brass safety pins. She pulls a stool over and sits beside my feet. "Now, this will not hurt one bit." She opens the wet wipe and starts to clean off the glue residue left from the plaster. It feels cold and delicious.

"That feels nice. Thank you."

"You're welcome. Now, you keep drinking your water. I'll have you fixed in no time." She finishes cleaning the area and then squirts a tiny dollop of colourless ointment from the tube onto the wound. She uses a cotton wool ball to spread the lotion, then takes a plaster from the box and places it on top. She reaches for the crepe bandage.

"Oh, that's fine, thank you. I don't think I'll need an actual bandage."

Margaret coughs theatrically. "Excuse me!" She points ostentatiously to the word *Nurse* sewn into her right breast pocket. "Now, who's the medical professional around here? And who's the patient?"

"Sorry, Margaret."

She makes quick work of strapping the ankle and uses the two pins to fix the end. "There!"

"It looks really neat and tidy. So much better. Thank you." She beams at the compliment but says nothing. I swing round so I'm sitting side-on on the trolley with my legs dangling. I slide off slowly and stand.

"Easy does it, Eilidh. How's your head? Do you feel dizzy, faint, or nauseous?"

I shake my head gently. "No. Not a bit."

"Good. That's real good. And your ankle feels okay?"

"Much better, thank you. The bandage feels really good, and it certainly looks a whole lot better."

Another beam of pride. "I'm glad. Now, Eilidh, there's something I'm going to have to insist on. No relative of Walt Buchanan is leaving my care until I'm sure they're ready. You have to drink the whole of that glass of water right now. I can't have you passing out again." She makes big eyes at me and smiles. She's lovely.

"Okay." I return her smile and drink the rest of the glass. I want to please her.

"Good girl."

I have to make sense of what's going on. To understand. "Margaret, are you going to Walt's thing too?"

Her face falls. "I can't, sweetie." She holds her arms out to her sides and gestures round the room with her eyes. "I've gotta work here 'til six." Then the smile returns. "But I'll be at the afterparty." She pauses, like a cartoon character having a lightbulb moment. There's concern on her face, and she looks at the watch pinned on her chest. "Eilidh! It's ten to four!"

I can tell she's surprised that I don't seem to comprehend the importance of the time. "I don't have my watch with me." I can't tell her I don't have a watch. That I use my phone. I can't say I don't have my phone with me—they might not have mobiles here. Now.

I can tell from her eyes that she's dubious. "Okay. You can probably still just about make it."

I freeze. Don't know what to say. I don't know what it is. Nor where I am. How am I meant to respond?

Margaret steps forward in front me. She takes my hands in hers and looks directly into my eyes, concerned. "Eilidh, sweetie. Are you sure you're all right?" My confusion must be evident on my face, but I don't say anything. "You don't know what the time is. You don't know where you're meant to be. I'm not sure you're okay yet. I think I maybe need to check you over more thoroughly."

I don't understand everything that's going on. But with sudden absolute clarity, I *know* that I need to be at Walt's thing. Whatever it is. "I need to be at Walt's thing." I'm slightly surprised by the firmness of my own voice.

"That's right."

"Margaret." I look hard into her face. "I'm fine. Honestly. I know where I need to be. I'm just confused about how to get there from here."

"Of course." She believes me! "We're at the far end of the mall from where you passed out. You need to go through that door there and turn right. All the way to the opposite end of the mall and out through the main doors there. When you get out, you'll see the studios about fifty yards further on the right. Up some big, wide steps. It's a big, white building. There's a flagpole on top. You can't miss it."

"Okay, thanks." It doesn't sound complicated. Whatever Walt's thing is, it's obviously at the "stoodios." And they're right next door.

"Well go, girl! It starts at four! Be quick, but don't run on that ankle. I'll see you at the party afterwards." She squeezes my hand and uses it to push me toward the door.

I shout my goodbyes as I exit into the mall. The heat is astonishing. I turn to my right. The mall is enormous. I'm at ground level. There are two levels above. The doors at the far end must be four hundred yards away. I break into a trot toward them. The people I pass don't seem to be dressed all that differently from how I imagine Americans dress today. I scan shops looking for clues as to where or when I am. Gloria Jeans, American Girl, Gadzooks, Sears. All very American. McDonalds, Haagen Dazs, Dunkin' Donuts—more familiar. Game Stop has Pokémon and Super Mario in the window. This can't be a million years ago.

I reach the end of the mall, push through the glass doors. The temperature outside is the same. I see the building Margaret described. Several storeys, with the letters KDBC at the top. It's actually more like another couple of hundred yards away. I up my pace, and I'm there and through the revolving doors in less than a minute. The air conditioning feels wonderful. I wipe sweat from my brow with the back of my hand.

A man in uniform approaches me. "Can I help you, miss?"

"I'm here for Walt Buchanan." He looks me up and down. He's hesitant, probably unsure about me. "I thought I wasn't going to make it."

"Follow me." He leads me across the deep foyer to a huge reception desk. There are three women stationed behind it. Uniform Man takes me to the woman on the left. "Someone here for Walt Buchanan."

The woman eyes me with even more suspicion than the guard. "Name?"

"Eilidh McVicar."

"McVicar?"

"Yes."

She's looking at a computer. A museum piece. There's a huge plastic box attached to the back of the screen. "How are you spelling that?

"M, small C, capital V, I, C, A, R." The clock on the far wall is showing five to four.

"No McVicar listed." Her suspicion confirmed, she exchanges glances with the guard, who turns to face me. This is about to go completely wrong.

"I was expecting to make it here for the afterparty. But my flight got in early, and so I thought I'd be able to get here for four o' clock. Then on my way here—" I use both hands to point out the length of my body: sweating, ripped jeans, bandage "—well, don't even ask. I come all the way from Scotland for Uncle Walt, and now I end up like this." I'm laying on my accent. Not so much that they won't understand it. But milking it.

"Okay, okay. George, can you show Miss McVicar straight to Studio 2? You'll need to be fast. It's scheduled to start at four."

I nod my thanks and follow George across the foyer, up a flight of stairs, and through a double door leading to a dimly lit corridor. We reach another smaller lobby, and George explains to a girl about my age who I am and why I'm here. She's got headphones loose round her neck and is holding what looks like a walkie-talkie in her hand. Cropped T-shirt, jeans, and trainers. She's looking at me as George talks to her, nodding. She comes across.

"Follow me." Through a door and up two flights of stairs to another door. She turns and whispers. "There's a single seat at the end of the row immediately in front of you when you go through this door. Sit down quickly and don't make a sound." She puts her finger to her lips to emphasize the point.

21.

INSIDE THE STUDIO, it's dark, but not pitch black. The seat is right in front of me. Maybe another ten or eleven beyond it. And two more rows in front. Every other seat is occupied, and all eyes are turned toward me. I feel my way into the theatre-style seat.

The man in the seat next to mine leans toward me, smiling, his white teeth just visible despite the gloom. "Just made it," he says. I smile a response.

We're in a gallery, looking down on a stage. A man comes on, microphone in hand. Sharp suit. He stage-whispers into the mic. "Welcome, ladies and gentlemen. Now, we all know why we're here. Donny is bringing Walt in any second now. Walt thinks they're meeting me to film a piece about the upcoming season. But we know different, folks! We're going to dim the lights in the auditorium and just leave this stage lit. I need everyone to be perfectly silent. Once they're in, we'll put the lights up, and I want you all to go crazy. Okay? Right, everyone. Shhhhhhhhh." The lights in the auditorium dim further.

There's a single cough from below. There must be more people in the audience underneath where I'm sitting. Silence. Paper rustling. Silence. Voices from off stage. Two men appear, and microphone man steps forward so they can see him. He uses his free hand to make an upward gesture. The lights come on in the auditorium, and those on stage brighten. Everyone in the gallery is on their feet. Cheering. Clapping. Whistling. I stand and clap along. One of the pair of men steps toward mic man. They're facing the now solitary figure and join in with the clapping. He's tall with a big Roman nose and thinning copper-red hair. He looks utterly bewildered. I can hardly believe it. It's Walter. Younger than he was when I went to bed. But unmistakeably him.

People start to sit, and I follow suit. The guy with the mic steps toward Walter. "Well, Walt. Bit of a surprise? How're you feeling?" He holds the mic out to Walter.

"Earl, what's going on? Donny and I were meant to be meeting you to film a piece about the new season. What's happening?"

"All part of an elaborate plan to surprise you, Walt. Today is, I believe, a significant birthday for you. We—" he makes a grand sweeping gesture with his arm toward the audience "—all of your friends, we decided we wanted to do something to show how much we all think of you. How much we love you."

The last sentence triggers more clapping and cheering from the gallery and below. I can't stop staring at Walter. He's moving his head slightly, taking in his surroundings. It's impossible to read his expression. He gestures to Earl, who holds the mic toward him. "Donny. You knew about this? You piece of sh ..."

Earl pulls the mic back sharply. "Whoa there, Walt. Women and children in the audience!" Donny steps toward Walter, and they embrace in a huge bear hug. Walter seems to be trying to jokingly wrestle Donny to the ground and, to laughter from the audience, mimes punches to his head. I'm laughing too.

"Walt," Earl says, "we knew that if we tried to involve you in the planning, you'd just say no. So we've got a fantastic party arranged for later on. But first we wanted to do something just a little bit special for you. I'm going to play the role of Ralph Edwards." There's a pause. Walter shrugs and pulls a face that suggests he has no idea what is going on. "This afternoon, Walt Buchanan, just like on the TV show *This Is Your Life!*"

There's cheering and applause again. Earl is obviously a pro, as he milks it just enough before continuing. "Given that he's right here on stage with us, I think the best person to talk first about you is your old friend—at least I think he's still your friend—Donny Handleson." There's polite applause as Earl passes the mic to Donny.

Donny is almost as tall as Walter, and his jacket clearly wouldn't button up if he tried. He talks about how he went to Europe to pursue his soccer career and ended up on the same team as Walt. How Walt was a good player, but that he was better—which gets a laugh. He explains they became best buddies and both moved to the States to wind down their careers with the local soccer team, the Wildcats. While Walter has managed to largely maintain the physique of a sportsman, Donny has been less successful in containing the ravages of middle-age spread.

A picture appears on a screen I hadn't noticed at the back of the stage. It's the face of a young black man, huge smile below bright, lively eyes. Donny tells us about Daniel. How the three of them became the closest of friends and teammates. About a trip to Ethiopia, Daniel dying in a traffic accident. "But I believe Daniel is here today," Donny says, a catch in his voice. "Or his spirit is. There's no way he'd miss this." Walter goes to Donny, and they embrace.

There's silence in the auditorium. But not inside my head. I can hear my blood pumping. *Whoosh. Whoosh. Whoosh.* My head feels like it's spinning. I'm not going to be sick. But I might faint. They were in Ethiopia. Walter was in Ethiopia. He was the man. The patient in the bed. Dubya is Walter. What's going on? How do I make sense of this? Walter was in Ethiopia, and so was I. Walter was at Dundo Point at the same time as me. And he was staying at my house overnight when I was going to my bed. And now we're both here. Why?

There's laughter and applause. Walter's shaking hands with Donny. Donny turns away and takes a seat on one of dozens of chairs arranged in rows on the other side of the stage.

"Thank you, Donny Handleson. Some moving and very, very funny recollections there." A picture of an armadillo is fading to white on the screen. Earl's addressing us. "Now, I think we all know that Walt originates from Scotland. It's not as though he goes on and on about it." Lots of laughter. He turns to Walter. "What I want to know is why, if Scotland is so wonderful, none of the Buchanan family seem to want to live there? Here's a message from Surrey. Which is in England. Your brother Andrew!" He turns to look at the screen.

A family group appears. A man, woman, and two girls. It's clearly Walter's brother. Anyone could tell, even if Earl hadn't introduced him that way. Same copper-red hair. Similar features. But much younger. Maybe ten years or more. The woman is glamorous. Short, blond hair and very beautiful. The two girls have the same hair as their father and uncle. They're quite young. Maybe five and seven? They call out a cheery *hello* to Walter. The girls voices are sing-song high and excited. Andrew talks. About how Walter might have the glamour of a football career and lots of international travel, but he's not jealous because he's got the brains and the good looks. Walter's grinning. Stories of playing together. How Walter was actually rubbish at football compared to him even though he was eleven years older. More gentle teasing. Walter's smile seems to get even bigger. The clip ends with the family promising to visit next summer while waving and yelling excited goodbyes.

Earl introduces a sequence of different guests who each pay tribute to Walter or share amusing anecdotes involving him. Some of it registers with me, and much of it doesn't. I can barely take my eyes off Walter. I keep asking myself why. What's the link between me and him? Why am I here? He's obviously some kind of minor celebrity here. Or he was.

Some of the speakers grab my attention. One lady is representing the American Dyslexic Association. She tells of how Walt—they all call him Walt—gives regular talks. She says he's an inspiration. Walter looks embarrassed and pleased at the same time, his head slightly bowed. Another man gives a very emotional speech about Walter's work promoting the Daniel Foundation and all the money it raises for the children's ward at the hospital. I'm focused on Walter. He's being polite. Gracious. And I can tell—I just *know* he'd rather be anywhere else. He's humble. He's putting up with all this because he doesn't want to let people down.

All the chairs on the other side of the stage are occupied. This thing must be about finished. But Earl builds up to yet another introduction. "Walt, we're almost done. There's a couple more folks who want to be here with you today." He turns and theatrically throws one arm wide. "Okay, Wildcats, on you come!" There's a sudden swarm of kids from both sides of the stage. All wearing football tops. Boys and girls. Ages from maybe twelve to late teens. All cheering and clapping. The audience are on their feet too, joining in. Maybe a hundred of them. Walt's going around shaking hands with every single individual. Smiling. Laughing.

Eventually, the hullabaloo subsides. Earl's on the mic again. "Don't they all look great? Every one of them in their soccer uniforms." That draws another burst of sustained applause from everyone, including those on stage. "Now, everyone is here to celebrate Walt's special birthday. But there's something missing. What do you think it is?"

"A birthday cake!" One of the younger kids can barely contain himself.

"No!" Earl makes a sheesh face to the audience. "There will be a cake later at the party. But what else do you think is missing?"

"Presents!" Another youngster is jumping up and down as she shouts.

"Exactly! We need a present for Walt. And we've got one we know he's going to love. *And* we've got someone extra special to make the presentation." Earl pauses for dramatic effect. "Folks, we're all here to honour a truly special guy. And we wanted to get another special guy to do this presentation. Best of all, this other guy was desperate to do it. Ladies and gentlemen, the greatest Wildcats player ever. The first Wildcat player to transfer to Europe for over a million dollars. Star of the USA Olympic soccer team this summer. Flown in all the way from pre-season training with his club in Spain. It's Mikey Wilson!" Earl's voice has been going up in pitch to the point he's almost screaming. Some of the others in the audience are screaming. Those that aren't are cheering, clapping, shouting, stamping their feet. A tall black man, six-foot-four or five, emerges from off stage behind the chairs and strides toward Walter. He's wearing a sharp charcoal suit and might be the handsomest man ever. He's got a square shaped gift-wrapped present under one arm, which he hands to Earl as he passes him. He cuts through the swarm of teens in football strips and pulls Walter into the biggest man-hug imaginable. All this amid an ovation that causes the floor beneath my feet to vibrate.

Finally, after well over half a minute, they part and Mikey steps back. Earl hands him the mic. "Coach. When Donny told me about this event, I told myself there was no way I'd miss it." His voice is like Morgan Freeman's, but just half an octave lower. And even sexier. He's younger than I first thought. Maybe twenty or so. He looks up, addressing all of us as well as Walter. "I guess everyone here knows how good my career's going. There's lots of reasons for that. Hard work. The love and support of my Mom. More hard work. Great teammates. Great management. Did I mention hard work? Oh, and of course, there's my good looks." He pauses to enjoy the laughter and applause. "But there's one man. Without that man I would have none of this." There's a crack in his voice. "That man believed in me. Worked me hard. Taught me self-respect. Stood by me when no one else would've.

When maybe he shouldn't have." Turns and addresses the kids on the stage. "You're all blessed to have this man coach you. I know you all cuss him sometimes when he's out of earshot. I know you all think he works you too hard. I know he goes on and on and on about Scotland." More laughter. "But he cares. About each and every one of you. Of us. And he's got our backs." He turns back to Walter. "Coach Buchanan, I don't have the words. Just thank you. For everything."

The applause is deafening. As it fades, Earl returns the gift to Mikey. "Now, Walt, Mikey has a gift for you that we hope you're going to love."

Mikey hands it over to Walter and holds the mic between them.

"You want me to open it now?"

"That's what we're all waiting for, coach!"

Walter tears the wrapping off to reveal an old-fashioned, long-playing vinyl record. He looks at it and smiles. "*Horses* by Patti Smith. Thank you."

"Coach, we know you must already have a copy. Man, you've probably got a hundred copies. Look at the back of it."

Walter flips the record over, squints at it, and breaks into a huge grin. His delight is obvious. "It's signed! You got me a signed copy of *Horses*! Thank you. Thank you, everyone. For this." He holds up the LP. "And for all this." The lights in the auditorium have been turned back up. He gestures to everyone on the stage, then to the audience. "I really don't deserve all of this. But I'm truly grateful. Thank you, everyone." His voice is the same. Younger and stronger, with an American twang. But the same voice.

From below, a solo voice pipes up with "For He's a Jolly Good Fellow." By the time the second line begins, the whole place is belting it out. I'm staring at Walter. He's slowly looking around. Drinking everything in with his eyes. A beautiful, warm smile adorns his face. The singing reaches a crescendo, then starts to repeat. Walter's gaze turns upward, and he's scanning the gallery. Finally, his eyes meet mine. My heart's pounding. He's looking right at me. Staring. The smile is gone.

He recognizes me! *He knows who I am*. I just know it. Each of us knows who the other is. The singing has morphed into "Happy

Birthday to You." Walter is frozen. Staring. Recognizing. Me too. Like we're both in a trance.

"Sure looks like you got Walt's attention." The spell is broken as I turn to see the man standing next to me. Some other people in the gallery have turned toward me too, curious to see what Walter is staring at. My head birling and my heart pumping even harder. I've got to get out. Got to get out now. I turn and push through the door. Run. Running. Down a flight of stairs. Turn. Trip. Fall. Falling. Falling.

22.

SHE'S GONE. SHE was there and now she's gone.

"Walt? You okay, man?"

"She was there."

"Who? What're you talking about? I can hardly hear you."

"Donny, she was there. Patti was there." I feel my eyes pricking.

Donny's arm is around my shoulder. "Stick with me. Stay close."
He's guiding me through the crowd, heading off the stage. "Excuse us,
folks. Walt's just going to get some air."

I can see him making a hand signal to Earl, and maybe some others.
We're through the wing and heading toward a staircase. The hubbub
behind is fading as we pass into a small, windowless room through a
door which Donny closes behind us. "Walt, are you feeling okay?"

"Donny, I saw Patti. I was looking around. I looked up, scanning
all the faces in the gallery. Right at the very back. In the corner. She was
looking straight at me."

"Walt, you know it can't have been Patti."

"It was her, Donny. Do you think I wouldn't fucking recognize her?
But …"

"But what?"

"But she was young. Like when we first met." I can hardly get the
words out as a massive dry sob earthquakes through my body.

Donny pulls me into a hug and squeezes me, holding me tight.
"Walt. Walt. It's okay. This whole thing today has been emotional for
you. Taken you by surprise. You *want* Patti to be here. Hell, I do too.
But she's not, Walt. You know that. You're seeing what you want to.
Not what's real." His hands are on my shoulders, and he's looking right
at me. "Walt, it wasn't Patti. You *know* that, right?"

I nod.

"Good. Like I say. The excitement. The emotion. Just your
mind playing tricks. Now listen. There's a hell of party back
downstairs that's waiting for its guest of honour. You've never let
anyone down in your life, and you're not going to let anyone down
now. Capiche?"

"Capiche." I'm back in control. Of course Donny's right. All these folks are here for me, and I can't spoil it. And I know he's right—that it can't have been Patti. Yet I also know, with even greater certainty, that it was.

August 10, 2019

23.

FALLING. FALLING. I'M not alone. I'm being followed. I turn my head backward. Or is it upward? There's a man. It's like he's swimming down toward me, rather than falling. I recognize him. He's Daniel, the person whose picture was on the screen. Walter's friend who died in Ethiopia. He seems to be smiling at me, beckoning me with his eyes. I can sense that I'm falling more slowly as he gets closer. As I begin to sense danger his kind face contorts, then his entire shape morphs into an inky black cloud, with fierce, fiery eyes. My fear somehow seems to propel me, and I'm falling faster again. Still falling. But not landing anywhere. Then I'm suddenly awake. In my bedroom. Not in America. Not in a studio. Definitely in my bedroom. Alone, with no one else here. Not being chased. Safe? It's daylight outside, and I can hear birdsong. I reach for my phone. It's quarter to six in the morning. Tenth of August. I feel my face with my hand and stroke my forehead. I'm sweating.

I'm lying on my back on my bed. Think! I had a headache last night. I came to bed early, plugged my phone in to charge, then lay down before going to brush my teeth and get changed. I must have fallen asleep. Then I woke up in that room with Margaret, before I went to the studio and saw Walter. Not like he is today. Not young. But younger. Oh God! That look on his face when he saw me. I ran out and tripped, and it felt like I was falling forever. Then I woke up here. This is the same as Ethiopia. I know it is. I know it was real, that I was there. In America. Where in America?

I push myself up into a sitting position. There's the sensation of someone walking over my grave when I look at my ankle. The crepe bandage is there, complete with two brass safety pins. There's no comfort in the confirmation. It just emphasizes the questions in my mind. When I went to Ethiopia, I was there for a whole day but only unconscious here for less than half an hour. Last night, I came upstairs early, just after seven, and must have fallen asleep pretty much straight away. I've been asleep for the best part of ten and a half hours. How long was I there? It couldn't have been much more than two hours. Three at most. There's no correlation. No logic. This just doesn't make sense.

What are the common factors? Doctors? Medicine? Hospitals? Walt was in hospital in Ethiopia, and I was too, nursing him. I woke up in hospital after I was knocked out. Then the big hospital for a CT scan. When I woke up in America, I was in some kind of medical facility. Walt does fundraising for the children's ward at the hospital in America. Is that the link? Or is it just coincidence? I can't work any of this out.

I lean forward and feel the crepe bandage and touch each of the safety pins in turn. I can see Margaret in my mind's eye, as clear as day in her uniform. I go to my top drawer and get the white envelope out from underneath my socks. I take Kia's button out and hold it between my forefinger and thumb, look at it for a moment and kiss it lightly. Then I put it back in the envelope and return it to its safe place.

What does all of this mean? What's happening to me? Who is Walter?

Walter's the key. He was the patient in Ethiopia. He was at Dundo Point yesterday. It was his birthday celebration in America. He's asleep now in George and Archie's room. That recollection sends electricity through me. He's here. Now. What did he say? When we were in Ethiopia? He called me Patti. He said he *loved* me! Oh my God! He said he loved me. He said something about being the one. What was it? I can't remember. Think. *Think*. He said he loved me. But he called me Patti. Who's Patti? Was he delirious? Confused?

Think! In America. That present they gave him. An old record. By Patti Smith!

I head straight to the computer and Google *Patti Smith*. There's a full page of listings. Tickets for her upcoming concert tour, merchandise available on Amazon, an official fan site, a Wikipedia entry. I click on that link and learn that she's a 72-year-old singer-songwriter, poet, visual artist, and author. She's been active from 1967 to the present day. Her debut album in 1975 was *Horses*. Did Walter think I was her, that I was Patti Smith? I click on a few images. I look nothing like her.

I search for *Walter Buchanan* and get 3,390,000 results, so I modify it to *Walter Buchanan Footballer*. That throws up *Walter Scott Buchanan, English international footballer*, which is clearly wrong. There's another result that looks promising. *Walter Buchanan (footballer) dating Dinah Washington*. Interesting! Apparently, Dinah Washington was a famous jazz singer. Never heard of her. But that Walter Buchanan passed away December 1963, so it's not him. A Wikipedia entry catches my eye. *Walter Anderson Buchanan. July 17, 1950—date. Journeyman Scottish professional footballer. Played in Scotland, various European countries and North America. Citation required.*

That must be him. Got to be. That would make him seventy now. Yes, that's him. That party must have been his fiftieth birthday. So I was in the USA on the17th of July, 2000. I don't know precisely where, but I do know when. Nineteen years ago. Before I was born. Much more recent than Ethiopia, but before I was born both times. Does that matter? Or is it just coincidence?

I read the Wikipedia entry again. *Citation needed*. You can say that again! Nothing about where in Scotland he was born, just the date. Can I use the date to trace where he came from originally? Maybe I'll try that in a minute. There's nothing about relationships. Was he married? He was wearing a wedding ring yesterday. But there was no sign of a wife or partner at the fiftieth birthday bash. There were all sorts of friends, colleagues—even his brother on video. But no wife or girlfriend. And no mention either. Not by anyone. But at Dundo Point yesterday, he mentioned his wife. That's right. He asked if I was his wife. But there was no sign of a wife in 2000. Maybe he married late in life?

I can hear the front door opening downstairs. Ten past six. It'll be George back from his work. There are voices. George's, of course. I can't make out what's being said. Female. English? It couldn't be Molly. Not this early. But who else could it be? I make straight for the bathroom to brush my teeth and smarten myself up, then head down the stairs.

24.

THE VOICES HAVE moved to the kitchen, and it seems like conversation is flowing easily. I don't know why, but I hesitate before pushing open the kitchen door. When I do, George is facing me. Standing looking down at Molly, who's seated at the kitchen table with her back to me. I know it must be her because of the copper-red hair. George looks up, and Molly turns at the sound of me entering. She gets up as George says, "Here's Eilidh now."

"Eilidh. It's so nice to meet you in person." She steps forward and leans in to hug me. "Thank you so much."

"Honestly, it's fine. You got here early." I'm looking up. She must be six inches taller than me.

"I know. I'm really sorry. I didn't mean to waken or disturb anyone."

"No, no. It's fine. You're not disturbing anyone. I was awake, and George was coming back in from his work."

"You're very kind. I was so worried that I set off last night. I knew I'd never get to sleep anyway. The roads were clear all the way. I arrived just after three this morning."

"Three! You must be knackered! Please, sit back down." I take a seat at the end of the table so I can look at her properly.

"Thanks. I'm not too bad, actually. I got a couple of hours sleep in the car. I woke up about half past five. Then, when George pulled up, I could tell from the way he was squinting at me that I'd parked where he would normally do. Right outside your gate. I guessed it might be him because you'd said he works nightshift."

"Aye, that's right." George has seen his way back into the conversation. "I was peering in through Molly's windscreen, as I could see there was someone there." He looks right at her. "I'm often troubled with glamorous women stalking me."

God Almighty, George! What possessed you to say something as stupid as that? Molly has gone bright red. I've got to rescue this. "In his dreams. You'll have to forgive George, Molly. He's usually that tired after a nightshift that his delusions take over."

"I think he was just being very gallant. Thank you, George. I'm sure you could use plenty of words to describe me. But *glamorous* isn't one of them."

She's right. She's in jeans and a shapeless jumper. There's not a trace of makeup on her. She's got bed-head. Not glamorous at all. But she is really good looking. Probably early twenties. Good complexion. Wide mouth that smiles easily. And eyes so green you'd think she was wearing contact lenses. I can see what was on George's mind when he made his idiot remark. He knows he's made an arse of things too.

"I was just boiling the kettle to make Molly a cup of coffee. Do you want anything, Eilidh?"

"Yes. I'll have a cup of coffee as well. And get the toaster going too." I flash him silent remonstration and warning. Molly sees the exchange and averts her glance. "Molly, I'm sure you're starving after that journey. Would you like some toast too?"

"Thank you. I wouldn't say no."

"Great." I get up and fetch three side plates, knives, and teaspoons. George is sorting the mugs. "Did you stop anywhere on the way up, Molly?"

"I stopped at Southwaite services to fill up."

I put jam, marmalade, and butter on the table and sit down again. "And did you manage to get anything to eat there?"

"No. To be honest, I wasn't hungry."

"You'll be starving now, then." Don't give her the chance to deny it. "George! Plenty of toast, and keep it coming."

"Aye, okay, missus. What did your last slave die of?" George places two mugs of coffee on the table. "You did say milk with one sugar?" Smiling at Molly.

"Yes. Perfect. Thank you." She returns his smile. George is beaming.

Best I intervene before he says something moronic again. "So will you look to head back down today?"

"I expect so." She's really polite. But she's distracted.

"George?" I feel I've got to say something to stop him from staring at her.

"What?"

"Have you checked on Walter?"

"Eh? No. No, I haven't. Do you want me to make toast, or do you want me to go up and check on Walter?"

Molly and I exchange silent smiles. "You can do both, you big lump. It'll take you ten seconds to pop upstairs."

"Okay." George puts a plate with four slices of toast down between Molly and me. No petulance in his tone. Because Molly's here. "Tuck into that. There's more in the toaster. I'll just pop up and check on Walter." He heads out the door.

"Thank you. He's probably sound asleep. He's never usually awake until half-seven or eight. But. You know ... with it being a different place."

"I do know. We understand. Help yourself to a couple of slices of toast, or you'll offend George."

She smiles and puts two slices on to her plate.

"Sound asleep. Breathing regular and even." Christ! He sounds like a nurse. He's trying to impress and glides toward the toaster. "Eat up, you two. More ready in a minute."

"Thank you, George." She spreads butter thinly and ignores the jam and marmalade. "I was just explaining to Eilidh that he doesn't usually waken until half-seven or eight. Is that going to put you out? What time do you like to get to your bed?"

"Oh, don't worry about that. I never usually bed down until half-ten or eleven."

Lying toad! Why's he saying that? I know exactly why.

"That's good. I really wouldn't want us to put you out even more than we have already. I know—" Molly is cut short by her phone buzzing. She pulls it from her pocket and looks at the screen. "Oh, sorry. Excuse me just a minute. Do you mind if I take this?"

"Not at all. Do you want to step into the garden for a bit of privacy?" I gesture toward the back door.

Molly nods and smiles as she heads to the door, phone pressed to her ear. "Hi. Yes. Fine." Pause. "A few hours ago. It was ..." The door closes behind her, muffling her voice.

"For God's sake, George. What's the matter with you?'

"What do you mean?"

"You know fine well what I mean! *I'm often troubled with glamorous women stalking me.* Or how about br*eathing regular and even, doctor*?"

"I never said doctor!"

"Might as well have done! You are a pure red neck sometimes, George."

"Hark at the Queen of fucking Sheba! *Make me coffee! Make me toast! Run up the stairs! Do this! Do that!* What gives you the right to be so high and mighty?"

Before I can annihilate him, the back door opens again. "Sorry about that."

"No problem. Bit of an early call?" I'm fishing for what I know I can catch.

"Yes. My boyfriend, Ben. Just checking up that everything's okay."

"That's nice." I flash a look at George. He's avoiding eye contact. And making a poor job of trying not to look crestfallen.

"He would have driven up with me, but he's on a business trip to Frankfurt. Not back until next week."

Better and better. "Sounds like a nice guy. And a glamorous job."

"Mmmm." A shrug of the shoulders. Shit. She's planning to finish with him. Even George spots it. He perks up.

"Where were we before the phone call?"

"I was saying that I didn't want to put you out anymore. George has been so kind, giving up his room. You all have." She smiles at George. He's like the Cheshire cat that got the cream. I swear to God he's going to purr. I don't think she's playing him. She doesn't come across at all like that. There's no affectation to her.

"Molly, do you mind if I ask how you know Walter?"

"Of course. He's my uncle."

I knew it! Knew it. She's one of those little girls that were in the video clip at Walter's birthday do. "And he lives with your family?"

"Just me. It's just Uncle Walter and me."

I can't read this at all. That's the first time she's actually called him Uncle Walter. She never called him that on the phone. Just Walter. Does that mean anything? Does she want to say more? Or does she want me to butt out?

Molly inhales slowly. Girding herself? "Just me and him. There was an accident. A car accident. Mum and Dad and my big sister died. Uncle Walter came back to look after me."

She's reporting the event but not engaging with the meaning of the words. Protecting herself from hurting all over again. I've started to do the same when I have to tell people who don't know about Dad. She's in control, but my head is spinning. I just saw that family on video last night. Andrew. His beautiful wife. Those two lovely, wee lassies. Now she's telling me that she's all that's left. "I'm so sorry to hear that."

The automatic response convention demands. But Molly hears the catch in my voice. Looks deeper at me. Sees the moistness in my eyes? Puzzled? Continues. "It was a long time ago." Still reporting. Then a tilt of her head. "A long time ago. August 2000. I was five. At a friend's birthday party. They were coming to fetch me. Pile up on the motorway and … "

I reach forward and put my hand on top of hers. "I really am so sorry." And I really am.

She uses the interruption to regain control. "Thank you. As I say, it was a long time ago."

"And that's when Walter came to live with you?"

"Yes. I had my granny, my mum's mum. But she was in a care home. And there wasn't anyone else. Just Uncle Walter. So he moved back to look after me."

"Moved back?"

"Yes. He was living in America. Working over there. He had been for years."

"There wasn't any question of you going to live with him? With his family?"

"To be honest, I had no idea what the thinking was at the time. I was only five, and my whole world had been turned upside down."

"No. Of course."

"Years later, he explained that everyone—the authorities, child psychologists, and the like—had said it would be better for me to stay put. The same home. Familiar surroundings, you know?"

I do know. Perfectly sensible. She's not picked up on the question about Walter's family. I can't repeat it without looking odd. "Yes, I know."

"Uncle Walter was a widower. No kids." Aha! "So I suppose it was relatively straightforward for him to come back." She pauses. "Not that I'm downplaying the sacrifice he made for me." There's sudden anxiety in her voice.

"Of course not, no."

"He's been wonderful. So loving and caring." She pauses and sits back slightly, more upright. "But you don't want to hear me go on about that."

I do! I really do! I want to know everything possible about Walter. And his family. His relatives. Anything at all that might help me understand. "Don't worry about it. You can say anything you like."

But the moment has gone. I can see she's uncomfortable and feels she's saying too much to virtual strangers. Bloody George standing there staring at her doesn't help. There are sounds of movement from upstairs, and the chance has disappeared completely.

25.

THE KITCHEN IS manic. The table is covered in mugs, plates, bowls, cereal packets, milk carton, sugar bowl, butter, jam, and marmalade. There're only six seats at the kitchen table and seven of us in the room. George is being "gallant" and continuing to stand. He's morphed into an oversize puppy, hanging on anything Molly says, unable to take his eyes off her. At least he's still supplying toast to the table. Walter's in great form. He's lucid, clearly delighted to see Molly, and is chatting to her about the journey back down south. I'm studying everything that passes between them. Watching. Listening. Gran is quiet, overawed. She's nibbling toast and sipping tea. Mum's in host mode, encouraging some conversations while trying to prevent others. Scott's being what Mum would describe as overexcited. I describe it as being a pain in the arse.

"Anyone for more toast?" George leans in with a plateful, smiling at Molly. She smiles back politely and shakes her head.

"Why are you still up?" P in the A demands.

"What do you mean? I'm making toast."

"I can see that. But why are you still up?"

"I've just tellt you. I'm making toast."

Scott doesn't know why. But he senses George's discomfort. I can see it in his face. Devilment. "Aye, very good, toasty boy. But why are you not away to your bed? You're always in bed by the time I get up."

George's face is glowing red. Teeth gritted. "I'm not always in bed when you get up." "Maybe not on a Sunday or Monday. But you are when you've come in from work."

Mum rides to the rescue. "Scott. What did I tell you about that football top last night? You've finished your corn flakes, so away upstairs and put that in the wash basket. Put on a clean one." Scott stomps off, face like thunder. "And mind and brush your teeth properly." She smiles at our guests as he half-slams the door behind him. "He'd wear that dirty shirt every single day until it disintegrates, if I let him."

Breakfast continues at a more leisurely pace, mainly because it started earlier than usual and Mum has plenty of time because she doesn't go to work on a Saturday. George has Scott's seat at the table, sipping coffee slowly and stealing glances at Molly when he thinks she won't see him. Discussion is polite. Superficial. How nice our kitchen is. Even Gran joins in and agrees how nice the kitchen is. I see Molly looking at her sympathetically. How pretty the garden is. The lovely yellow rose by the front door. The best time for Molly and Walter to set off to miss the worst of the traffic. Using the M6 toll road to avoid congestion round Birmingham.

"Patti, will you be happy in the back seat?" Walter is looking right at me.

"I'm sorry?"

"When Molly is driving us home. Will you be happy in the back seat?"

He thinks I'm this Patti person again.

It's Molly's turn to perform a rescue act. "Uncle Walter! This isn't Patti. This is Eilidh. Remember?" Walter nods, deferring to her. Molly leans toward me. Whispers. "I'm so sorry, Eilidh. Patti was Uncle Walter's wife."

"It's fine. Funnily enough he thought I was his wife yesterday too."

Molly looks at me differently—appraising, quizzical. "I think you do look a bit like her, actually. There are only two photographs of her that I've ever seen. One in profile at a bit of a distance and the other really blurred. Apparently, she was very camera shy." She breaks off as George asks whether she wants more bloody toast.

I want to get Molly on her own. Corner her somehow. Ask more about Walter. Why didn't she refer to him as uncle on the phone? What does she know about his late wife? How did she die? When? See if she knows anything that might be useful. Anything. But there's no way. Then she asks to use the loo. It's my chance. I'll make an excuse to go upstairs when she's on her way back down and speak to her alone on the stairs. I need to time it right. What will I say?

The kitchen phone rings, startling everyone. Who would ring at twenty-five past eight on a Saturday morning? George gets it. "Hello." Pause. "Yes. Yes, she's here." Pause. "Okay." He turns to me. "It's for you." I get up and go toward him. He hands me the receiver. "It's the surgery."

"Hello?"

"Is that Eilidh McVicar?"

"Yes. Speaking."

"Hello, Eilidh. It's Doctor McKenzie at Kilmadden Surgery."

"Yes?"

"Eilidh, try not to be alarmed. But I'd like you to come in to see me."

"Okay. Why?"

"As I say, try not to be alarmed. I've got your CT results here, and I'd just like to chat them through with you."

"Aye. Okay. When?"

"As soon as you can."

"What? Like on Monday? Do I need an appointment?"

"I'd like you to come in this morning. As soon as possible, please. You don't need an appointment."

"This morning? Okay."

"Thanks, Eilidh. As I say, please don't worry."

"Okay."

"Oh! And one other thing, Eilidh. Do you think there might be somebody free to be able to accompany you?"

"Probably."

"Good. All right, then. I'll see you soon."

"Yes. See you soon."

Click.

I replace the phone and turn. Everyone's looking at me. Molly's back in the room, standing by her chair. Walter's seated, smiling at me. Gran has her head tilted to one side. George has taken a couple of paces back. Standing at the end of the table. Mum is staring at me. I can see she's frightened. More than frightened. Maybe as frightened as me? Got to hold this together.

"That was Doctor McKenzie. She'd like me to go in and see her at the surgery."

"It sounded like she wants you to go now." Mum's being the grown up, but I can see she's struggling.

"Yes. She says its nothing to worry about. Said it three times. Just wants to talk through my CT results. That's all."

"Okay, love. Would you like me to drive you there?"

"Yes, that would be great. Thanks." Yes. Yes, please. Please come with me, Mum. She knows. I could walk there easily. She knows.

"Great. Well, we'll clear all the breakfast things away, then we can head off." She looks at Molly. "Of course, there's no rush for you and Walter to go. You should still plan to leave at the time that suits you best for your journey back."

Molly doesn't get the chance to reply before George. "Why does Doctor McKenzie want to see you so urgently? Surgery's only open on Saturday mornings for emergencies. And she never works Saturdays anyway. She's got young kids, remember? And telling you three times there's nothing to worry about sounds to me like there *is* something to worry about."

For fuck's sake, George! You absolute fucking plum! We're all thinking that. Well, most of us. Mum and me at least. But we're not fucking saying it! Not out loud. Because we're not fucking morons.

"Now, George. Let's not get into idle speculation." Mum to the rescue again, her voice calm, authoritative. "Let's get the breakfast things cleared."

Gran and Walter sit quietly at the table. Molly helps George load the dishwasher while Mum and I put everything else away.

As we're finishing, Molly pipes up. "Mrs. McVicar, you've obviously got a lot going on this morning. Uncle Walter and I will get his things together and shoot off out of your way."

"Really, Molly. There's no need."

"Honestly, it suits us to leave soon. It means we can take the journey at a leisurely pace. We can be back well across the border before stopping for lunch."

"Only if you're sure."

"We're sure. Honestly." She turns to Walter and nods. "That's right, isn't it, Uncle Walter?" "That's right." Walter nods enthusiastically. I'm not sure if he knows what he's agreeing with. The spark he had at the breakfast table seems to have gone. Molly shepherds him toward the hall and the stairs.

I need them not to go. Need them to stay. Need to know what it is that connects me to Walter. I need there to be nothing wrong with my CT scan. Need there to have been a mix up. Need not to die. Need … Mum is hugging me. Firmly but gently. Cooing *wheesht* and *there, there* in my ear. Her hand free, wiping the tear from my cheek with a tissue. I'm scared. Scared like when the doctors said there was nothing they could do for Dad. Scared.

"Stay strong, Eilidh." Mum's eased her hold and inched back, looking straight into my eyes. "I'm here. I'm with you. Can you stay strong?" I nod because I don't trust my voice. "Good girl." She turns to George. "Will you stay up for a while? Look after Gran while Eilidh and I go to see the doctor?" George nods. He never really knows how to act in emotional situations, and I can see on his face that he's grateful for direction from Mum. Despite my upset and fear, I can't help but smile. "Fine. Thank you." She looks back to me. "Are you up to saying goodbye to our guests?"

"Yes."

"Good."

On cue, Molly reappears in the doorway, Walter a step or two behind her. "I think we've got everything. Thank you. All of you. You have been so wonderfully kind." She comes forward, round the table, embraces me and whispers in my ear. "Thank you, Eilidh. So much. Good luck with the doctor. I'm sure everything will be fine."

"Thank you. Do you mind if I call you later? Just to make sure that you've got back home safely?"

"Of course. I'd like that." She steps back, smiling, turns to George, and shakes his hand, still smiling. The same with Gran. Then to Mum. "Mrs. McVicar, thank you. You and your family have been so kind. I don't think you'll ever know how grateful I am."

Still framed by the doorway, Walter's watching with a satisfied smile. Beatific almost. He catches me looking at him. His smile widens to a grin, and he throws me a huge wink. I'm grinning back. Fear banished temporarily. What is it about him?

Molly goes to Walter, followed by Mum, out into the hall and then to the front door, before more goodbye noises and the sound of the front door shutting.

26.

MUM STARTS THE car, and we pull away. "Molly seemed like a lovely girl."

"Yes."

"I hope she's okay to make that drive. It's such a long way. And she's bound to be tired."

"They've got plenty of time. No need for them to rush." I know she's just trying to distract me, to kill some time. But it's not working. "Why is George *such* an arse?"

"He doesn't mean anything by it, Eilidh. You know that. He's just clumsy that way. He just blurts out what he's thinking, without consideration of the consequences."

She's right. "Did you see his face in there when I was crying?" The memory makes me smile again. I look over at Mum. She's looking straight ahead, concentrating on the road. But she's smiling too. She won't say anything, out of loyalty to George. "You'll never guess what he said earlier."

"What?"

"Before you got up. He told Molly that he keeps getting stalked by glamorous women."

"No!" The car shudders slightly as she eases off the accelerator and glances over at me, incredulous. She's appalled.

"Honest to God, Mum. I couldn't believe it. I just wanted to curl up and die."

"He actually used the word *glamorous*? Who says that these days? He said he gets *stalked*?"

"It's not something I'd make up."

"I don't suppose for a minute it is." She's shaking her head ever so slightly. And grinning. "What did poor Molly have to say to that?"

"She was really good about it, actually. Denied being glamorous. Said George was just being gallant. I'm sure she was as mortified as I was, but she carried it off well."

"She's a nice girl. It sounds like George got off lightly."

"Aye. He definitely did. Honestly, Mum, he's an absolute weapon."

"He's just worried about you."

"I know."

We pull into a parking bay outside the surgery. Mum yanks on the handbrake, switches off the engine, and takes a deep breath. She's preparing herself to be Mum. Supportive, protective Mum rather than frightened and worried Mum. I'm so pleased she's come with me. She looks me in the eyes. "Ready?"

"Ready."

She leans over and kisses my forehead. "Let's go, then."

We go through the front doors, through the vestibule, and into reception. There's just one other patient sitting waiting. Hannah Lennox is on reception. She went to school with Dad. She smiles as we enter. Why is she smiling? Does she know something? She catches my eye. "Hello, Eilidh. Doctor McKenzie's expecting you. She's in Room 7. Please go straight through."

I lead us along the corridor to Room 7 and knock on the door.

"Come in." I push the door back and step inside. "Good morning, Eilidh." Doctor McKenzie smiles at me, then looks over my shoulder at Mum. "Good morning, Kirsty." She beckons to a pair of chairs by the side of her desk. "Please, take a seat. Thank you both for coming in at such short notice."

She pauses as Mum and I take our seats. I'm terrified. Absolutely bricking it. I don't want to be here. But I'm glad it's her if it has to be anyone. She was so good with Dad when he got his diagnosis. "I know that you'll be worried. You both will. Being asked to come in like this. As I mentioned to you on the phone, Eilidh, I wanted to discuss your CT scan results." She looks over, flicking a glance first toward me, then Mum. "Now, the first thing I should say is that I'm sorry you didn't get feedback sooner. The scan was taken on Tuesday. I should've had the results next day at the latest, but there was some kind of software problem. They didn't come until yesterday, and I didn't actually review them until I got home in the evening."

"No need to apologize, doctor." At least that's what I try to say. My lips are moving, but my tongue isn't. It's like my mouth is full of dry sand. No sound comes out.

Doctor McKenzie sees. "But we can talk about that later, if you like. The important thing now is to discuss your CT scan." Her left hand reaches out to the computer screen in front of her. She turns it ninety degrees so Mum and I can see it. Her right hand is on the mouse on the pad on her desk. "Can you both see the screen clearly?"

"Yes." Mum speaks for us both. I nod. There's an irregular white oval with fairly symmetrical light and dark grey shading inside.

"Eilidh, this is the scan taken of your skull on Tuesday. It was taken purely as a precaution following your fall and your being knocked unconscious. Essentially, it was a check to see that your skull hadn't been damaged. The skull is the white circle enclosing the grey. The scan shows it to be intact, with no apparent damage."

"But?" I've found my voice. Doctor McKenzie's eyes flick to engage with mine. I feel Mum's hand on the back of mine. I clasp it and squeeze.

Doctor McKenzie's eyes return to the screen. She moves the mouse so the arrow hovers over an area to the top right of the image. The area is lighter than its surroundings and isn't matched on the left-hand side. "There appears to be an anomaly in this area, the dorsolateral prefrontal cortex."

"Go on." It's my voice. But it's separate from me. Like the image on the screen. That's mine too. But it's like they don't belong to me. I feel present and removed at the same time. But strangely calm.

"You see this lighter patch? It would normally be the same darker shade and indistinguishable from the area around it."

"So what does that mean?" I feel Mum's hand tighten.

"It's not possible to say with any degree of certainty right now, Eilidh. It could simply be a glitch in the scan, or it could be an indication that there's something wrong."

"When you say *something wrong*, what do you mean? Like a tumour?" Mum's hand tightens more.

"As I say, it's not possible to be certain at this stage. And it could be nothing. There's no point in speculating."

"But you don't think it's nothing. If you thought it was nothing, we wouldn't all be sitting here." I can almost feel the calmness seeping away.

Doctor McKenzie wheels her chair slightly closer to me, leans forward, and puts her hand on my shoulder, looking me in the eye.

"Eilidh, I simply don't know. It really might be nothing, but equally, it could be important. There are a few tests that I can do now that will help me get a better idea. Are you happy for me to run through those with you?"

"Yes. What kind of tests?"

"I'd like to test a number of different things. Reflexes, muscle strength, vision, eye and mouth movement, coordination, balance, alertness, and a few other functions. Nothing invasive. Are you okay with that?"

"Yes."

"Okay. Good. Now, the first thing I'd like you to do is to place your palm against my fist here. Good. Now try to push my fist backward. That's right. Harder. Okay. Good. You can stop. Now I'd like you to do the same with your other hand."

And so it goes on. Various tests. Questions. Lights being shone in my eyes. Doctor McKenzie scribbling notes at every stage. Being attentive. Encouraging. Mum sitting silently by, giving the occasional nod of support. And throughout it all, the strange calmness has returned. It's not like what I imagine an out-of-body experience is. But it's like I'm observing something happening. Not experiencing it. I can't think of a word. Dislocation? I hear myself answering Doctor McKenzie's questions almost like I'm an eavesdropper. Is this how my mind protects itself? Distancing itself from a body that's diseased? Like it's—

"Eilidh?"

Doctor McKenzie's insistent tone snaps me back into the moment. "Sorry, I was away with the fairies."

"Are you okay?" Concern on her face. Mum's too.

"Aye. Honestly. Just day dreaming."

"Okay. That's fine. That's all of the tests done. Just a few more questions. Is that all right?"

"Fine. Fire away." The calmness has gone again. We're getting near to the end. The verdict. Got to stay composed.

"Have you experienced any unusual symptoms? Anything out of the ordinary?"

"Not that I can think of?"

"What about yesterday? When you dropped the knife?" Mum's right on it. She nods at me. Doctor McKenzie looks expectant.

"Oh, yes. Sorry. I forgot." I look straight at Doctor McKenzie, then flick a glance at Mum. I need to be honest. Not play it down like when I told Mum. "It was yesterday afternoon. I was going to put a knife into the dishwasher. Then there was this sudden pain in my head."

"Whereabouts in your head?"

"I don't know exactly. It felt like it was everywhere. Maybe the front half of my head?"

Doctor McKenzie leans in. "Can you describe the pain?"

"It was really sudden. Inside my head. Ferociously sore. Bad enough for me to drop the knife."

"How would you rate the pain? On a scale from one to ten, where ten is high."

"Ten." I see Mum's eyes widen.

"I see. And how long did the pain last for?"

"I'm not sure. When I dropped the knife, it cut the skin just above my ankle." I nod toward the bandage. "I remember being really dizzy. Still having the headache, but maybe a bit less sharp. I put a plaster on the cut and took paracetamol for the pain in my head. I think that helped to ease it, but the headache stayed with me until I went to bed."

"She looked terrible, doctor. Very pale. Ended up having to go to bed really early." Mum's trying to be helpful without sounding anxious, and doing a poor job of the latter.

"When you say the paracetamol helped to ease it, can you describe how it felt?"

"Like a dull thumping headache. Just less severe."

"And that continued until you went to bed?"

"Yes."

"How much later was that?"

"I probably first felt the sharp pain about four o' clock. I headed up to bed about seven." I look to Mum, who nods confirmation.

"And after the original sharp pain, there was a dull thumping that continued until you went to bed?"

"Yes."

"That's good, Eilidh. Thank you." She's jotting furiously. Noting down everything I say. "And how much paracetamol did you take?"

"Two."

"Two five hundred milligram paracetamol tablets." Saying it out loud as she writes it down.

"I don't know what size they were."

"Don't worry. If you bought them over the counter, they're pretty much guaranteed to be that dosage. Tell me more about the headache."

"There's not much more to tell. I went to bed and fell asleep before I'd even got a chance to get changed."

"So the headache didn't keep you awake?"

"No. Not at all."

"And how about now? Any headache? Any trace?"

"No. Nothing at all."

"When you woke this morning, there was no headache? It had gone?"

"Yes. That's right."

Doctor McKenzie finishes writing on her pad and looks up at me. "That's really helpful, Eilidh. Thank you. Now, is there anything else that might have slipped your mind? Anything at all different or unusual that you can think of?"

I look at her. Then at Mum. Then back. "Well …" What do I say? How can I avoid sounding like anything other than a total moon howler? They're both looking at me. They know there's something.

"Go on, love. Anything you can tell her will help the doctor."

And so I tell them. About Ethiopia. The different people there. How they are all real. Or were, all those years ago. About Kia. About America. Margaret. *This is Your Life* for Walter. About him recognizing me. Being twenty years younger. How Walter is the key to the mystery. Him thinking I'm his wife called Patti. How it's all linked. And then I stop. Conscious that I've been babbling—my words like a river in full spate, drowning my listeners in nonsense. Doctor McKenzie's expression is attentive. Mum's is bewilderment.

She turns to Doctor McKenzie. "She told Doctor Naismith about the same hallucination—the stuff about Ethiopia—the day she was admitted after she was knocked unconscious. All this stuff about America and Walter is new."

"I'm *not* hallucinating!"

I can see fear all over Mum's face. I don't want to frighten her. She exchanges glances with the doctor. "Eilidh, remember the last time? We agreed it couldn't possibly be real. That it was a nightmare. Remember?"

I *do* remember. But that was then. When I was suggestible. Now I *know* what I experienced. But there's no point. They're never going to believe me. It doesn't make any kind of sense. Not even to me. "You're right, Mum. It just seems so real to me. But I know it can't be."

There's partial relief in her eyes and the smallest of smiles. "That's right, love. Sometimes we can have the most vivid dreams." She turns to Doctor McKenzie. "Doctor, these halluc—" She catches herself. "These dreams. Could they be connected to her fall or to the dorsolateral cortex thing on the scan?"

"The possible anomaly in the dorsolateral prefrontal cortex area." Doctor McKenzie's correction is gentle, supportive. "I don't know. It's a highly specialized area of medicine, not one I feel comfortable speculating about. However." She pauses to check she has my full attention. "I'm friends with someone who is an expert in the field. Elspeth and I studied together. I'm going to refer you officially, and also approach her unofficially. I know she'll move heaven and earth to see you as soon as possible."

"Where is she based, doctor?" I'm glad Mum's speaking for me. I'm not sure if I can.

"She's at the Beatson, in Glasgow. So not too far to travel."

"The Beatson? The cancer centre?"

"Yes." A pause. "Look, I'm not going to tell you not to worry. Of course you're going to worry. What I will tell you is not to jump to conclusions. Elspeth and her staff will be able to provide a diagnosis as quickly as possible. If everything is clear, you'll know as soon as you can." Another pause. "And if there is something that needs further investigation, you'll be in the best place possible."

She's looking right at me. A quarter-smile of reassurance, and benevolence in her eyes, like those pictures of Jesus in the *Children's Illustrated Bible* at home. She's straight as a die, Doctor McKenzie. This is real. This is happening. I know I should say some words of acknowledgement, but I still can't speak.

"So, doctor, are you sure your friend will be able to see Eilidh quickly?" Thank God for Mum.

"Her name is Elspeth Cooke. Our families spent our holidays together last month in Tuscany. Elspeth and I were chief bridesmaids at each other's weddings."

I'm going to be a priority.

"Is there anything more you want to ask me, Eilidh?" I shake my head. She turns to Mum. "Kirsty, any questions from you?"

"I don't think so, doctor. No."

"All right. You've still got my mobile number?" She's looking at Mum. "From before?" Mum nods. "Good. If there are any other questions that do occur to you, just give me a call. Any time."

"Thanks, doctor." My voice is back. Really small, but back.

"I'll be in touch once I've contacted Elspeth. It's likely to be Monday, once she's had a chance to review her schedule. Meantime, please remember what I said. Don't pre-judge things. It's easy to jump to conclusions, but you should try to stay positive." She shifts position in her chair to signal it's time for us to go.

Mum and I both get to our feet, making goodbye and thank you noises. We make our way out. Hannah Lennox nods to us but doesn't say anything. Out through the vestibule and the front doors, me a pace ahead. Outside, I turn to face Mum. She's ready to cry, but she's holding it back. Being strong for me. I'm ready to cry. But I'm holding it back. Being strong for her. We hug each other. Tight. I convulse slightly as I refuse to let a sob escape. Mum squeezes tighter. We stay like that for ages. Eventually, Mum asks, "Are you okay, big girl?" I nod, and she kisses me on the forehead.

27.

BACK IN THE car. I buckle my seatbelt and wonder if there's any point. Then immediately shake myself out of that thinking.

"When we get back, George and Scott will want to know how you've got on."

"I know."

"Do you want me to tell them for you?"

"Are you sure?"

"Only if you'd prefer me to do it."

"Please."

"Will you go and sit with Gran in the living room, if I take them into the kitchen to tell them?"

"Aye. No bother. It'll be easier for me if I'm not there when you tell them."

She looks across at me. "Easier for them too." A soft intake of breath. "And me." She pauses. "And I'll phone the shop and tell them you're not coming in today."

The shop! I'd completely forgotten it was Saturday. I'm already late for my shift. "I can't let them down at such short notice, Mum. I've got to go in."

"Eilidh McVicar, for someone with four A's at Advanced Higher, you can be really stupid sometimes. I said I'd phone to tell them you're not coming in."

No arguing with that tone. And she's right. As usual.

We get home, and Mum parks in the spot where Molly and Walter's car had been previously. As we go through the front door, I can already hear the elephant stomp of George's footsteps on the upstairs landing. I divert into the living room. Gran is sitting in front of the TV and turns to look at me. As I pull the door closed behind me, I hear George thundering down the stairs and Mum calling for Scott.

Gran gets to her feet. Her eyes are lasering mine as she comes toward me. It's like before. Purpose. Awareness. "Did you see our Suzy?"

"What?"

She grabs both my shoulders in her hands, pulling me toward her. "Don't mess me about, lassie! You've travelled. Again! Did you see our

Suzy?" She's so close I can feel the breath of her words on my face. I can also feel the longing. The yearning.

"No, Gran. I didn't see Suzy."

Her grip loosens, and she takes half a step back. Her eyes are still vibrant but now filled with tears. My answer wasn't the one she wanted. "Gran, if I do meet Suzy, is there anything you want me to tell her? Or to ask her?"

No hesitation. "Ask her if she's happy. If she says yes, then tell her I think she made the right decision. That I'm happy for her." Then she's gone. Just like that. Not physically. But the eyes are tired again. Seeing, but only partially understanding. I guide her back to her seat, and her attention returns to the TV.

I hear the front door close and catch a glimpse of George heading out the front gate and turning left, in the opposite direction from his car. I recognize the scurrying pattern of Scott's footsteps running upstairs. I ease the living room door open and make my way along the hall to the kitchen. Mum is filling the kettle.

"How did it go?"

"Oh!" Mum flinches, and some of the water spills. "I didn't realize you were there."

"Sorry. I didn't mean to sneak up on you."

"No, you're fine."

"So how did you get on?" I'm not going to tell her about Gran. There's enough going on already.

Mum puts the kettle on the counter and switches it on, then turns to me. "Fine, as far as I can tell. I told them that the doctor had identified something that looked a wee bit odd on your scan and was going to ask her specialist friend to have a look at it."

"And they were fine with that?"

"Scott never said a word from start to finish. George asked questions."

"What did he ask?"

"Where exactly the odd bit on your scan was. I said it was in your brain, at the front."

"Oh."

"He asked where Doctor McKenzie's friend would see you, and I told him it was at the Beatson."

"What did he say?"

"He just said *right*. Then he paused and asked if we should tell Archie."

"There's no need for us to say anything to Archie. We can wait until I've seen Elspeth Cooke. Then, if there's any news, we can maybe contact him."

"That's exactly what I said. I also said that Doctor McKenzie had emphasized that there's no point in speculating unnecessarily. Oh, and I also said to them that they should treat you just the same as usual. No tiptoeing round you."

"Good. Thanks, Mum."

"Then George said he was going to go for a walk."

"Not to his bed? He must be exhausted."

"No. Said he was going for a walk, and off he went. Scott just said he was going back upstairs. And that was it. Off they both went." The kettle clicks off as it comes through the boil. "Do you want a cup of tea, love?"

"No thanks. I think I'll pass, Mum. Would you mind if I went up to my room for a while?"

"Of course not. Give me a shout if you need me or if you think there's anything special you'd like for lunch."

I go over and kiss her gently on the side of the head. "Thanks, Mum. But I'll just have whatever it is that everyone else is having. No tiptoeing round me, remember?"

She smiles and gives me a knowing look. I turn and head toward the stairs. I reach my bedroom and close the door behind me. A huge sigh escapes. Being brave is exhausting. But it's the right thing to do. I decide to stretch out on my bed, shoes still on—how cavalier am I? I'm just starting to try to get my head round things when there's a soft knock at the door.

"Come in."

The door opens slowly, and Scott's head pokes round. "Can I come in?"

"I just said so, didn't I?"

He doesn't rise to the bait. "Can I talk to you?"

"If you want."

He comes and positions himself at the bottom corner of the bed. I adjust my feet to make more room for him. "You've got your shoes on. On top of the duvet."

"Is that what you want to talk to me about?"

"No."

"Well, what is it, then?"

"I want to ask you some questions."

"Go on, then. I'm waiting."

He's not looking at me. Staring back at the door. "Are you going to die?"

Jesus! I did not see that coming. Try to think of something funny to say. But my brain's not at it today. Got to be quick. The silence is excruciating. "I …" The word chokes in my throat. I cough and swallow, grasping for composure. "I hope not."

"I hope not too."

"Thank you."

"Do you believe in heaven?"

Oh my God. "I don't know."

"Kids at school say it's just a made-up fairy story. It's not real."

"And what do you think?"

"I don't know either. The minister at Dad's funeral said he was in heaven now. But other people say it's not real."

"Different people believe different things."

"They can't all be right."

"Maybe they can."

"That's just stupid."

"If you believe in something and it works for you, then it's true for you."

"That sounds like shite."

"Scott McVicar! What sort of language is that?"

"I've heard *you* say it. And George. And Archie. I even heard Dad say it when his horse fell in the Grand National."

"That doesn't mean it's all right for you to say it."

"Everything turns to shite."

"Scott!"

"It's true. Everything." He's still refusing to look at me. Face firmly directed toward the door. He's struggling to keep his voice level.

"Why are you saying that?"

"Because it's true. Archie went away to university. Then Dad died. Now you're going to die. And Jacob is moving to England next week with his dad's work."

I'm appalled and amused at the same time. Appalled he thinks I'm going to die. Amused that it's less of an issue than his best pal moving away. "Why are you saying that I'm going to die?"

"Because you are!"

"I never said that. I said I hoped not."

"See! If you weren't going to die, you would've said so. But you just said you hoped not. Because you think I'm a baby and I can't take it."

"Scott! That's not true."

"Yes it is. Everybody lies to me. Because I'm the youngest, everybody thinks I'm a baby. You all treat me like a baby. But it's George who's the real baby!"

"What do you mean?"

"After Mum told us what the doctor said, I followed him into the hall. I was going upstairs, but he had said he was going out for a walk. When I went past him at the front door, he was crying. My big brother was crying. Like a shitey big baby."

"Scott! Stop saying that word. And don't say bad things about your brother."

"It's true! Everything is turning to shite. Archie. Dad. You. Jacob. And George is a crybaby." He turns to look right at me. Eyes ablaze, blinking back tears. Defying me to tell him he's wrong.

"Oh, Scott!" I lean forward to embrace him, but he pushes me away with his hand. He leaps to his feet and dashes out the door, letting it slam behind him.

I can't take any more of this. The weird stuff with Walter. The brain scan. The Big C. Gran giving me messages for her dead sister. Scott thinking I'm going to die. The family falling apart. I roll onto my side on the bed and curl into the foetal position, close my eyes, and squeeze them tight. Make it all go away.

October 31, 1969

28.

I'M COLD. REALLY cold. And my bed is rock hard below me. I was being chased again—definitely chased rather than followed. The same inky black cloud with fiery eyes as before, and I could sense how much raw hatred it had for me. I've got a pounding headache. I can taste vinegar. Shit! I know what this means. I open my eyes slowly. It's daylight. My face is right up against a wooden expanse. I feel the solid structure beneath me with my hand. Also wood, I think. I sit up. I'm on a bench in a shelter. I get to my feet unsteadily and press my hand against the shelter for support. I take a step forward. There's a pole in front of the shelter with a Bus Stop sign. I've woken up in a crappy bus shelter!

Where am I? And when am I? There's nothing to provide a clue. No information or timetables in the shelter. No numbers below the Bus Stop sign. Nada. There's a rubbish bin at the bottom of the pole. Empty. Not even a plastic liner. I step forward and look both right and left. The road is pretty straight for maybe a quarter of a mile in each direction before it bends. Lots of trees and bushes both sides. No street lights. No traffic.

The trees and vegetation look familiar. So does the Bus Stop sign. And it's in English. I'm pretty sure I'm in Scotland. Or at least the UK. Definitely not Ethiopia or the States. But where are the people? There were people around the last two times. This place is deserted. Am I meant to wait here? For a bus maybe? I feel my pockets. No money. Should I just start walking? Which direction?

To the right I hear a loud engine. A motorbike coming, maybe? A car comes into view around the corner. It sounds like a tank. And it's going at a fair lick. Instinctively, I step forward and hail it like it's a cab. But I'm still a bit unsteady and have to quickly stretch out for the Bus Stop pole for balance. The car stops about ten yards away, and the engine cuts. Actually, it's a van. Vintage. Maybe 1950s or 1960s. The door opens, and the driver gets out. Really tall. Longish hair in an old-fashioned feather cut. Dark copper. Huge bushy sideburns like a Dickens character. "Are you all right?" The voice is unmistakeable. Younger, but definitely him. Walter looks the same age as me, or as near as makes no difference. I feel my legs give and grip the pole harder.

"Can you hear me? Are you okay?" He's covered the ground in a twinkling and has hold of my wrist. Firm. Gentle. Supportive. Looking right into my eyes. Obviously concerned.

"Yes. I think so."

"Are you sure? You look a bit unstable on your feet. Do you want to sit back down?" He doesn't wait for an answer. One hand still on my wrist. The other under my elbow. He guides me back to the bench.

"Thanks." What am I going to say to him?

"Where's your coat? Or your jacket?"

Shit! What should I say? I pretend to look around. "I don't know."

Walter looks about for the non-existent coat, then gets up and looks around the outside of the bus shelter. He turns back to me. "Wait there a minute."

"I'm not going anywhere."

He smiles. The first time he's dropped the concerned face. He turns and goes back to his van, reaches in across to the passenger seat, and retrieves something. Think! Think! Think! What am I doing here? What do I say to him? He's coming back. It's something denim. A jacket. He holds it wide as he gets near me. I lean forward. He drapes it round me. Over my shoulders. "That might help keep the chill off you."

"Thanks again." Got to be ready for the inevitable inquisition.

"So what's the story here?"

"Sorry?"

"What's going on? What's someone doing in the middle of nowhere, without a coat, hanging onto a bus stop and waving down a random van?"

"I don't know." Second time I've said that. It's not going to wash a third time.

"What do you mean, you don't know?"

"Maybe I was mugged. Ripped off. You know?"

"Eh?" His face is the epitome of bafflement. Shit. If he's the same age as me, this is fifty years ago. How do people talk?

"Like, maybe I was robbed?"

"Somebody robbed you and ripped your coat off? Here? Jesus Christ!" He's hunched down in front of me, so our faces are level. The worried look is back. "We need to find the nearest police station and get this reported."

Shit! Shit! Shit! No! This is a nightmare. I'm losing control. "No! Not robbed. I don't know why I said that." Worry morphs to confusion. "I fell. Banged my head. Was unconscious." He's looking right into my eyes, but I think he's going with it. Keep going this way. Tell him the truth. Or a version of it. He's much more likely to believe something that's at least on nodding terms with reality.

"Go on."

"A few days ago, I had an argument with my boyfriend. My ex-boyfriend. I slipped and fell. Got knocked out. Since then, everything has been really weird. Strange."

"How do you mean strange?"

"I keep wakening up and finding myself in strange places. Not knowing how I got there."

"And that's what's happened now? You've woken up here, and you don't know how you got here?" He believes me. I can tell. So he should. It's the truth.

"Yes." I let it hang. Watch his big, wide eyes. Kind eyes.

"And are you feeling all right now?"

"Yes, thanks. A wee bit of a headache. But that's fading. And I was cold, but this jacket's helping."

"Good. And do you know where you are?"

"Honestly? No."

"You're in Drumchastle Wood."

"Where?"

"Between Kinloch Rannoch and Balmore. On the road to Pitlochry."

"The Highlands?"

"Aye." He grins. Then the serious face returns again. "Where are you meant to be?"

Don't answer straight away. Think. Still okay to stick with the truth? "Kilmadden."

"You're at it!"

"What? Do you know it?"

"I should do. I'm there every second Saturday." His smile is boyish. Open. Sincere.

"What do you mean?" I'm smiling back, despite myself. He's just a likeable guy.

"I play for Kilmadden Primrose. And I did a bit of work there a year or so back. I live in Ardnahuish."

"Get away!" I feign surprise, as I remember old Walter telling me he played for the Primrose. "What are the odds?"

"Well, they do say it's a small world." I can see it coming as he pauses. Surely he's not going to? Then he does. "But I wouldn't like to have to paint it all."

I'm smiling despite myself. It's a howlingly bad joke, but there's just something about him. He sees my smile and grins with pleasure.

"So how often have you told that one, Walter?"

"How do you know my name?"

Shit! I break eye contact and look away. He follows my gaze. To his van. Walter Buchanan—Bricklaying and General Building Services. Thank you, God! "Because in another life, I'm the female Sherlock Holmes."

It's his turn to smile at my feeble joke. He takes me by surprise by thrusting his hand out. Very formal. I shake it instinctively. "Wattie Buchanan, at your service. Walter is my Sunday name."

Oh no. I don't like that. "Well, I'm going to call you Walter."

He's obviously taken aback and almost double takes, like a cartoon character. Maybe he's wondering if I'm mad. Then he shrugs. "Okay. If you want."

Good. I don't know why, but that felt important. I don't want him to be a Wattie. I want him to be Walter. He's still looking right at me. Waiting. Smiling encouragement. What does he want now? He nods. What is he waiting for?

The penny drops. I extend my hand, and he grips it. Not too firmly. "Patti. Patti Smith." I say it without thinking.

"Very pleased to meet you, Patti Smith." His grin widens. "Or should I call you Patricia?"

"Certainly. If you want a smack in the face."

"Patti it is."

"I'm glad we've got that sorted."

His expression returns to one of concern. Like the class joker who realizes he's forgotten his homework again. "That's all fine and well, Patti, but we have to get you back home. People will be worrying about you. We should get to the nearest phone box and let them know that you're all right."

"We don't have a phone at home." I hope that's credible. Seems to be.

"What about a neighbour?"

"Nope."

"Maybe we should phone the local police. In case they're looking for you."

"They won't be."

"How do you know?"

Shit! Shit! Shit! "Because! Because it's a surprise visit. I live in Renfrew. I was meant to be visiting my auntie in Kilmadden."

"You've been finding yourself lost in strange places since you were knocked out, and you thought it was a good idea to travel alone from Renfrew to Kilmadden?"

Shit. I need to get him to back off. "My dad's dead, and my mum works full time. We agreed it would be good for me to go to Auntie Isa's. She doesn't work. No kids of her own, and I've always been a favourite of hers."

"Aye, okay." I can tell from his tone he's still sceptical. But he's going along with it. I feel bad about using Dad. "So how do you want to play it?"

"What do you mean?"

"Look, I'm happy to give you a lift to your auntie's. But there's a problem."

"What kind of a problem?"

"You must've heard me coming before you saw me."

"Oh, yes. Your van was making a bit of a racket."

"That's putting it mildly. My exhaust finally fell off a few miles back. I'll have to stop in Pitlochry or Perth or somewhere to get a new one fitted. That could easily add another hour to the journey."

"I don't mind."

"Or I could put you on a bus or a train and maybe get you there sooner."

"No. I'd rather go with you." Shit! I want to stay with him to learn what I can. But that came out wrong. I sound pathetic.

"Okay. If that's what you want." I can tell he's pleased. "Are you okay to get into the car now? There's no rush, if you need a bit longer sitting here."

"I'm fine, thanks. No time like the present. Actually, what is the time?"

"Nearly quarter to one. Why?"

"No reason. Just asking."

We walk toward his van. He takes the lead, gets there slightly ahead, and opens the passenger door for me. I take my seat—leather. Everything else is unbelievably spartan. Almost primitive. A few dials in front of the driver's seat. A gearstick and a handbrake. I reach instinctively for my seatbelt. There isn't one.

Walter gets into his seat and slams his door. Looks round and smiles. "This is the end of conversation for a while." I give him a quizzical look. He turns the ignition, and the noise from beneath us is almost indescribable. "See what I mean?" He's literally shouting, and I can barely make out what he's saying above the racket. I nod in response, and we pull away. The next twenty-five minutes are like being inside an oil drum with someone trying to break out using a pneumatic drill. Eventually, Walter taps me on the shoulder and points to a sign: *Johnstone Tyre & Exhaust*. We pull in and park.

Walter smiles across at me. "That's a relief. Just wait here a minute, and I'll see if they can sort us." He gets out the van, closes the door gently behind him, and strides purposefully toward the office. Straight back. Broad shoulders. Slim waist. Fantastic arse.

29.

THE "WAITING ROOM" is pretty basic. Four battered metal and plastic chairs along one wall. Opposite is a table bearing a kettle, some mugs, a tin of Nescafe, sugar bowl, and a half-full bottle of milk.

"How do you take your coffee, Patti?"

"Just milk, please. No sugar."

He looks at me as though he's not sure he heard correctly. "No sugar?"

"That's right. Just milk."

"Okay." He picks up the sugar-encrusted teaspoon. Looks at it for a few seconds. The kettle boils. He shovels three heaped spoonfuls of sugar into one mug. Three! Then he drops the spoon in the mug, pours boiling water in, and stirs. He pulls out the clean spoon and smiles to me before using it to spoon Nescafe into his mug, then into a separate mug. He pours boiled water into the second mug, adds milk, stirs, and brings it over to me. "How's that?"

I look into the mug and smile up at him. "Fine. Thank you."

"You're welcome." He pours milk into his own coffee. Stirs. Brings it back to sit beside me.

I sip my coffee. It's hot, but drinkable. Only instant, but it tastes good. Quite rich. Full fat milk. Can't remember the last time I had that. He's looking at me over the brim of his mug. Like it's my turn to say something. He's got beautiful eyes. Really beautiful. Lashes I'm jealous of. But I can't tell him. "So how long did they say it would take?"

"They said it would be up to an hour. But they'll be done in three quarters, no bother. They just say up to an hour so that you're pleased when it's sooner."

"Expectation management."

"Sorry, what?"

"They're just managing your expectations so that when they do better, you'll be pleased. I'm agreeing with you."

He smiles at me again and pauses. Thoughtful. "I like that. *Expectation management.* Nice way of putting it."

He's going to start asking me questions. I need to get in first. "Lucky that they had the right exhaust for the van."

"Not really. I suspect every exhaust place in the country carries a supply for Morris Minors, they're so common. Mine's a '57 model, so twelve years old. You'd expect it to need replacing."

That's closed that one down. But now I know it's 1969. Walter must be nineteen, given that it was his fiftieth birthday surprise party in 2000. Quick. Think of another question. "What're you doing in the highlands if you live in Ardnahuish?"

"I've been working on a job up there." He can see from my expression that it's not a sufficient answer. "I'm a time-served brickie. I set up as independent contractor and got my own van, as you know. My pal Bert is a signwriter—did the van for me. I've even got my own listing in *Yellow Pages*."

He's not boasting. But he's trying to impress. To impress me. That pleases me, makes me feel good. "Doesn't explain why you're travelling this far to find work."

"I had a mate up there working on the job. He got in touch. Said they were in trouble—needed a reliable brickie. Willing to pay top dollar. That was five weeks ago. I've been up here Monday to Friday since then. I've probably got less than a week now until the job's finished. I'm a subbie. I go where the money's best."

"So how come you knocked off early today?"

"Part of the deal. I drive up Monday morning and finish lunchtime on a Friday. I prefer to be back down early on a Friday so I can prepare properly for the game on the Saturday. I stay in a B&B during the week. It's boring there, so I tend to work later to fill time. I get well paid, but they get their money's worth out of me."

"Looks like you're doing well for yourself. Own van, self-employed, and what? Nineteen or twenty? What will you do when the job you're on finishes?"

I'm genuinely interested. And he can sense it, just like I can sense his pleasure. "I'm nineteen, seeing as how you ask. And I suppose I have done well, but I've worked for it. It helps that I take the football seriously enough that I don't drink. That saves a fortune—helped me save for the van. I'll get work back nearer home as soon as I'm free. Already got a couple of offers."

"On your van, it said general building services as well as bricklaying."

"Aye, well. To be honest, Patti, you have to serve four years to finish your apprenticeship and get your papers. The truth is that you can learn everything in less than a year. The rest is just experience. Serving time. I made it my business to help the other trades whenever I could, so I could learn from them. It helped keep me from going mental with boredom. I hope that doesn't sound big headed. I'm just telling it straight."

"It doesn't sound big headed at all." It really doesn't. I'm going to ask how he got into it in the first place. But he takes the initiative.

"What about you? Do you have a job?"

"Aye. A part-time job. I work in a supermarket on a checkout."

"Part time? What age are you?"

"Eighteen." I'm judging from the cold and the light that we're well into autumn, maybe November time. Can't say I'm about to go to uni. "I'm on a gap year. Working to save enough to go travelling."

"A gap year?"

"Aye. Before I go to university next year."

He shuffles uncomfortably on his chair. "University?"

"Yes. I'm going to St. Andrews to study history."

"So a bit of a brainbox, then? A bit posh?" He's avoiding eye contact.

"I'm not a brainbox. I'm just interested in history and lucky enough to be able to study it."

"Hmmm." Still no eye contact.

"And I'm certainly not posh."

Me going to university has certainly changed the dynamic. The easy flowing conversation is gone. He's not resentful. At least I don't think so. But he's uncomfortable. "What will you do with a history degree? Teach?"

"I don't think so. Teaching's never really appealed to me."

"So what will you do with it?"

"Nothing in particular. It probably just helps open up other opportunities."

"Like what?"

"I don't know!"

"Like making you more appealing as a wife to some posh boy?"

"What?"

"You heard me."

"I certainly fucking did, you cheeky bastard. Who says I want to marry a posh boy? Who even says I want get married at all?"

"Well what's the point? Swanning off to spend years studying something you're not going to use. A complete waste. What *are* you going to do?"

"I told you I don't know. Maybe when I'm finished with that, I'll do an apprenticeship. Become a brickie like you. Or a plumber."

"Now you're just taking the pish."

"What? Why?"

"Who ever heard of a woman brickie? Or a woman plumber? It's just stupid."

"Why? Why is it stupid? Why can't a woman be a brickie or plumber?"

Walter gets up from his chair, walks across to the table, and places his empty coffee mug down. He turns to look at me. Look down at me. "Patti, I don't know if you're just at it. Taking up an unbelievable point of view just for the sake of an argument. But can we just drop this, please?"

Fuck just dropping it. Who does he think he is? Sexist bastard. "What's unbelievable about it? Are you saying women are too stupid to do men's work?"

"Not too stupid, no. Just inferior."

"Inferior! Who the fuck are you calling inferior?"

"So you think you can climb up three ladders to the top of a scaffold in the freezing rain carrying a full hod of bricks? Or replace a boiler pump that's rusted in place when you can barely get one hand in to locate it? It's common sense. Men are bigger and stronger. We're built to do man's work."

He believes it! He actually fucking believes it! "There's no such thing as man's work. There's only work that men monopolize so that women have to do the rubbish, less well-paid jobs. If a man can do something, so can a woman."

"I play football. Can a woman play football?"

"Yes. And rugby. A woman can do boxing, karate. Anything a man can do."

He's grinning down at me. "I get it." He nods at my tits. "Are you going to burn it?"

"What?"

"Your over-the-shoulder boulder-holder."

"What are you talking about?"

"You know. Your tit sling."

"I said what the fuck are you talking about?"

"Your bra! Are you going to burn your bra?"

"What? Why would I want to do that?"

"Isn't that what you do? You women's libbers? That's what I've heard."

"Brilliant! I suppose making lewd comments is funny for a moron like you."

Oh shit.

I've crossed a line. The grin has disappeared, and I can see he's upset. Angry as well, but more upset. "Walter, I'm sorry."

"It's fine." Said in a tone that confirms it's anything but fine. "I'm just going to see how they're getting on with fitting it." He walks to the door and out without looking at me. I watch through the window as he strides toward the workshop. He doesn't look back.

How can I have been so stupid? I've really, really pissed him off. Why can't I be smarter? Why do I have to react to everything like it's a personal insult? He was just being someone of his time. Just saying what most folk believe. Probably trying to make a joke out of it. And I have to go and insult him.

I wait. And wait. I study the spoon he used to make the coffees. And wait some more. He's clearly decided to stay outside, in the workshop or office. Anything rather than be stuck in here with me. Maybe he'll just pay up once the work's done and drive off without me. I feel my stomach somersault at the prospect. The door opens, and he's back in the room. "All sorted. We're ready to go." He turns straight back out and walks toward his van, which is now in the courtyard. I follow him and get in. He turns on the ignition, and we pull away.

30.

WE'VE BEEN DRIVING for five minutes without a word spoken between us. Patti's staring straight ahead, obviously avoiding any sort of eye contact with me. The silence is amplified by the fact that the new exhaust means the car is a million times quieter than before.

This is awful. I can't let it go on like this. I have to say something.

"Patti, I'm sorry—"

"Look, Walter, we're—"

We both start to speak at exactly the same time. Like in those unbelievable scenes from movies or TV shows. What made me think that? Anyway, I'll defer to her. Let her go first.

There's an awkward pause as each of us waits for the other. Eventually, she says, "Go on, then."

"No. Please. You go first."

Another pause. "Okay, then. I was going to say that it's ironic that now we can hear each other in the car, neither of us is speaking. I don't know what went wrong back there, but I'm willing to apologize and put it behind us if you are."

"No." I pause for effect and she takes a sideways glance at me. "I won't accept your apology because I don't think I deserve one. It's the other way round completely. I owe you an apology. I'm sorry that I lost my temper. I really regret it, and I wish it never happened."

I steal a quick look at her. She's still looking straight ahead, but I can sense that her demeanour isn't confrontational the way it was a minute ago. I also register again just how good looking she is. I let a couple of seconds pass before continuing. "Patti, I'll only accept your apology if you accept mine. Deal?"

"Deal."

I'm pretty sure she's as pleased as I am that relations have thawed. I think it's okay to ask her the question that's been gnawing at the back of my mind since we stopped to get the exhaust replaced. "I don't want to prod a fresh wound, but is it okay if I ask you something about what happened back there?"

"Why?"

"Look, if you'd rather not, then it's fine. No problem. Honestly."

"No. It's all right. What do you want to ask?"

"You said that I made lewd comments."

"Yes?"

"What does *lewd* mean? How do you spell it?"

She turns in her seat to look at me, as if she's weighing up whether I'm serious, before replying. "L, E, W, D. *Lewd.* It means crude or offensive. In a sexual sense."

I didn't anticipate this! She thinks I was trying it on, telling dirty jokes. God Almighty! I really messed things up back there. "I didn't mean it in a sexual way. I was just trying to be funny. To take the heat out of things. I honestly never meant anything by it."

"I realize that now. I overreacted. One of my many flaws. I rise to the bait too easily. Lose perspective. I know you weren't trying to be crude."

"Good. But I'm still sorry it came across the way it did." I'm relieved, but still feel awkward.

"I thought we were done with apologies." Patti pauses, as though she's considering what to say next. "Walter, can I ask you something back?"

"What?"

"When I had a go at you back at the exhaust place, I really upset you. I didn't mean to be hurtful. I was just lashing out. But I was surprised at how much it seemed to affect you."

I didn't anticipate her saying that, and I feel completely wrong-footed. I can feel all the old emotions welling up inside of me as I consider its implications. Part of me is thinking, *Who the hell is this lassie? What right has she to poke about in my business?* But another part of me wants to answer, to tell her. Somehow, it matters to me what this virtual stranger, this Patti, thinks about me. "I overreact to some things too." My voice is low. Quiet. "All my life as a kid, I was the stupid one in school. The idiot. Bottom of the class. The thickie. The dunderhead. I'm quite good at shrugging it off, but sometimes it just gets to me. When you called me a moron … well, you know."

"Walter, I had no idea. And I'm really, really sorry."

"It's done. My problem, not yours. And I thought we agreed we were finished with apologizing." We drive on for a moment in silence.

"Walter, is it all right if I ask you about school?"

"What about it?" I can feel myself tensing up involuntarily.

"No. It's okay. If you'd rather I didn't."

"No. Go ahead and ask."

"Well, what it is I'm struggling with is this. You tell me that you were the stupid kid at school, yeah? But the person I see sitting beside me isn't the least bit stupid. In fact, the total opposite. He's nineteen. Time served. Set up his own business and got his own company van. He's bright, good at conversation, and funny enough to be able to make me smile at absolutely crap jokes."

She stops just when I don't want her to. I feel flattered, although I don't think she's intentionally trying to charm me. I think she's just saying as she sees it. At least I hope so. But I do wonder if she also fancies me. "Don't stop. I like the sound of what I'm hearing. You forgot to add in the bit about how good looking and noble I am."

She smiles and punches my arm gently. "Piss off, you!" We drive on for another twenty seconds or so. The mood is transformed. She continues, "Seriously though—if you even know how to be serious—it just doesn't add up."

"Thank you. You won't understand how nice it is to hear somebody say something like that. Especially a brainbox like you."

"I'm *not* a brainbox, you!" She delivers another mock punch to my arm.

"So they let dunces into university, do they?"

She ignores my question. "Why did you get called stupid at school?"

I feel my stomach clench. Then I take a long, shallow breath. "I was rubbish at reading and writing. Really rubbish. I tried hard at first. But I just couldn't do it. When we did tests in class, I was always bottom. Different teachers all told me I was slow, or lacking in application, or just not suited to school work." The words have been tumbling out, and I pause, partly to take a breath but also to marshal my thoughts. "When lots of different people tell you you're stupid—however they dress it up—then you just believe them. The other kids cottoned on and started to tease me about being thick. So I became a joker. The class clown. Better to have people laughing at my jokes than laughing at me. And I was good at football. That got me respect. Made me fit in. I was happy to be the guy that was funny and good at football."

I stop because I don't think there's anything more to say—and because it feels strange to have said all this to her. We drive on in silence for maybe a minute.

"Are you okay?" she asks.

"Yes. I've never really spoken about that before. Never said it to anyone."

"Maybe because no one's ever asked?"

"My mum and dad both did. But I could never explain it. I just used to get angry with them. In the end, I think they just had to believe the teachers when they were told I wasn't any good at school work."

"It seems so unfair."

"It's just the way things are, Patti. No point in moping about it. Just get on with things and show what you can do."

She pauses, as though she's considering what I've said.

"Walter?"

"Yes?"

"Have you heard of dyslexia?"

"Now who's being lewd?"

"Sorry? What do you mean?"

"Sounds like one of those posh names they have for VD. Like gonorrhoea."

"Walter, you are such an arse!"

Her third punch is firmer than the previous two. "Ow!"

"You deserved that."

"Go on, then. What is it?"

"It's the medical name that they've come up with for word blindness."

My heart misses a beat, and I suddenly feel like all of my senses are supercharged. I'm trying to take in what she's just said whilst at the same time willing her to say more, which she does.

"It's a recognized condition."

"Say what it's called again. And spell it."

"Dyslexia. D, Y, S, L, E, X, I, A."

"And it's a condition? A proper medical condition? Word blindness?"

"Yes. Just like some people are colour blind. Other people can be word blind."

"And where did you hear about this dyslexia condition?" It's not that I don't believe her or think that she's making it up. It just seems completely incredible to me. I might have a condition. Something properly recognized by doctors. Something that might explain so much, provide the answer to so many questions. Why haven't I heard about this before?

"It was on the radio. They were talking about research that was being done on it in America."

"And what else did they say?"

"Not much more than that."

"Did they say there was a cure?" I can hear the tension in my own voice. Oh God, please let there be a cure.

"No, they didn't. But I suppose if it's like colour blindness, then there probably isn't an actual cure as such."

"Okay." Her answer sounds sensible, but it's not what I want to hear. I can't believe how deflated I feel. For just a moment, I suddenly thought that there might be an answer, a magic solution for a disease or condition that I hadn't even realized I had. Then, just as suddenly, the hope was snuffed out. We drive on for several minutes without conversation. There's no bad atmosphere. It just seems like there's not a lot to say. After quarter of an hour or so, I take my own advice—no point moping, just get on with it—and break the silence. "Where is it that you want to go travelling?"

"Sorry?"

"Earlier. You said you were on a gap year. Working to save money to go travelling."

31.

I CAN TELL from a slight alteration in Walter's demeanour that my previous mention of travel genuinely interests him. He seems animated.

"Oh yes, that's right," I respond.

"So where, then?"

"Not really decided. Maybe just round Europe. Maybe something more adventurous. Southeast Asia or Australia maybe."

"Wow. You'd want to be careful in Southeast Asia."

This is where being a history student is useful. "I certainly wouldn't go near Vietnam or Cambodia. Thinking about it, I probably wouldn't risk going anywhere in the region just now."

"It's not like there isn't plenty to see closer to home anyway. I've always really wanted to see Europe. Maybe America."

"Any plans?"

"Yes and no. It kind of depends."

"On what?"

"Promise you won't laugh?"

"Probably not. But no guarantees."

His huge grin is back. "Fair enough. It all depends on the football."

"You're going to have to explain that one to me."

"All right. Look, I don't want to sound big headed. But I'm a pretty good player. I've had a fair few offers to go senior at some very decent clubs. But I've stayed part time with Primrose until I finished my apprenticeship. I wanted something to fall back on if the football doesn't work out. But now I've served my time, I need to make the move into full-time football."

"Sounds very impressive. But what's it got to do with you going travelling?"

"The offers I've had have come from Scottish clubs, plus two in England. I'm a decent player, and I'll get better once I turn full time. But I'm under no illusions that I'm a world beater. I'm never going to play for Scotland or anything like that. I'll be able to get a reasonable wage as a footballer. Probably much the same as I can earn on the building sites. Enough to get by."

"Interesting, and I'm sure you're being modest. But I still don't see the link to travelling."

"I want to play my football abroad. Nothing against Scotland, or even England for that matter. I just fancy trying a different lifestyle. I'd be happy to go to a lower division team in Spain, Italy, West Germany—some place like that."

"And what are the chances of that?"

"Funnily enough, there's a strong rumour that a scout with continental connections will be at tomorrow's match."

"Who are you playing tomorrow?"

"Away to Mintry Victoria, in the Qualifying Cup."

"Are they any good?"

"Very strong outfit, apparently. But we're a good side ourselves."

"Well, good luck for tomorrow."

"Thanks. I appreciate it."

The conversation moves on, switching topics frequently and easily. I'm aware that I need to be careful not to say anything that would sound too out of place in 1969, but it doesn't inhibit the flow between us. We talk about our respective families. He's sensitive when I talk about Dad. We exchange notes on annoying little brothers, although he describes his brother, Andy, as "another brainbox like you." I talk about school and my friends. He's impressed that Seonaid is going to be a doctor. He tells me tales from the building sites that make my hair curl. The hours pass, and I soon recognize familiar landmarks, although there are fewer buildings than in 2019.

"I should get you to your auntie's before it's too dark and all the weans are on the street."

"Why would there be weans on the street?"

"Because it's Hallowe'en."

"Oh yes, of course." It's October 31!

"Patti, can I ask you something?"

"That sounds ominous."

"You know you said you broke up with your boyfriend?"

I stiffen at the memory. "Yes?" I can hear the strangled tension in my own voice.

"Well, I was just wondering if you were doing anything on Sunday?"

OMG! He's asking me out. Shit! Never saw this coming. What do I say? "That's really nice of you, Walter, but I think I should spend the first couple of days just recovering and resting up at Auntie Isa's. Is that okay?"

"Sure. Of course it is. I wasn't thinking."

I feel terrible. I really, really like this guy, and I don't want to hurt him. But what can I say? "Maybe another time?" What a shitty cliché.

"Aye, maybe." Walter makes a point of concentrating on the road. There's a touch of frost inside the car. "We're just coming into Kilmadden now. Where's your auntie's house?"

"Oh, just drop me at the cross. I can walk from there." I want to get out before he quizzes me on where my auntie lives. On what I'm going to do for clothes given that I've no coat and no travelling bag with me. At least the tension between us now will spare me some awkward questions.

"Are you sure? It's no bother."

"Honestly, it's fine."

We draw into the roadside some twenty yards short of the cross. "Patti, what're you going to do for clothes, toothbrush, and a coat?"

Shit! "I've got some changes of clothes already at my auntie's. And a spare toothbrush." How implausible does that sound?

"Fair enough, then. But take that Levi jacket with you. Keep the chill off you until you get to your auntie's."

"Thanks, but I couldn't. How would I get it back to you?"

"A week tomorrow, after the home game, most of the lads go for a few pints at The Tassie. I sometimes go in and have a couple of lemonades with them. If you're still staying at your auntie's, you could maybe pop it in to me then?"

"And what if I've gone back to Renfrew?"

"Then I'll buy a beer, cry into it, and start saving for a new jacket." I *love* his smile.

I get out of the car and wrap myself in the denim. "Thank you. For everything." I flash him my biggest, best smile and blow him a kiss. I turn and start walking toward Meikle Close. I feel his eyes on me and turn. He waves and then pulls away in the van.

What now? I keep walking and pass a huge tree that isn't there in 2019, or at any time I can remember.

"Boo! Whoooooooooooo. Whoooooooooooo." From behind the tree.

What in the name of God? I turn around to find myself confronted by an Olympic athlete and Count Dracula. Both about eight or nine years old.

"You're too old to be out for your Hallowe'en." The athlete urchin's tone is a masterclass in disdain. "And what are you meant to be anyway?" He points to the denim jacket, which reaches below my knees and whose sleeves are only three-quarters filled by my arms and hands. "The Incredible Shrinking Woman?" They both laugh heartily. Little bastards.

Count Dracula fishes in a bag he's carrying and pulls out a hazelnut, still in its shell. He takes aim and bounces it right off my forehead.

"Ouch! You little bastards!" They're off and running, and I'm in full pursuit, murder in mind. As we reach Quarry Edge, I almost grab the athlete, but he wriggles free. My foot slips and I fall sideways. And fall. And fall.

August 10, 2019

32.

FALLING. FALLING. I look upward behind me, and I can see Dad, smiling down at me. *Don't worry, Eilidh*, he shouts. *I'll save you.* He stretches his hand out, reaching for me. Instinctively, I do the same, and our fingers almost touch. His kindly smile morphs into a predatory grin, and his shape dissolves into a black, inky cloud with two fierce red eyes glowing with malevolence. I'm genuinely fearful for my safety. Suddenly, I'm awake. In my bedroom. Eyes open. I try to feel my face, but my hand's smothered in something. A denim sleeve. I'm wearing Walter's jacket! I sit bolt upright, slowly swing my legs round, then stand up and step over to the mirror. You could fit two of me inside this jacket. There's sweat on my forehead. I take the jacket off slowly and hold it up wide in front of me. He really has got incredibly broad shoulders—I didn't notice them on old Walter. I go to the wardrobe and put the jacket inside on a spare hanger.

I sit down in front of the desktop on automatic and fire it up. Walter fancies me! Or fancied me, all those years ago. He must, if he asked me out. Gave me his jacket too, so he'd have a chance to see me again. Joked he'd cry into his beer if I didn't take it back. Definitely fancies me. Do I fancy him?

I start by Googling *1969*. There's all sorts of stuff, which is no surprise. Some of it I'm familiar with or have at least heard of. There are also references that mean absolutely nothing to me. The Beatles gave their last public performance on the roof of Apple records. Concorde had its first test flight in France, and the jumbo jet made its debut. Richard Nixon was the US president. These are all things that I have definitely heard about, or at the very least, they ring a bell.

Four hundred thousand rock and roll fans gathered at some place called Woodstock. Calling them rock and roll fans sounds so old fashioned. Someone called Bobbie Gentry had a UK hit with "I'll

Never Fall in Love Again." I've never heard the song, and I presume that spelling means Bobbie is a female, but who knows?

"Suspicious Minds" was a hit for Elvis Presley in America, which is a surprise. My parents have an old 45 RPM vinyl disc of that song by Fine Young Cannibals, but it looks like Elvis did it even before them. I'm also surprised to see that people were watching *Monty Python's Flying Circus* on TV that long ago. Who knew?

I don't really know what I'm looking for, but this kind of generic search isn't getting me anywhere. I type in *Walter Buchanan Scotland 1969* and click. I'm rewarded straight away when the first result returned is an article in the Brothmulloch and Ardnahuish Press and Argus, dated the 5th of December, 1969.

Buchanan Goes Low as He Aims High

Kilmadden Primrose starlet Wattie Buchanan caused something of a surprise when it was announced that he had signed a deal to play his football in the Belgian second division next year. The talented nineteen-year-old had been attracting interest from a host of clubs both north and south of the border. There was rumoured interest from Kilmarnock, Motherwell, Aberdeen, and Heart of Midlothian as well as enquiries from down south where Nottingham Forest and Fulham were known to have scouted the tall, pacey forward. So there was some astonishment when it was announced he was joining KFC Diest in Belgium's second tier. Wattie explained to the *Press and Argus*. "It's flattering to be linked to all these big clubs, but I've always had a notion to try my hand on the continent if the chance arose. Diest are going well in the league and pushing for promotion. I hope to help them achieve that. There was apparently interest from France as well. But I don't drink, so all that French wine didn't appeal to me. Whereas I understand Belgium is full of chips and chocolate," he joked. So young Buchanan is setting his sights high as he begins his career in the Low Countries.

Clichéd sports reporting has obviously been around for at least fifty years. Walter got his move abroad, then. And not long after we met at Hallowe'en. He's obviously a good player. Or at least he was back then. I get my tenses confused. Fifty years back was just fifteen minutes ago for me. I can't get my head round all of this. I reread the article and smile. I can just hear his voice saying the bit about French wine and Belgian chocolate and chips. And I can see his big, daft grin. And the image makes me smile.

It's almost half past twelve. I remember it was just after ten when Scott came into my room earlier. When he'd gone and I fell asleep, it couldn't have been later than half past. I've been awake for fifteen or twenty minutes. So I must have been out for an hour and a half, maybe an hour and three quarters. But I was with Walter for maybe five hours in 1969. Each time I've gone back, I've spent more time in the past than has elapsed in the present. But there doesn't seem to be any other relationship. Nothing proportional. It's not like two hours there exactly equals one hour here. Unless there's some relationship that I'm missing. Or maybe it's just random.

I still just can't get my head around all of this. It's obvious that Walter is the key. But key to what? Why do I keep encountering him? Am I meant to do something with him? Go to his home in Cobham? Is there some secret that he's meant to tell me? That he can't because of his dementia? Or is all of this just in my head? Is it a symptom of whatever's wrong with my brain? Am I really just imagining everything? Even the physical things that I bring back? Is that jacket really in the wardrobe, or do I just think it is? Is Kia's button just any old button I've picked up? Did I put this bandage on myself? Am I going mad? Did I just meet an old man at Dundo Point and my fried brain started to dream all sorts of crazy thoughts about him? My head is starting to hurt.

My phone rings on my bedside table. I stretch to grab it. Seonaid. "Hi, Seonaid."

"Eilidh. Didn't you get my texts?"

"Sorry, no. I've been a bit distracted today."

"Is everything okay?"

Should I say anything? "Seonaid, there's all sorts of shit going on in my head."

"What do you mean?"

"Doctor McKenzie called me this morning. Asked me to meet her at the surgery to discuss my CT scan. I went to see her, and there's something wrong in my brain."

"Fuck! Eilidh. Oh my God. What sort of something wrong?"

"She couldn't tell me. It's not her specialism. Just said there's an anomaly on the CT. She said it might be nothing to worry about. But she's referring me to her specialist friend at the Beatson to get an expert opinion. Seonaid, I think I might have a tumour." The word catches in my throat.

"Shit. Fuck. Eilidh, I don't know what to say."

"And I've been having dreams. Like really, really vivid dreams. But they're not dreams. They're actual reality. Mum and Doctor McKenzie think I'm having hallucinations, but everything seems so real to me. Seonaid, I'm scared. Really, really scared."

There's a tiny pause. "Right, Eilidh, deep breath. You said Doctor McKenzie said it might be nothing to worry about. Right?"

"Yes."

"What else did she say? Exactly."

Deep breath. "She said there was a bit of the scan that was a lighter shade than she would've expected. She said it could be a glitch in the scan or it could mean that something's wrong."

"Anything else?"

"She asked if she could do some tests on me. Reflexes, vision, eye and mouth movement, coordination, balance. That kind of stuff."

"And?"

"She did a load of tests and made piles of notes."

"Then what?"

"She asked about any other symptoms."

"And are there any?"

"I had a sudden, blinding headache yesterday afternoon. And …"

"And what?"

"The really vivid dreams that I mentioned. She called them hallucinations."

"Doctor McKenzie called them hallucinations?"

"Actually, no. It was Mum who said that. The doctor didn't."

"Right. Did she say anything else? What was her advice?"

"She said it was natural for me to worry. But that I shouldn't jump to conclusions. That I'll probably hear from her colleague at the Beatson on Monday. And that I should stay positive."

There's a pause before Seonaid speaks again. "Okay. Eilidh, you rate Doctor McKenzie, don't you? She was the one with your dad, wasn't she?"

"Yes, she was. And yes, I do rate her."

"Good. And she says that there might be a problem and that there might not? That it's natural to be worried but not to jump to conclusions?"

"Aye. That's right."

"So if this conversation were the other way round—if I told you all of that about me and that I was scared—what advice would you be giving me?"

I've seen Seonaid do this before. Help people try to see something from a different perspective. "I'd tell you that I could understand that you're worried. But that you've taken professional advice from someone you trust. And that someone has told you not to jump to conclusions. To wait until you're referred to a specialist after the weekend."

"And how would you feel if I gave you that advice right now?"

"Like you're a total smartarse."

"You're welcome. Look, Eilidh. Do you think that if Doctor McKenzie was convinced there really is a serious problem, she'd wait until Monday?"

"I guess not."

"Of course she wouldn't! She'd have had you admitted somewhere immediately."

"I suppose so."

"So pull yourself together, McVicar."

"You're going to have to work on that bedside manner of yours, Doctor MacDonald!"

"Aye, very good. Look, Eilidh, do you want me to come round? Spend some time with you? I'm meant to be going with my mum to visit Auntie Aileen in Ardnahuish later on, but I can easily cry off."

"No. Thanks, gorgeous girl, but you don't need to do that. To be honest, I've got a bit of a headache, so I'll probably just take it easy for the rest of the day."

"Are you sure? I honestly don't mind."

"No. Really it's okay."

"Fine. I'll maybe give you a call tomorrow and see how you're fixed."

"That would be good."

"All right, then. I'll let you go now."

"Hang on. What was it you wanted to ring me about in the first place?"

"It's just a bit of gossip. It can wait until tomorrow. You've got more than enough on your plate."

"No. Go on. To be honest I'd welcome any distraction."

"Are you sure?"

"I just said so, didn't I?"

"Okay, then. But be prepared to have your mind blown."

"Get on with it!"

"Alice has finished with Sandy."

I think she just said that Alice has finished with Sandy. But that's obviously not right. I must have misheard. "What?"

"You heard me. Alice has finished with Sandy."

"Fuck off!"

"I'm not shitting you. It's the gospel truth."

"She finished with him? When? Why?"

"Yes. She finished with him. She told him last night. Texted me this morning and asked me to call her."

"But they've been an item for three years, for God's sake. They were even going to uni in Glasgow together. Christ, she could probably have got in last year, but she wanted to wait for him."

"I know, I know, I know."

"So what's going on? What's happened?"

"That's what I asked her. She says that it's not felt right for months now. She means from her point of view. Says she still loves him, but not the same as before. She says she feels terrible. Really guilty. He's done nothing wrong. She says she just stopped fancying him. She says she became a right cow."

"How? What does she mean?"

"She says that she began to pick faults with things he did. Never said anything to him, like. Just inside her head. Criticizing some of his habits, the way he acted sometimes. She got annoyed at him just for being himself. And then at herself for being such a cow."

"How long has she felt like this?"

"She says since Easter. Maybe even longer."

"Easter! Why didn't she say something sooner?"

"She says she felt she couldn't. He had his exams, and she didn't want to put him off. She felt trapped. They'd told everyone they were going off to Glasgow Uni together. It was like she wasn't in control."

"So what's changed now?"

"Getting exam results. The prospect of going off to uni with Sandy becoming imminent. Alice says she realized it was all wrong and she had to do something before it became too late. So she told him last night. Face to face. Was honest but trying to be gentle at the same time. The old *it's not you, it's me* speech. She said it was the worst thing she's ever had to do."

"Oh my God. How did Sandy take it?"

"Terrible. Cried. Kept asking her to explain. Wanted to know what she wanted him to do differently. Begged her to change her mind."

"That's horrible. For both of them."

"I know. She said that in the end, she had to be brutal. Told him it's over forever. She's happy if they can be friends, but they will never be more than that in future. She also told him she'd gone through clearing and switched to Edinburgh Uni—her grades were so good it was easy for her."

"Jesus! That is pretty brutal. And it can't have been easy for her. Why didn't she talk to us? To you and me about all of this?"

"I asked her that too. She says she wanted to but felt it would be an even bigger betrayal of Sandy if she talked to us before him."

"I get that, although I'm not sure I could've gone through something like that without talking it over with my besties first."

"Me neither."

"So how is she now?"

"She says she feels strange. Says she barely slept at all last night. Feels bad for Sandy. Wonders how he'll tell his pals. How he'll tell his folks. But she says she also feels free. She knows she's done the right thing. Wishes she'd had the courage to do it earlier but pleased she's faced up to it now."

"Should I talk to her? Give her a ring?"

"She said this morning that she felt bad telling me without telling you at the same time. But she was worried after you being knocked unconscious. Wasn't sure about how to play it."

"Typical Alice. Always more worried about everyone other than herself."

"You're dead right there. How about I give her a call and tell her about your news? Would you be okay with that? Then maybe we can touch base tomorrow. See where everyone's at. Maybe get together?"

"I'm fine with that. I'll drop her a text so she knows I'm thinking about her."

"Good idea. Look, I'll let you go now. Promise you'll take care of yourself, and we'll catch up again tomorrow."

"I promise. Speak again tomorrow. Byeee."

"Byeee."

I message Alice: *Just spoke to Seonaid. Told me about you and Sandy. So, so sorry for everything you're going through. Thinking about you. If you want to talk—anytime— just call me. Love you lots. Speak soon. XXX* 🖤 🖤

My phone battery's low, so I plug it in to recharge. My headache's getting worse. I hear Mum calling upstairs about lunch and make my way downstairs into the kitchen.

Mum turns as she hears me enter. "Hello, love. I just wondered if you want anything for lunch? Scott's already eaten and skedaddled off somewhere, and I've just stuck sausage rolls in the oven for Gran, George, and me. Do you fancy one too?"

"I think I'll just make a sandwich and take it to my room. Got a bit of a headache. Maybe take a couple of paracetamols and have a lie down." I see her eyes widen with concern. George, who's sitting at the table, mirrors her expression. "Nothing to worry about you two, for God's sake. It's just a headache." Neither of them looks convinced as I get the bread, butter, and tuna mayo out.

"Okay, love." Mum's got her *everything's normal* voice on. I spread the butter and dollop on some tuna. "Did I hear you on the phone earlier?"

"Yes. Seonaid called." Put the second slice of bread on top and cut in two.

"That's nice. How is she?"

"She's fine." I place the sandwich onto a plate and reach for the paracetamol. "You'll never guess what's happened though."

"Go on. What?"

"Alice has finished with Sandy."

"Never! What's happened?"

"She just didn't feel it was right any more. She only told him last night, so the whole thing is pretty raw."

"Such a shame. For them both. Both such lovely people."

"I know."

George has been all ears. Any hint of fatigue banished. Now he can't contain himself any longer. "So that's Alice single is it? Back on the market?"

"George! You absolute fucking prick!"

"Eilidh! I will not have language like that in this house. And I will not have you speak to your brother like that!"

"I'm sorry, Mum. But that ... that *vulture* brings out the worst in me. I'm off upstairs!" I storm out with my sandwich and the paracetamol bottle. I can hear Mum remonstrating with George as I climb the stairs.

I reach my room and put the sandwich and pills on my desk, then fetch a glass of water from the bathroom. My head is really pounding now. I take two paracetamol and eat one half of the sandwich. I'm not really hungry. I lie down on my bed and roll onto my side.

March 11, 1972

33.

THE INKY BLACK cloud with the fiery eyes is almost upon me. It emits a banshee-like howl and is suddenly joined by a companion. I think they're going to catch me. Faint headache, fading. Vague taste of vinegar. It's happened again. I'm warm. Comfortable. Headache gone already. So comfortable. My head's sunk into something soft. A pillow. Snuggled inside something warm. I'm in bed. Content. I feel wonderful. It's definitely happened again. But it's different from other times. I feel safe. Happy. Good. But that's not why it's different. I can't explain what it is. This isn't quite the same as the other times. But it's definitely good.

I'm not alone! There's someone else here. Right here! Right beside me. Breath on my neck. Flesh in contact with the length of my naked back and legs. Something hard, insistent, pressing on my bum. I know it's an erect penis. A hand stroking my hip. Moving over it and downward. Stroking. Stroking. Rubbing. Rhythmically, gently. Soft kisses on my shoulder. Warm breath on my ear. I'm paralyzed, confused, aroused. This is real. It's happening to me. *To me*. I'm not in control. That's not right.

I flip one hundred and eighty degrees in a single movement, faster even than I'd imagined. Changing behind-me-person into facing-me-person and pushing them back all in the same instant. His face is surprise and delight in the semi-darkness. It's Walter's face, of course. I knew it would be. He looks pretty much like when I saw him in 1969. Except he's got a moustache. Same wide smile. Same eyes. He doesn't say anything. Nor do I. My hand reaches for his penis. Holds it. I lean forward. Press my lips to his. My tongue searching, insistent. I want him. Indicate with a nudge that he should roll on to his back. I climb on top, guide him, then gasp involuntarily. I look down to see him beaming back up at me. Bliss. Bliss.

Half an hour later, we're both flat on our backs. Side by side. I've never felt like this before. Ever. So fulfilled. Euphoric. Because of the orgasms. No, not just that. Everything is as perfect as it can be. This is the answer to the mystery. Walter and I are destined to be together. This is so clear in my mind that it's beyond question. I just know it.

"Thank God I'm not playing in Belgium anymore."

"What?"

"No sex the night before a match. Remember? Coach said it took all the strength out of a player's legs. Good job the Dutch are more enlightened."

"Hmmmm." I do remember that. How?

He rolls over. Kisses my cheek. So tender. "Shouldn't push it, though. Best get to sleep." Another kiss, gentle as a paintbrush flick. "I love you, Mrs. Buchanan." He rolls away onto his other side.

Mrs. Buchanan! Mrs. Buchanan! Oh my good God! Oh my God! I want to sit up. Shout. Run around the room. Shout some more. Not let him sleep. Hold him. Squeeze him. Look at his face. At his eyes. Touch him. Feel him.

But I don't. I roll to him. Whisper. "Hold me." I roll back. He turns. Spoons me. Nuzzles my neck. I feel his breath gradually become shallower and more regular, as his hold on me loosens.

He's asleep, and I'm a universe away from joining him. What do I know? We're married. We're in Holland. We were in Belgium together, maybe. Makes sense because I know he signed to play there. This experience is different. Every other time I've had an episode, I've woken in the past dressed in my 2019 clothes. This time I was naked. Unless my clothes are nearby. But somehow, I know that's not the case. How do I *know* that? When Walter reminded me about the Belgian coach banning sex the night before a match, I remembered it. It was a real, bona fide memory. How? What else can I "remember"? Getting married in a registry office with just two witnesses. In Belgium. The tiny flat we lived in in Diest. Me working part time stacking shelves. Walter's football going so well. The friendliness of the people, despite my struggles with Flemish. How pretty the streets and buildings were.

I remember our surprise when, after less than six months in Diest, Walter was offered the chance to move to the NAC club here in Breda.

We've been here a little under two years now. And life is perfect. Walter's wages are good, and we have a lovely apartment in a good area near the city centre. We have friends. I work in a supermarket, and I'm proficient in Dutch—enough to read the papers and novels, although most people can speak English too. I sing in a choir.

How do I know these things? Have these memories? I play the questions over and over in my mind. How do I *know* things? As tiredness eventually embraces me, a new, calming knowledge descends on me. An understanding. I have travelled back here—to Breda in 1972. *But I was already here.* Somehow, I have inhabited myself. Inhabited my own body and mind. I can't explain and don't really understand the how or why. But as much as I know so many other things, I also know this to be true. And I'm fine with it. I remember Doctor McKenzie telling me about the issue with my CT scan, meeting Walter in 1969, Seonaid telling me that Alice had finished with Sandy. And I remember being in Belgium with Walter, moving to Holland, all the details of our lives here together. But I don't remember anything in between. And I'm fine with that too. I think.

May 7, 1972

34.

I'VE BEEN HERE eight weeks now. Going about my life. Working. Socializing. Laughing. Loving. Being loved. Living. Really, *really* living. I sometimes forget that I've woken up here. Inside myself. That doesn't even sound strange to me. I know what I mean, and I'm still okay with it. When I say sometimes, I mean most of the time. Sometimes I remember that I'm just visiting, which is the word I've chosen to describe it. Most of the time I'm just too involved in living my life to even think about it.

On the occasions that I do think about it, I realize there are some answers I know and others I don't. I do the how, why, what, when inventory. I don't know how this all works and don't imagine I ever will. Why is easy. Easiest of all. It's because Walter and I just have to be together. What's the same as why. The two of us are simply meant to be together, and we are. When's not so clear. Sometimes I think it obviously must be forever and always. Other times, I think it just means right now, as it's happening. But as I say, I don't spend much time reflecting on it.

I do think about Walter and me. I know I'm besotted with him. And although he doesn't drink, he's intoxicated with and by me. It's not all hearts and flowers, lovey-dovey, make-everyone-else-sick saccharine (although some of it is). Sometimes his jokes are cringeworthy corny, and sometimes he is stupidly, annoyingly over-optimistic. (I know that sometimes I can be spikey, and sometimes I'm a really huffy cow.) We spar, tease, wind each other up. We disagree when he's wrong or when he's too pig-headed to see that I'm right. But most of all, we laugh.

He's fun and interesting and exciting to be around. We have a brilliant social life, and he sparkles in company. And when we're alone, just us two, he sparkles even more. He always makes an effort, while making it seem effortless. We talk. And really listen. And I'm interested in everything he has to say. The big stuff. The little stuff. All of it. Same for him.

Then there's respect and trust. Absolute trust. He knows how Findlay hurt me, and I know Walter could never do that. Would never do that. He gives me space. There's so much mystery about me. Questions that I know he has. *Why don't I ever want to go back to visit family in Scotland? Why don't I let myself be photographed? Why do I sometimes speak oddly, use strange words? Don't I want to do my degree course?* But he doesn't pursue it. I tell him what's off limits, and he accepts it. There's a memory from when we were first together in Belgium. I asked him to have the tattoo done. The one with Dundo Point 8.8.19. He asked why. I told him I could only say that it really mattered. So he just had it done. He never asked about it again. Absolute trust.

Right now, I'm drying dishes in the kitchen. Today's a big day. Walter's playing this afternoon in a home match. He's unusually nervous. He's been told that there's a scout from a big Spanish club attending specifically to watch him. I've agreed to go to the match as a spectator. I rarely go, unless Walter makes a point of asking me. Which he has. I like watching football, but I find it too tense to enjoy when he's involved.

There's a knock at the door, and I go to answer. There's a kid, maybe sixteen or seventeen, all hair and acne and utterly focused on avoiding eye contact. "I was told Walter Buchanan lives here." Mumbling, directed towards my midriff.

"That's right. Come in." Mumble-boy shuffles past me, clearly concerned that he might trip over, given how concentrated he is on looking at his shoes.

"Wim! Welcome, welcome." Walter comes into the hall and shakes Wim by the hand, then turns to me. "Patti, this is Wim. He's been selected for today's squad. First time in the senior squad. Big day for him. He only lives a couple of streets away, so I told the boss I'd bring him to the stadium with me."

Wim turns to face Walter briefly, then looks back to the floor. But his presence has invigorated Walter, banished the nerves that were apparent earlier. "Wim, you've obviously met Patti, my wife." Pause. "And I know what you're thinking."

Oh God! Not again. Not with a kid.

"You think I'm punching way above my weight. That I'm well out of my league."

I see the grin spread from Walter's face and infect Wim. I catch Walter's eye and draw back my hand, as if to throw the dishcloth I'm still carrying. I'm warning him. *Don't! Don't you dare.*

"She's virtually the perfect woman."

He is. He's bloody well going to say it again. I draw my arm back further.

"I say virtually, because she has just one flaw. She's not intelligent enough to realize how much better than me she could do!"

Every time! He says this every time. And every time my toes curl with embarrassment. And my heart skips with joy. Wim is grinning. I hurl the cloth, and it flies a yard wide of Walter.

"Two flaws! Her aim is absolutely dreadful!" He signals to Wim, and the pair race through to the kitchen, laughing like naughty schoolboys.

I pick up the dishcloth and follow them. "Do you guys want anything before you head off?"

"Thanks, darling. But no. We'll be having the team lunch shortly after we get there. Unless ..." He looks to Wim. "Would you like something now? Maybe a drink? Even just a glass of water?" Wim shakes his head forcefully while at the same time studying the pattern on the linoleum flooring intently. Desperately hoping, no doubt, that the heightened risk he might have to speak will prove transient. "Looks like that's still a no then."

"Fair enough. When will you set off?"

Walter checks his watch. "Actually, if we leave now, we can catch the earlier bus. That'll get us to stadium fifteen minutes earlier and give us more time to prepare. It'll let Wim get a feel for the senior match-day prep."

"Fine. Have you got enough for your fares?"

Walter takes out his wallet and opens it to show it's full of notes. He makes an *Are you satisfied, Mum?* face. I remember recognizing that wallet in a shop window and buying it for his last birthday. I also remember when I first saw it. When old Walter fished out the grubby cloth bag he kept it in to protect it. Bittersweet. I snap myself back into the moment. "Okay, smartarse—just checking. It's not as if you've gone out without any cash before."

I see he remembers. "Touché. We'd better dash now if we're going to get that bus. I'll look out for you in the stand later. Wish me luck!"

I blow him a kiss, and he winks back. Then the door slams, and he and Wim the Mute are gone.

I'm going to the match with Martha Weiss. She's Donny Handelson's girlfriend of six months. American, like him, and great fun. Donny and Walter are best pals, and I know that's a lifetime friendship because I saw Donny on stage at Walter's *This-Is-Your-Life* birthday thingy. I didn't notice who, if anyone, was Donny's partner at that event. So I don't know whether Martha will turn out to be a keeper. I hope so because she's so likeable. But you can't tell with Donny and relationships. The split with his last girlfriend, a Dutch girl called Lieke, was pretty cataclysmic.

Martha and I meet for lunch at a café about half a mile from the ground. It's funny that when I'm with her, we talk miles. When I'm with my Dutch friends, I naturally talk kilometres. She calls Walter *Walt*, a habit she's picked up from Donny. I hate it. It's even worse than Wattie. I've told them both. Several times. But despite some half-hearted efforts, they always lapse back into it. I'm learning to live with it, and I'm more tolerant of it with Martha because she's picked it up from Donny. I spent a few weeks calling him Don, and then Donald, but it didn't seem to bother him.

Anyway, after ten minutes walking, we're at the stadium. It's warm and sunny, a perfect spring afternoon. The smells of the various street vendors are heavy in the air, and the numbers queueing for entry suggest it'll be a big crowd. Martha and I make our way to the turnstile indicated on our ticket, less busy than most others, as it's reserved for officials and people, like us, who are associated with players and staff. We climb the stairs inside the grandstand and make our way to our seats, only four rows back from the front and just to one side of the halfway line. The view of the pitch is great. I must force myself to relax and enjoy it. It's only a game. Except it's not. It's Walter's job. His career. His living. The ground is pretty full, and kickoff is only minutes away. I stand and turn to scan the other spectators round me. Looking to see if I can see the Spanish scout. Pointless. What am I looking for, someone in a matador outfit?

The buzz of the crowd erupts into a mighty roar as the two teams come out onto the pitch. Walter looks up and catches my eye, smiles and waves. I wave back. Martha is doing the same with Donny. The referee calls the two captains together for the coin toss, which NAC win and elect to play right to left, as I look at it. The game kicks off, and the noise ratchets up further. The young men and boys on the Spionkop generate a phenomenal noise, creating an atmosphere intended to intimidate the visiting team.

The match is compelling and keenly contested. Walter's playing well. He's beaten his direct opponent three times in the first half-hour and raced forward to create dangerous opportunities for teammates. I see the opposing captain speak to one of his defenders and point to Walter. After a couple more minutes, it's clear that Walter has been identified as a threat and that two defenders are now doubled up on him. Walter has drifted wide onto the right wing, looking for space. A long clearance by the NAC goalkeeper lands ten yards in front of Walter, who's off like a whippet after it, his marker in close pursuit. The second defender is charging forward from a deeper position, hoping to intercept the ball before Walter can reach it.

All three reach the ball simultaneously. All going full pelt. Each with a leg outstretched trying to get the ball first. No one holding back. I hear the crack from here. Hear Walter's scream. See his agonized expression as he pirouettes through the air. See the top of his head land with his full weight on the knee of one of his opponents. Hear that guy shriek. Then everything stops. The crowd is virtually silent. All three of them are on the ground. One opposition player is waving furiously for assistance. The other holding his knee with one hand while beating his other fist repeatedly on the turf. Walter is totally still. Prone. I can see that his left leg is at an impossible angle.

Players from both teams are running toward their stricken comrades. Trainers from both teams coming on from the side, the referee racing to inspect the situation. Still the crowd is quiet. They know this is bad. Donny and another teammate reach Walter and crouch over him. Donny steps back and holds both hands to his head. Recovers and signals frantically to the touchline. The other teammate wheels away, crouches, and throws up on the pitch. I can see a couple of players walking away from the scene. Unable to look. One is crying. I want to scream, but no sound forms. The image on the pitch is blurred as my eyes fill. Martha's arm is round me, hugging me tightly.

35.

"Are you sure you don't want anything to eat?"

"Honestly, Martha, no. Maybe bring me a coffee when you come back."

"If you're absolutely sure."

I nod. She touches my shoulder, smiles down at me, then turns away to head toward the cafeteria. She stops and turns back. "Donny, what about you?"

"Coffee is fine for me too."

Martha nods, turns, and continues on her way.

Donny shuffles in his seat. He stands up, then moves to the other side of me and sits down in the seat Martha just left. He doesn't say anything, because there isn't anything to say. We've said it all, sitting here waiting. Walter's in theatre. Been there hours. Resetting his leg is apparently not straightforward. Something to do with the nature of the break. But I'm more worried about his skull. *The X-ray shows a fracture to the skull. This further complicates the procedure. We'll let you know more as soon as we finish in theatre.* The doctor wasn't lacking in compassion. But he had sounded robotic, impatient that he was talking to us when he could be getting on with Walter's treatment. *This further complicates the procedure.* I keep playing it over in my mind. What did he mean? How complicated was it already? How much worse? A broken skull! Will he die? Was the doctor in a hurry because time is critical? I should've asked more questions. But I didn't. Just listened. Nodded when he asked if I understood. I know I've seen Walter in the future, and he's all right. But what if this changes that? What if he doesn't make it? Does a fractured skull cause dementia in later life?

Now I'm sitting here waiting. Not just me. Donny and Martha have stayed with me. And there have been others. Other teammates. The manager, coach, physio. Even some fans. All concerned. Wanting news. Keen to show support for me. Local sports journalists wanting news. Donny handled them brilliantly. Thanked them all. Explained that it would be kinder to leave me space—that he and Martha would stay with me. Took notes of telephone numbers. Promised to call whenever there was any news.

"You know he'll be all right, don't you?"

"He's got a broken skull, for fuck's sake! The procedure is *further complicated*, whatever that's supposed to mean. So no. No, I don't know that he'll be all right, Donny."

I feel tears threatening to overwhelm me. Donny places his hand over mine. Shuffles round in his seat so that he's looking right at me. "He'll be fine, Patti. Really, he will."

"You don't know that. How can you know that?"

"Patti, he'll be fine because of you."

"What're you talking about?"

Donny leans in closer. Holds my hand more firmly. Face a mixture of compassion and pain. "You remember Lieke?"

"Yes."

"You remember how it was? When we finished?"

How could I forget? "Yes."

"How bad I got with the booze?" I nod. "I got suspended from the team. Probably on my way out anyway." He pauses. "Not just out of the team. Out altogether."

It was bad, I remember. But I didn't realize it was this bad. "Mmmm." Non-committal encouragement.

"One night at home, I'd drunk two bottles of rum instead of dinner. I decided to take a bottle of aspirins." A pause. Pained. "Dubya—sorry, *Walt*—found me. I don't know how he knew. I still don't. He made me be sick and sick and sick again. Slapped me around. Poured coffee into me."

Walter's never told me any of this. I'm confused and scared for Donny. "Go on."

"He got me sober. At least, sober enough to talk."

"About what?"

"The point. The point of living. The point of going on. We talked and talked and talked some more. We talked about Lieke. Walt said how sorry he was that I was so upset. But that I'd get over it. He said that Lieke wasn't the one."

"Not the one what?"

"Not the one for me. Not the one I'm meant to be with." There's a slightly distant look in Donny's eyes. "He said I'd find the one for me, and I'd know. He said that when it happened I'd know—I'd understand."

There's a natural lull. Neither of us speak for several seconds. "You'd understand what?"

"What it's all about. What it's all for." His eyes are passionate now. He's back in the room and looking right at me. "He told me how you had transformed his life. How he had thought he was happy until he met you, then realized he'd merely been content. The way he talked about you—I don't have the words to explain it. You're all the joy in the world to him. And that's how I know."

"Know what?"

"Know that he'll be all right, dumbass. There's no way on Earth Walt Buchanan isn't coming back to you, Patti. No way on Earth."

He squeezes my hand and smiles. I pinch back tears. "Thanks, Donny. Oh, and by the way." Pause. "His name's *Walter*."

He smiles in response. A smile that takes on a different complexion as he sees Martha come round the distant corner, carrying a plastic cup in each hand. It's my turn to smile. Whisper. "Is Martha the one for you?"

Conspiratorial. "I haven't told her yet."

The intimacy is broken as Martha arrives with two vending machine coffees. Simultaneously, the doctor appears from the opposite direction, behind us. His face is fixed, unreadable. My heart freezes as he approaches.

"Mrs. Buchanan."

"Yes."

"The operation was complicated. As you know, the fracture was severe, and the bone had broken through the skin." GET ON WITH IT! "However, I am able to inform you that it has been completed successfully. We're optimistic that, once it's healed, your husband will eventually be able to play football again. Of course, there will be extensive scarring, but that's unavoidable. Do you have any questions for me?"

Completed successfully. *Completed successfully.* Thank you, God! "But what about the fractured skull?"

"Yes. Your husband has a linear parietal fracture without any depression." He sees my blank expression. "This means that there's no serious damage. We've checked extensively. It's likely that the skull will heal itself. Are there any more questions?"

"So the fractured skull isn't serious? Isn't life threatening?"

"No. No danger to life."

"Can I see him, please?"

"He'll be moved into a side room close to the nurses' station once he's brought down from theatre. He won't be conscious for some time, but you'll be able to see him."

I don't even say thank you to the doctor before I'm engulfed in a pincer hug by Donny and Martha.

Donny relaxes his grip and leans back slightly. "I knew there'd never be any danger of damaging that thick skull of Walt's."

I glower. "He's called *Walter!*" Then I pull the pair back into our tight hug again.

May 8, 1972

36.

I FEEL LIKE I've been put through a mangle, but Patti looks like she's had it even worse. Once they told me she was here, I asked them to prop me up with pillows so I could see her. I've been watching her for the last hour, shifting restlessly in her sleep as she tries to get comfortable in the unforgiving wooden-framed hospital chair. Her hair is all over the place, and her eyes look puffy, as though she's been crying. Her forehead seems creased into a permanent frown, and she snores intermittently, depending on what position she's in. But she's still the most beautiful creature on this Earth. I feel terrible that she's so obviously been worried about me, and I'm fearful for what the future holds for us both if whatever injury I've suffered means the end of my football career.

Anna, my nurse, lowers the plate toward the mobile table positioned over my lap. She's a big woman, with a ruddy complexion and dark hair scraped back severely into a bun behind her nurse's cap. Despite her size, there is something graceful about her movement, and she places the plate in front of me with a delicate flourish.

She leans forward, cutlery in hand, and begins to cut the *uitsmijter* into dainty forkfuls. The sound of the knife and fork striking the porcelain wakens Patti, and I watch as she stretches her arms and legs while blinking the sleep from her eyes as they adjust to the daylight.

"So this is what you call looking after your husband, is it? Having a kip in a chair while your wounded hero has to rely on his nurse to feed him?" My voice sounds strange to me. It's slightly thick—perhaps as a result of whatever drugs they've given me, or maybe the anaesthetic?

Anna looks round at Patti when she realizes that's who I'm talking to and signals that she can approach. Patti's at the end of the bed in a twinkling.

My leg's encased in plaster from above the knee to my foot and elevated by a pulley. There's a drip on the other side of the bed, attached to my left arm. I know that my head is swathed in bandages because

Anna told me so when I commented on how it felt odd when I rested it against the pillows behind me.

Patti leans slightly toward me. "You look terrible."

"You're one to talk! You look like you've slept in a chair overnight."

She squeezes past the nurse, leans into me, and kisses me on the cheek. "You gave me a fright, you big eejit."

"You can hardly accuse me of doing it deliberately." My voice sounds like I've smoked forty fags in a row.

"How're you feeling?"

"My head hurts when I move it. Don't know if I'm more tired or more hungry. Anna here—" I glance toward her "—says it would be good if I could eat something."

Patti turns to Anna. "Would it be all right if I were to feed him?"

"Of course. Be sure to give him small mouthfuls and plenty to drink to wash it down." She nods in the direction of the glass of water with the straw.

"I will. Thank you."

"Would you like me to give you some time alone together? I will call back in—" Anna's hand lifts the watch pinned to her chest so she can read it "—about thirty-five minutes. Before the doctor does his rounds. Are you happy with that?"

"Thank you. Yes."

Anna turns back and addresses me directly. "Walter, please be sure to eat as much as you can. But do not force yourself. I will leave you both now." And next thing she's gone.

"What have they told you?" I ask Patti, hoping my voice doesn't betray the anxiety I feel.

"What do you mean?"

"About what happened. How they've patched me up. Anna said they were pleased but that the doctor would explain more when he comes round."

Patti spears a portion of the fried egg, melted cheese, ham, and bread onto the fork and offers it up. "Last night, they said that the operation on your leg had been successful. They said that there would be quite a lot of scarring. But they said they were optimistic that you'll be able to play football again once it's all healed."

I stop chewing as the relief floods through my body like a river in full spate, then slowly resume chewing before swallowing.

Patti looks right into my eyes. "They said that your skull should heal itself."

"My skull?"

She places another portion of breakfast on the fork and steers it into my mouth. "Yes. You fractured your skull as well as your leg. Had us all pretty worried." She moves the glass to my mouth, and my lips take the straw. "But it turns out that you've got the thickest skull known to medical science." I hold her gaze as I suck on the straw. "The doctor used a lot of jargon. What was it he said? Something about a parietal fracture, whatever that is. Oh, and something about bone density. Dense—that's it! He said he'd never met anyone more dense than you."

I let the straw go and smile up at her. "It's a relief to learn that he's someone who clearly knows what he's talking about. A proper expert."

The silly banter continues between a few more forkfuls of breakfast, until I can't avoid confessing how tired I am.

37.

WALTER'S SOON ASLEEP. I realize that I'm tired too. I could sleep for a week. Fight it. Stay awake for the doctor's visit.

The voices waken me. Anna and the same doctor as last night are by Walter's bed. Making finishing-up noises. The doctor steps back, realizing I'm awake. "Ah. Good morning, Mrs. Buchanan."

"Good morning."

"I have just finished examining your husband." He adjusts his stance so that he's addressing both Walter and me. "It is obviously very early, but I can confirm what I said last night. The operation was a success. The recovery period will be long—many, many months. There will be much physiotherapy. But that is some way off. For now, we must focus on you recovering from the trauma."

"Thank you, doctor." Walter pauses. "You told my wife that I would recover enough to play football again?"

"The recovery period will be long, like I say. But yes, there is no reason that you will not be able to resume your football career." He hesitates before breaking into an unexpected smile. "After all, what kind of NAC fan would I be if I did not fix one of our star players?"

"You're a fan? Were you at the match yesterday?"

"No. I could not go. I had to work here. Bad news for me, but good news for you, I think." The doctor smiles for a second time. Then he's business-like again. "If there are no more questions, I must attend to my other patients."

"Thank you, doctor."

"Yes," I echo. "Thank you."

A final brief smile of acknowledgement, and he leaves.

Anna steps forward. Addresses me. "I have explained to Walter the regime for medication, meal times, and visiting times. There have been many phone calls last night and this morning. I think there will be many visitors this afternoon. You should manage them so they do not tire him too much."

"I will. Thank you, Anna."

She smiles. It's the first time I've used her name. "Mrs. Buchanan, Walter is not in any danger. It would be good for you to go home. Get some rest and then come back."

"Honestly, I'd rather stay—if that's all right. I gave my friend the keys to our flat last night, and she'll pop in later this morning with fresh clothes and a few other odds and ends."

"Okay. But you will go home tonight."

"Yes, I'll go home tonight. Thank you."

Anna gives me a meaningful look, then turns, presumably to catch up with the doctor.

"Patti, you really don't need to stay. I don't mean to be funny, but you look shattered. Maybe you should go home and get some proper rest."

"Are you looking to pick a fight?"

"Okay, then—stay. But I'll probably be asleep most of the time."

"I'm banking on it. Conversation with a panda half-encased in plaster doesn't exactly hold much appeal."

"What do you mean, panda?"

I retrieve my little mirror from my bag and take it to him. Hold it in front of his face. "See? Panda!"

"Jesus! How did I get those?"

"Dunno. Maybe something to do with your cracked skull. Or maybe somebody gave you a couple of smacks."

He smiles weakly. I feel my throat catching and turn away. I get the chair and manoeuvre it across closer to his bed, then sit down in it so that we can both look at each other without him having to move his head. I hold his hand, resting on the mattress.

"I love you, Patti Buchanan."

"Look, Walter, the doctor said you're going to recover. You're not going to die, so you can cut out the sentimental crap."

"Still love you. You stubborn, contrary, women's libber, beautiful mentalist."

"That knock to your head hasn't improved your chat-up lines."

"Love you, love you, love you."

"Love you too." I try to make it sound grudging, but I'm not fooling him.

"Any chance of a drink?" He nods toward the glass, and I gather it from the table and hold the straw to his lips. He takes several sips. "Thanks."

I return the glass to the table. "You're welcome." I resume my position holding his hand.

"Patti?"

There's that tone in his voice. The *I want to speak to you seriously, properly* tone that always surprises me when it comes. "Yes? What is it?"

"Are you happy?"

Where has that come from? Why's he asking that? "What?"

"You heard me. Are you happy?"

"What do you mean? With this? With you all broken and in hospital? Of course I'm not happy! That you're going to be okay? Make a full recovery? Of course I'm happy about that. What is it you're asking me?"

He gently squeezes my hand. "About us. Are you happy about us?"

"Jesus, Walter! Where has that come from? Of course I'm happy about us. I love you, you moron. Where has this come from?"

"I worry sometimes about us. About what us means for you."

"Now you're just talking in riddles."

"Sometimes, when I think about us, I worry that I'm selfish. I want to play football. To move around and see different countries. And I just expect you to come with me."

"Walter, you're the least selfish person I've ever met."

"No, I'm not, Patti. I'm living my dream. Being with you. Playing football. Seeing the world. But what about you? What about you fulfilling your dreams? What about going to St. Andrews? Doing your degree?"

"*This* is what I want. Being with you. Us. Together. God Almighty! What's brought this on?"

"I got lucky this time, Patti. Another time, that could have been my career over. Gone. Just like that. And where would that leave us? You hitched to a crippled ex-footballer who can't earn any money. You've sacrificed your education and your prospects, and you're lumbered with me."

"You silly bugger. I *want* to be lumbered with you."

"I'm serious, Patti. We both know you're different. You're special. There's stuff you don't want to tell me, and I'm okay with that, if that's what you want. But if I ever thought I was holding you back. Stopping you fulfilling your potential. Stopping you being happy. It would kill me. If I thought that, it would be better if we'd never met. If you'd never known me. You could go on and be everything that you could be."

Why is he saying this? Doesn't he realize that none of that stuff matters? What matters is us. Him and me. I get up from my chair. Lean forward and rest my cheek softly on his.

I whisper. "I'd be nothing without you." I hold my position for only a few seconds, and already I can tell from the rhythm of his breathing that he's asleep. A gossamer-light kiss to his cheek, and then I settle back into my chair. I need to keep awake for when Martha arrives with my things.

August 10, 2019

38.

FALLING. FALLING. Two of the creatures are in pursuit, both yowling and shrieking in a way that freezes my blood. I know they want to kill me. I mustn't let them catch me. Still falling. Suddenly awake. Eyes open. Back in my old bedroom in Scotland. It's kind of familiar, but it also feels strange. I've been away for so long. So very long.

Instinctively, I reach out for my phone. It's still the tenth of August. Half past two. When did I come to my room? There's half a sandwich on a plate beside a glass of water and a box of paracetamols. I remember. George was being an arse, and I had a headache. Came to my room to eat lunch. Then I lay down for a rest and woke up with Walter in 1972. I lay down just over an hour ago at most. It couldn't have been longer than that. But I was gone for so long. I was there for weeks. Must have been a couple of months. I can remember everything. Details of my day-to-day life. Our flat. My job. Friends. How could I absorb all of that in less than an hour? Actually, I remember more than that. I remember years' worth. Living in Belgium before we moved to Holland. The excitement of new places and friends. I remember the joy of my wedding day.

I sit bolt upright. I'm married! To Walter. My name is Patti Buchanan. I feel my left hand. My wedding ring's missing! Where is it? Why isn't it on my finger? Stop! Don't panic, Patti. Think! Think this through logically. Slowly. In my mind I know that I'm Patti Buchanan. But here, in this time, I'm Eilidh McVicar. I'm Eilidh McVicar, and I'm eighteen years old. I've got something showing up in a CT scan of my brain that needs further investigation. I'm still living at home with Mum and the boys. I'm due to go to St. Andrews for the new term.

Except I'm not Eilidh. At least, I'm not just Eilidh anymore. I might be here, back in her time. But I'm Patti too. I've got my memories and experiences as Patti. I'm not going to kid myself that I'm all sophisticated and mature because I've got those extra memories and experiences. I'm still the same me, at my core. I don't know what words to use to describe it myself. And it doesn't matter because I know what I mean. And most important of all, I know what this is all about. What really matters. Walter and me being together. I've got all the memories of our time together in Belgium and Holland. But I can't remember how I got there. I don't have a memory of us both getting together. I need to go back. I need to return to 1969. I need to see Walter at The Tassie after he plays in the match on the Saturday. I *know* that's what I have to do.

I get up and go to the wardrobe. His jacket's still there. What will I need when I go back? What do I need to live there? What do I need to live *then*? Think logically. I check my phone. My online account shows I've got £856.33 in the bank. Good. I go to my laptop and fire it up.

A search for how to find the death certificate for someone who died in 1951 returns a rather daunting *58,962 death records found*. View Records. When I click to view, it tells me that I need to be a member to view the records. Shit! Every site is going to be the same. But as I scroll down I see that membership's free for the first seven days, so I register. When I access the site, I'm confronted by 8.7 billion records and scanned images. Shit! Where do I start? I select *United Kingdom*, then *deaths*, and then *1951*. I type in *Smith*.

Smith is a blessing and a curse. A curse because there are so many to trawl through. A blessing because I'm more likely to find something suitable. I scroll for twenty-odd minutes. All of these died in 1951. The death certificates don't record the dates of birth, just the year. I'm looking for 1950 or 1951. Eventually, I find Patience Smith, born 1951, died April the 16th, 1951. Cause of death—carbon monoxide poisoning. There's an address in Manchester. I should feel like a ghoul. But I'm actually excited.

I search for *Patience Smith Manchester April 16, 1951*. There's one article. "Family Die of Smoke Inhalation" in the *Manchester Evening News*, which I click on. It's horrific. Patience was two weeks old, first born of Horace and Esther Smith. A fire occurred on the ground floor of their end-of-terrace home, and all three died of smoke inhalation. They were found in the same room, looking like they were still asleep. A shudder passes through me. At least they didn't suffer.

I flick back out of deaths and into births, where I locate Patience's certificate. It has the full date, the address of the hospital, and details of her parents. I screenshot it. When I get back to 1969, I'll be able to use her identity. I can get a National Insurance number, or whatever they had then. And a passport. I should feel bad about this. And maybe I do. A bit.

Think. What else will I need? Money. I Google *1969 money*, and using the inflation calculator I find, I learn that £100 in 1969 is equivalent to £1,632 today. Okay, so let's work on a fifteen-to-one ratio. I type in *Buy 1969 Money*, but the search just returns more inflation calculators. I try *Buy 1969 Cash* and get results about someone called Johnny Cash at San Quentin. Who? Some singer, it looks like. I feel my stress levels rising as I enter *Buy Vintage Money* and click. Bingo! You can buy old banknotes on eBay! Who knew? There are a range of filters and I select: *Scotland, £1, £5, £10, Elizabeth II (1952–now)*. Most of the results returned are too recent. There's a British Linen Bank £1 note in Edinburgh dated February 29, 1968, for £2.41. But it's four days until the auction ends. There's another one dated January 25, 1966, for £1.45. Same seller. Same auction end date. This isn't working.

I refresh the whole search and try English notes, ticking the buy-it-now filter. This throws up a much wider selection, and most with more than a single note allow the option to choose by cashier. A quick search for *Bank of England Cashiers* provides a list that includes 1962–1966 Jasper Hollom and 1966–1970 John Standish Fforde. I'm not concerned about condition and buy from three different sources who all offer next-day delivery (including Sunday, for a premium). I've got £267 in used 1960s English banknotes arriving tomorrow for the princely sum of £380, including packaging and delivery. Sorted.

What else do I need? Clothes, of course. I Google *Vintage 1960s women's clothes for sale*, only for the screen to advise me that there are *About 95,200,00 results*. I start to look at the images. Dear God! Did people really dress like that? I go back from Images to All and begin another trawl. I'm looking for something my size that's not too hideous. Something that's probably okay for 1969 Scotland. That also offers next-day delivery. Eventually, I settle on an outfit, a smartish overcoat, and shoes from a company in Leeds. Over a hundred pounds!

I can buy anything else I need when I get back there. What else haven't I thought of?

My phone rings.

"Hello?" I'm too distracted to check caller ID and just press it to my ear.

"Eilidh?"

"Speaking. Who's this?"

"It's Molly. Is now a good time?"

"Molly, hi. Of course. It's a really good time."

"Great, thanks. I was phoning about a few things. First, just to let you know we got back safely, like I promised. But really I wanted to know how you'd got on with the doctor."

"Glad to hear you got back safely. It's kind of you to ask how I got on. There's no big deal regarding the doctor's visit. There was a bit of an issue with a scan, and they'll probably need to redo it. But the doctor said that I shouldn't worry."

"Oh, right. Good." She doesn't sound convinced. Maybe because I didn't either. Trying too hard, probably.

"How was your journey down?"

"Really good, actually. Surprisingly so." The briefest of pauses. "Eilidh, there's something I wanted to say."

"Go on."

"Well, you know how Uncle Walter kept confusing you for his wife?"

"Ye-es." Oh my God. Where's this going?

"Well, he kept repeating it every so often during the journey back. He seemed almost fixated. Anyway, when we got home, my curiosity was piqued. So I went and got out the photos of Patti. You know, Uncle Walter's wife?"

"Yes." My heart is pounding. Absolutely pounding.

"Honestly, Eilidh, I can see why he keeps saying it. There are only two photos. They're both small. In one, you can see Patti in profile. She looks quite young. Dressed in seventies clothes and dancing with Uncle Walter. In the other one, she's full face on to the camera, but it's really grainy. But if I screw up my eyes to look at it, it becomes much sharper. The thing is, Eilidh, Patti honestly is almost your double. I really can see why Uncle Walter keeps getting confused."

"That would explain it."

"Tell you what. Would you like me to scan the photos and text them to you? So you can see what I mean?"

"Oh, don't go to any trouble on my account."

"It's really no trouble. Wait until you see them. You'll be amazed."

"All right, then. That'd be nice. Thank you." There's only one thing I care about. "And how is Walter?"

"He's fine. Absolutely fine. He's here in the room with me now. Would you like a quick word?" She doesn't wait for my answer. I can hear her telling Walter that I'd like a word. The sound of the phone changing hands.

"Hello?"

My heart's racing. "Hello, Walter. How are you?"

"Patti? Is that you, Patti?"

It's old Walter's voice. But still Walter. I can hear the age and vulnerability. But more than that. Loss. Loneliness. Longing. "Yes, my darling. It's me."

"Patti, Patti. Why didn't you come with us?"

"Don't worry. I'll be with you as soon as I can. I promise."

"I miss you, Patti. I love you."

I'm just going to tell him that I love him when I hear Molly's voice talking to him in the background. Then on the line to me. "Oh, Eilidh, I'm so, so sorry about that. I hope that didn't upset you."

I want to scream down the line at her. For stopping me telling Walter that I love him. But I don't. "No. No, not at all. I completely understand."

"You're so kind. I'm going to go and make us something to eat now. I'll send through those photos later, or perhaps tomorrow. Then maybe ring to see what you think of them. Would that be okay?"

"Of course. Perhaps we can have a catch-up later in the week."

"I'll do that. I'll ring back on Tuesday or Wednesday. Eilidh, thank you for everything you've done. Honestly, you're a star. Speak again soon. Bye."

"Yes, speak again soon. Bye."

I press the red end-call icon. A huge sigh escapes involuntarily.

I can feel the headache returning. Too soon to take more paracetamol. Maybe I'm dehydrated. I drink some more water and go to my bed to lie down. Hands behind my head. Try to get comfortable. Try to think. How do I get back to Walter? Can I control this . . . I don't know what to call it. Travelling? That was Gran's word. Am I able to control it? So tired.

May 3, 1941

39.

I'M BEING CHASED again. There are three of the creatures this time. Two of the familiar inky black clouds with burning red eyes and another ball of yellow-orange flame with empty black sockets where I imagine it should have eyes. I know I mustn't let them catch me, but I feel certain that this time they will. They're close, and I'm scared. It's like I'm in a dream that's turned to the very worst nightmare. Except I know this is real. But now, suddenly, I've escaped or eluded them. There's a dull ache in my head. And the hint of a taste of vinegar. It's happened again. It's dark like nighttime, and it's hot. Really, really hot. The smell of smoke, a pungent mix of wood and paint burning. Muffled noises. Like they're coming from several rooms away. They're above me. Other sounds. Indistinct, except for a piercing scream. There's a fire. I'm in a building that's on fire! Shit!

I'm lying on my side. I try to sit up, but I bash my head on something hard and smooth. I roll onto my front. Try to feel with my hands and my feet as my eyes adjust to the darkness. My feet press against something solid. I raise them off the ground, and they immediately meet resistance. Whatever I banged my head on must slope down to my feet. So there's no way backward. It's clearer in front because I can see faint light about three metres away, upward. I start to crawl forward. There's a loud crashing noise just to my left, and I'm choking. Coughing. Blinded, with eyes stinging. I feel the dryness of dust, almost grit-like in my mouth. And I taste the smoke, acrid and sharp like the terminal of a battery, and I gag involuntarily. It's so, so hot. Dear God, don't let me die like this.

I half scramble, half crawl toward the light. There are voices directly above. Male voices. I can't make out what they're saying. Scream. Scream for help. No sound. Mouth and throat thick with dust and smoke. No sound. My tongue is like carpet in my mouth. Scream. Scream! Scream!

"Bill! Stop. I can hear something."

Scream! Scream!

"Over here. There's someone under this door."

Thunderous crunching and scraping from above my head. A whirlwind of dust and grit and God knows what. Something hard and heavy, perhaps a brick, hits my shoulder and bounces away. I shriek as much with fright as pain. Suddenly, there's light above. Two faces looking down at me. Men in tin helmets.

"Are you all right, love? Are you injured?"

I'm mouthing a soundless answer. Please, please. Get me out. Please.

"Can you move toward me, love? Nice and easy. Try not to disturb anything."

I ease forward. Reach up with my right hand.

"That's it, love. Well done. Just a little more."

"Jack! For Christ's sake! The rest of the place is going to come down any second."

"Just a little more, love. That's it. Stretch. Good. Just a little more."

Two hands grab me. One firmly on the wrist, and the other under my oxter. I'm being pulled with surprising strength. My knee crashes against some jutting masonry, and I feel a sharp, stabbing pain as I'm hauled up. Up and out. Two uniformed men have one of my arms each over their shoulder as they race as fast as the sloping rubble underfoot will allow. There's an almighty crash right behind us. Then a deafening, explosive bang and a blinding flash ahead. All three of us are thrown to the ground.

I'm prone on a pile of rubble as vision gradually returns to my stinging, teary eyes. I can see one of my rescuers crawling to the other just two metres in front of me. Hand signals, ending with mutual thumbs ups between them. Each confirming to the other they're uninjured. There's no sound, just a loud hissing. And a wooliness inside my head. The man who pulled me out—Bill?—crawls toward me. Points at me. Mouths, *Are you all right?* in an exaggerated way. I nod instinctively. He gives me a thumbs up sign, which I return. He signals for me to stand up.

All three of us get to our feet. Bill offers me his arm for support. I grab it. There's dust everywhere, hanging in the air, on my clothes and skin, even through my hair. I take in where I am for the first time. On a street. Or what was a street. Behind is a huge pile of burning rubble. That's where I was. Where these men saved me from. Opposite is a row of terraced houses, except that four houses to the right, there's a half-demolished house completely ablaze. The houses either side of it are alight too. Further to the right, there's a jet of flame half the height of the houses. Coming from a crater in the road. Maybe a burst gas main.

Bill has his hands on my shoulders. He's shouting at me. The hissing in my ears is receding. I can hear his voice. But I can't make out the words. His helmet has the letters ARP on it. He's an air raid warden. This is the Blitz. I'm in the Blitz! Maybe I'm in Clydebank. Or London or Coventry? "You need to get to a shelter, love!" I can hear him. And the roaring of the flames. Little tinny bells in the background. Maybe a fire engine? Other voices shouting in the distance. Thrumming of aircraft engines high above. A woman screaming somewhere. A dog barking. "I said, you need to get to a shelter, love!" He's shouting.

I nod. "Which way?"

He looks along the street in both directions. Then points in the opposite direction to the burning house. Shouting to make himself heard. "Go to the end of the street. Turn right, then second left. There's a bakery further along. They've got a cellar."

I nod again, signalling comprehension. But I'm paralyzed. Terrified.

He shakes my shoulder roughly. "You need to go. Now!"

I'm off. No acknowledgement. No thanks. Just head toward the end of the street in the direction he pointed. There's noise everywhere. Aeroplane engines droning and what sounds like artillery fire provide the soundtrack to images softened by smoke and dust and the smell of burning. Everywhere. People shouting. A tiny old-fashioned fire engine, alarm bell defiantly protesting hope, heads in the opposite direction. Toward the fires. I don't even look back as it passes. Head down and on to the end of the street. Turn right as instructed. Next left is only fifty metres away. I turn again. It's less dusty now. Easier to see. Where's the bakery?

I hear the whistle of a bomb. It's close. There's a loud blast, and the gloom is banished for a few brief seconds. It's landed behind the houses to my left. In the adjacent street. I start to run. Where's the bakery?

Which side of the road is it on? I stumble as I run. Grateful to grab the unlit lamppost and avoid falling. I'm crying, making it harder to see. I've reached the end of the street. I didn't see the bakery on either side. Did I miss it? I look back as the hideous flute note builds to a crescendo, heralding another mighty explosion less than two hundred metres down the street. Where I was less than half a minute ago, there's now a gaping crater in the road, where the fires of hell leap furiously upward.

I turn right, onto a slightly wider road. And I run. I've got to get away. Away from these bombs. Away from this hell. After less than a hundred metres, there's a shop doorway on the other side of the road. I stagger across, lean against the door, and slump to the ground. I'm panting, on the verge of sobbing. Tears are running down both cheeks, and my hands are shaking. Like, properly shaking. I can't stop them. I hunch into the fetal position and roll onto my side on the cold, hard entryway floor. I close my eyes tight. Squeeze them. Black all of this out. Please, God, please. Take me away from all of this. Save me. Make me wake up back in my bed. Safe.

Voices waken me, and I open my eyes, slowly. It's daylight, and I'm still in the shop doorway. My shoulder pulses low, dull throbs of pain, and my knee sends occasional stabbing reminders of its trauma. I draw myself up into a sitting position, gingerly, and try to focus.

"Yer all right, love?"

I look up. I think it's English. But spoken so quickly. And the accent. What is it? The woman is holding the handle of a big, old-fashioned pram. She's wearing a headscarf and a lightweight coat. Two small girls peep out from the folds of her coat.

"I says, yer all right, love?"

Definitely English. Scouse? "Where am I?"

"Sorry, love. What?" She's stepped forward from the pram and is leaning down toward me.

"I said where am I?" I put my hand on the doorknob above for leverage and pull myself to my feet. Then sway a bit.

"Whoa, love. Take it easy, take it easy." Her hand rests gently on my wrist. "There now, that's better. Where's that accent from? Are you Scotch?"

"Scottish. Yes."

"Thought so. You're a long way from home, love? What yer doing here?"

My ear's getting attuned to her accent. "Visiting. Visiting my auntie. Where exactly am I?"

"Inkerman Street, love. Or what's left of it." She must see my blank look. "In Bootle, love. Town centre's quarter of a mile that way." She points the direction with a flick of her head. "Where's your auntie live?"

I gesture with a nod in the general direction that I ran from last night. Palls of smoke are visible above the rooftops. "Over that way."

She gives me a sympathetic look. "They gorrit bad down there last night. Closer to the docks."

"The house got hit. Came down. Two ARP men got me out." I shudder involuntarily at the recollection. "I'm lucky to be alive."

"You poor love. Listen, see down there?" She points back down the street in the direction she has come from. "Go down there 'til yer come to The Kings Head, then turn left. Go along forra bit to the church hall. The WVS are serrup in there. They'll look after yer. I'd take yer meself, but I've got these." She nods at the pram and the two little girls, who are both studying me intently.

"No, that's fine. Thank you." I step forward and smile to emphasize my gratitude.

"A'right love. You take care now." She returns my smile, then ushers the girls onward, following on with the pram.

I watch briefly as they head off. Then set off in the opposite direction. I pass various men coming the other way. Probably dockers from the look of them. I'm quickly at The Kings Head and turn left. After less than a hundred metres, there's an enormous red brick church with a matching hall almost three-quarters the size attached to the side, like a younger sibling. The doors are open and I walk in, slightly anxious for some reason that's unclear to me.

There are sleeping bags the length of one wall—most occupied, some not. Tables and chairs are sporadically set along the other wall, and people—mainly women and older men—are drinking tea. Knots of children sit or kneel on the wooden floor, playing board games with dice. Two ladies approach me. Both quite matronly, grey uniforms and matching wide-brimmed hats with maroon bands. WVS Civil Defence badges sewn on their arms. At the far end of the hall, a small queue of women is waiting for tea being dispensed from a huge urn by a third uniformed WVS volunteer. They're side on to me, and the last person in the queue is Suzy. I recognize her instantly. She looks so much like Gran, but when Gran was younger. Even younger than I remember her— maybe mid to late thirties. Hair jet black, tall, upright and in animated conversation with the woman in front of her in the queue.

"Suzy! Suzy!"

A few heads turn at my shout, but hers isn't one of them. The WVS women have reached me, and the slightly taller one is looking at me, concern on her face. "Are you all right, love?"

"I'm fine, thanks. I just need to talk to Suzy." I point to the back of the hall and head toward her, not waiting for any reply.

"Suzy! Suzy!" Everyone in the tea queue has turned to look at me now, including her. "Suzy. Can I please have a word with you?" She's looking right at me. Taking everything in, assessing. I can see her mind working furiously behind those familiar, piercing eyes. "Your sister, Jenny. She sent me with a message."

The woman beside Suzy turns to her. "Why's she calling you Suzy?"

"It's a family nickname I had back in Scotland." She turns back to me. There's anger in her eyes. "Let's go outside. We can chat in the fresh air."

She strides past me without any more eye contact, heading back toward where I came in. I follow, almost at a half-trot to keep up. I'm spooked. Why's she angry? We come out of the hall and go round to the side. There are some steps leading up to a padlocked door. She points. "Sit down there." I do as she says.

She's looking down at me. "What do you think you're doing?" Her voice is low. She doesn't want others to hear. And harsh.

"I just wanted to speak to you."

"And you thought it was a good idea to march up to me in front of dozens of people and call me Suzy? Dressed like that?" She looks me up and down as her eyes accuse my filthy, torn hoodie and jeans and battered trainers.

"I'm sorry. I just saw you and was so relieved to see someone familiar."

"But you didn't think to dress appropriately? Thank God you're covered in dust and dirt. You didn't think I'd have an identity to protect?"

She's blazing mad. Usually, if someone's up for a fight I'll go toe to toe with them. But not this time. I'm frightened, tired, sore, and confused. This woman who looks so like my lovely gran is furious with me. I didn't ask to be here, and I don't want to be. I feel my eyes welling up. "I was trapped in a house that was on fire."

"What?"

"When I woke up last night, I was trapped in a burning house. Two ARP wardens got me out just in time."

"A burning house? Why did you aim there?"

"I don't understand. What're you talking about?"

"It's not a difficult question! Why did you aim for a burning house?"

"I don't understand! I lay down on my bed. I must've fallen asleep. Then I was awake in a burning house."

Her body adjusts, almost imperceptibly. But I can sense her entire demeanour shift. She bends forward into a semi-crouching position. "Is this the first time something like this has happened to you?"

"No. It's happened before. Four times."

"And you don't control it? It just happens to you?"

"Yes. I fall asleep. Or get knocked unconscious. Then I wake up, and I'm somewhere else. In the past."

She sits down beside me on the step. We're close, at an angle so we can see each other's faces. She places her hand on mine. "What's your name?"

"Eilidh. Eilidh McVicar. Except when I travel, I'm sometimes Patti Smith."

"And you're Jenny's daughter?"

"Her granddaughter."

"Granddaughter?" Her eyes widen. Then she smiles. "It's hard to think of her as a granny." A second's hesitation. "Is she well? Is she keeping all right?"

"She's keeping well for her age. She and I like to go for walks together. We quite often go to the Stoorie Burn."

"Oh. That's good. I'm glad to know she's well." There's a distant look in her eyes.

"Suzy?"

"You mustn't call me that. I'm Margaret. My name's Margaret."

"Sorry, Margaret." My turn to pause. "She asked me about you?"

"What?"

"Gran, sorry, Jenny. She said she could tell I'd been travelling, and she asked if I'd seen you. She told me that, if I did see you, I had to ask if you were happy. She said if you were happy, I'm to tell you she thinks you made the right decision and that she's happy for you."

Suzy-Margaret sighs. I can see it's her turn to tear up. Her hand is squeezing mine. "Tell her." Her voice is barely above a whisper. "Tell her, if she asks again, that everything is fine and that I am happy."

"Anything else?"

"Just that."

"Okay."

There's a long silence. It's not for me to speak next. She seems to be gathering her thoughts. Eventually, her hand loosens from mine, and she looks directly at me again. "Listen to me now, very carefully. We do not have very much time at all, and there's a great deal that I must tell you." Her voice is earnest, tinged with concern. Her accent is clearly still Scottish, but different that way that folk speak when they've lived down in England for a while.

"Why don't we have much time?"

"I'll explain, but let me ask you some things first."

"All right."

"When you travel—when you're asleep or knocked out—tell me what it feels like."

"Do you mean what has happened to me? Where I've been? What I've seen?"

"No. Those episodes are just possibilities. Glimpses of what might've been. What you choose to do can change things. I want to know what happens when you're actually travelling or just arriving."

"Well, when I waken up, I usually have a fuzzy head or a slight headache. But that passes quickly. Oh, and I can taste vinegar."

"And that's all? Nothing else?"

"Usually, it feels like I'm falling. And when I'm falling I can see monsters, creatures, who are trying to catch me. Each time I travel I see more of them, or they seem to be closer to catching me. It's really, really frightening." I shudder at the recollection. I see alarm in her eyes, and it scares me. "What? What is it?"

"When you feel like you're being chased, have you ever actually been caught?"

"No. Not caught, just chased. Why? What is it? I can see that it worries you."

Suzy—I can't help but think of her as that—takes both my hands in hers. Her expression is hard to read. Serious? Concerned? A mixture of both, maybe? "Eilidh, you must listen very carefully to what I tell you next. Don't ask for explanations, because I don't have them. Just listen. Do you understand?"

Shit! Shit! Shit! "Yes, I understand."

"Some women in our family can travel. Not all. Just some. And there are women in other families too, but never any men. The ability appears in some second daughters of a family. Jenny was born three minutes before me." A shudder passes through me as I remember Nora, Mum's first child, who died within hours of being born. But I need to concentrate on what Suzy is saying. "We travel to different places and the same places—always in the past. What we do when we travel has an effect—we can change things. When we travel, we experience love. And then we have to choose. Choose whether we'll stay with that love or return to the love of our families. Once we make that choice, we can never change it. If you choose to remain with your family, the ability to travel disappears. If you return to the one you love in the past, you physically die in your original time."

I recognize what she's saying and nod affirmation.

"Most of us can target where we're travelling. I'll explain how in a minute. You're unusual in that you haven't done it. You also haven't realized the dangers."

"Like arriving in a burning building? I think I've got a fair idea about the dangers."

Her frown signals my flippancy isn't appreciated. "No, Eilidh. Travelling like we do upsets things. Chasers try to catch us when we're doing it. If they catch us, we die."

"We die?" She nods and lets it sink in. "How do you know that? Who or what are Chasers?"

"I don't know. I'm repeating what I was told. I believe it, even though I don't understand it. And the danger's heightened when two travellers are together, as we are now. The longer we are together, the easier it is for the Chasers to catch either of us if we try to travel again."

I'm trying to make sense of this. It all sounds so far fetched. But then everything else that's happened to me is just as unbelievable, even though I know it's true. "You say you were told this. Who by?"

"My cousin. I travelled and met her. Many years before now. She explained everything, as I'm now doing to you. Sometime, you may need to explain it in turn."

My head is swimming with all of this. "I can't take all this in."

"Eilidh, there isn't time to dwell on this. I'm telling you the truth, and you have to believe it. Now, let me explain how to target where you travel. You must focus on a sense of where and when you want to be. That sense will be an image, sounds, smells. It'll feel tangible. You might even taste it. You must keep focused on that sense, irrespective of any other distractions. Maintain that focus, and then you'll find yourself there."

"How does it work?"

"I don't know, and it doesn't matter. It's enough that it works. If you choose to stay in your own time, then you must never talk of your experiences travelling. And if you choose to go back, you need to become someone else. Blend in and become anonymous. Don't leave any footprint that people from your original time could track. Forget about your old life and times. What I did ... what I did when I asked about Jenny." Her voice catches slightly. "That was wrong. If you leave your old life, you must never mention it and try never to think about it. Do you understand?"

I have so many questions. But I know she doesn't have the answers. "I think so."

"Good. Now there really is no time to lose. You have to decide where you want to aim for."

"Sorry?"

"Eilidh, there's no time to waste. You cannot stay here. Where do you want to go?"

"I want to go to Walter. To our wonderful life in Holland. Or back to 1969 and meet him in the pub. Give him his jacket back. But I'm not ready. Not prepared."

"Eilidh!" She shakes my shoulder hard. "No time to daydream, girl! You have to leave now. Where do you want to aim?"

"Home. My bedroom. Where I was before I arrived here."

"All right. That's good. Now picture it in your mind. See it. The objects and shapes and the colours. If you're sitting on a chair or lying on a bed—feel it against your body. Feel the temperature in the room. Listen and identify the sounds you can hear. Can you smell anything? Cooking? Soap? Flowers in a vase? Have you eaten or brushed your teeth? What can you taste in your mouth?"

I concentrate. I think about my room. No, it's more than that. More than imagining. I sense my room. I can hear the washing machine thrumming in the utility room below. The smell of newly mown grass comes through the window from Mr. Anderson's lawn next door. I feel the familiar contours of the mattress against my back. I see the glow-at-night moon and stars that Dad stuck on the ceiling when I was wee.

"Can you sense where you want to be?" Suzy's voice sounds distant. My eyes are tight shut, and I don't want to break my focus. I nod. Suddenly I'm being pushed off the steps. Violently. And falling. But not hitting the ground. Still falling. And being chased! They're close. Really close. More than one. Definitely two. Maybe three. I sense one reaching for me. I've never felt terror like it. *If they catch us, we die.* I can't let them catch me. Focus. Concentrate. Sense my bedroom. Sense it!

August 10, 2019

40.

I MUST FOCUS—I need to sense my bedroom. There's a shout from behind me, and I recognize the voice. I look upward and back and see him swim-falling toward me. It looks like Dad. And he's calling my name. But I know instinctively that it isn't Dad. Two other figures are close behind him. One of them looks like Daniel, but again I know it's not him either. After all, they tried to trick me this way before. They must think I'm an idiot. As I recognize him, he morphs into a swirling black cloud again. The same thing happens with the thing that resembles Dad and the third figure. There are three separate, seething black clouds and three pairs of murderous fiery eyes arrowing toward me. I'm going to die! I need to sense my bedroom! Sense it!

I sit bolt upright. Are they still there? I look back over my shoulder. Are they behind me? I'm not sensing my bedroom. I'm seeing it. Feeling it. I'm here, back in it. I've made it! I'm safe. But my heart's still drumming fit to burst. I'm sweating. My hands are shaking. Shaking like when I was in the shop doorway during the bombing. And I'm scared. Scared of what was chasing me. I could sense it. No. I could sense *them*. There were definitely three, and they were close. Really, really close. And they were wanting me to sense them. As if by sensing them, I couldn't sense my bedroom. Couldn't reach it. And they'd catch me. I know they nearly did. Suzy said I'd die if they caught me. But it was more than even that. When I could sense them, I could feel their malevolence. My presence seemed to fuel their frenzy. My entire body shudders at the recollection.

Think! I'm in my bedroom. They didn't get me. I'm safe here. I need to calm down. To think straight. I look at my hands, which are filthy. I get off the bed and go to the mirror on the wardrobe door. My shoulder and knee both ache. My reflection takes me by surprise. I am absolutely mockit. My clothes are thick with dust, my shoes scuffed, and my face and hands smeared with soot and grime. I need to clean myself up. I take my clothes off, slightly haltingly as my knee and particularly my shoulder fire painful reminders of my wartime trauma. The shoulder looks okay in the mirror, but I can see bruising already starting to form just below and to the side of my knee.

I shove my dirty clothes into the washing basket. I'll put them in the machine when Mum's next at work, so she doesn't see the state of them. I get my dressing gown from the hook on my bedroom door and slide it on, then go through to the bathroom, lock the door, and get into the shower. The water feels wonderful on my body. My hair is so filthy that the shampoo barely raises a lather. I rinse and shampoo again. There's so much grit and clag coming off me that the plug hole starts to block, and I have to bend and stir the debris with my finger to push it through. The soap feels good against my skin. I'm surprised at how dirty my skin is, even where it was covered by clothes.

The soft water here means that the only way to properly remove the soap is with a cloth. The stiffness in my shoulder makes reaching some parts of my body difficult. But this is good. Having to focus on properly cleaning myself, ensuring the plug hole isn't blocked, stretching in ways that are least painful—it all requires concentration. Usually, having a shower's something I do on autopilot. This time, it feels like therapy. Helping to banish the fear I felt. Giving me a sense of perspective. Rooting me in the here and now. I'm home. I'm safe.

I take the shower hose out of its bracket and direct the head to rinse round the bath, chasing reluctant dirt toward the plug hole. I replace the attachment, draw back the shower curtain, and step out on to the bath mat. Then I reach for the white bath sheet and towel myself off. The aches in my knee and shoulder are still there, but diminished as if diluted by the shower. I fold the towel over the rail and slip back into my dressing gown.

I unlock and open the door. "Oh my God!" Gran is on the other side of the threshold, hand outstretched like she'd been reaching for the handle, confused eyes on the door. "Gran! You startled me. Do you need to use the toilet?"

"I was going for a wee." She's still looking at the door.

"I was having a shower, sorry. But it's free now."

She looks at me and I see the transformation take place in her eyes, the switch being flicked to on. Awareness. Like before.

"You've travelled." A statement of fact. Delivered with confidence in the stronger, firmer voice that was normal for her when I was younger.

I don't want this conversation here, on the landing. "Come with me, Gran."

She follows me back to my bedroom and follows my gesture that she should sit on the bed, as I close the door behind us. Her eyes are locked on mine as I sit beside her.

"You have, haven't you? Travelled."

"Yes, Gran. I've travelled."

"And did you see her? Did you see Suzy?"

"Yes, Gran. I saw Suzy."

You see TV shows where people have been looking for long-lost relatives for years and years. Then a presenter from the show tells them that the lost relation has been found. It's like that. Gran goes completely quiet. Then a long, quiet sigh. Her eyes moisten, then focus back on mine. "How is she?"

"She asked me to tell you that everything's fine. And that she's happy."

"Good. That's good to hear. And did she look well?"

"Yes, Gran. She looked really well."

"Where is she? Where did she go?"

"England, Gran. She went to England. Near to Liverpool."

"England. Well, well." She goes quiet.

"Are you all right, Gran?"

"Sammy—the fellow that Suzy fell for—he wasn't English. She said he was from the east coast. Somewhere near Dundee. I never thought she'd be in England."

"Well, that was where I met her."

"And did she say anything else?"

"She was asking after you. Wanted to know if you were well."

She smiles. "That's nice." Nods encouragement for me to tell her more.

"She was surprised that I was your granddaughter. Said it was hard to imagine you as a granny."

Gran smiles. Wistful. "We were both young when she went. So young. Was she old, like me?"

"Older than when you last saw her. But maybe not quite as old as you are now."

"And what else did she tell you? What more did she say?"

"I'm sorry, Gran. We hardly had any time together. I've told you everything."

"She didn't say if she had children? Grandchildren?"

"Sorry, Gran. As I say, we only had the briefest of time together. But it was really important for her to know that you were well. And for me to tell you that she's happy."

She's quiet again. Eyes distant now, but still aware. "It nearly killed me, you know."

"What's that, Gran?"

"When Suzy went away. I nearly died of a broken heart. We were like that." She holds up crossed fingers. "We shared everything. Hopes, dreams, disappointments, plans. Everything. No secrets between us. And we had such fun. We would tease boys by pretending to be each other. Go to the dancing together. Double dates." She pauses, and I think she's finished. But she continues. "Then she started travelling. Met Sammy. And I knew. I knew straight away when she first talked about him. She would choose him. And I wanted her to choose him because I knew that was what she wanted. That's what I told her. What would make her happy." Another pause. Blinking back tears. "But I was broken hearted for myself. She was my sister, my twin, and my best friend. I knew how much I'd miss her. How lonely I would be." A tear spills down her cheek.

"Oh, Gran." I lean toward her and squeeze her hand. "You were the best sister you could be. And you were right. She's happy, and she wanted you to know that."

Gran wipes the tear away. Sniffs. Takes a deep breath. Brings her other hand across to sandwich mine between hers. Lasers my eyes with hers. The smart, vibrant woman I remember is back. "And what about you?" Her voice is low, calm. But earnest. "What are *you* going to do?"

I know what she means. And she understands that. No point in anything but the truth. "I want to go to him."

Her lips tighten almost imperceptibly. Like I remember them doing when I did something to make her cross. When she still had all of her faculties. I used to hate it when I knew I'd disappointed her. Even more than if I upset Dad. I feel a knot in my stomach.

"No."

"What?"

"No."

"But Gran."

"No buts. When Suzy went, it almost killed me. Losing a sister was the worst thing imaginable. Except for losing a child. You cannot do that to your parents. You can't do that to your mum and dad."

"Dad's dead! Don't you remember?" Oh God! Look at her face! She doesn't remember. She doesn't know that her son-in-law is dead. Bewilderment. Horror. Grief. She's shaking her head. Tears streaming. Me too. We fall into each other's embrace. Hold her. Hold her. She's holding me. Both crying silently, we stay like that for ages. The crying subsides. Gradually, her embrace relaxes, and she sits back. I see from her eyes that she's not in there anymore.

"I need a wee. I want the toilet."

"Okay, Gran. Come with me." She comes with me to the bedroom door. I point to the bathroom. "Over there, remember?" She heads toward it, wordless and without a backward glance.

I close the door behind me, cross to my bed and lie down. I can't cope with all of this. Maybe whatever's wrong with my brain has turned me into a headcase. None of this makes any sense. Maybe I'm imagining it all. Like some sort of weird dream. I roll onto my side and wince at the pain in my shoulder. That's certainly real enough, nothing imaginary about it. But perhaps I fell out of bed and banged my shoulder when I was asleep. And my knee as well? Even as the thoughts present themselves, I'm dismissing them as nonsense. I know that what's happening to me is real. Maybe it's related to whatever's wrong in my brain in some way, but it's not a hallucination.

A knock on the door.

"Come in."

The handle moves slowly, then the door swings gently toward me. Mum comes through carrying a tray. "I wasn't sure if you felt up to coming downstairs, so I brought you something to eat." She places the tray on my desk. Two rolls with bacon, a steaming hot cup of tea, and a strawberry cream tart from Hastie's bakery. My favourite comfort food in all the world.

"Mum, you're spoiling me!"

"Don't worry—it's rolls and bacon and strawberry tarts for everyone tonight. No special treatment for you."

We both know fine well the menu is entirely for my benefit. "That's as may be, but thank you all the same."

"You're welcome. When it got to half past six—" my God! I hadn't realized the time "—and you hadn't come downstairs, I thought I'd bring this up to you."

"That's really thoughtful, Mum."

"It's no bother. Did I hear you in the shower earlier?"

"Aye. I just felt the need to freshen up. I've been lying about most of the day."

"Of course. And how are you feeling now? Has your headache cleared?"

I hear the fear in her voice. This morning, she learned that there might be a problem with her daughter's brain. Then I've been complaining about headaches and staying in my room all day. While I've spent years travelling to different countries and continents, she's spent the whole day worrying about me. "It's definitely improved. To be honest, I might've been better going out for some fresh air, but I just didn't feel like it. I just wanted to spend some time by myself. Is that selfish of me?"

"Don't be daft! You got a bit of a shock this morning. It's completely understandable if you want some time to mull it over. But just remember that I'm always here to talk to if you want."

She sounds slightly reassured. "Thanks, Mum. I know."

"Will you be down later, or will you just stay up here?"

"I'll probably eat this and then maybe get an early night. If that's all right?"

"Of course it is. Probably best that you rest. Do you need any more paracetamol?"

"No, I'm okay thanks."

"All right, then. You sleep well, sweetheart." She comes over and kisses me on the temple, smiles, and looks into my eyes.

"I'm really okay, Mum."

"I know." Another temple kiss and she turns, leaves the room, and closes the door gently behind her.

I sit down at the desk, pick up the roll, and take a mighty bite. The bacon is lean with the fatty edge crisped and still warm, and the butter has melted and soaked into the bread. There's no greater culinary joy than this combination of texture, flavour, and aroma. A slug of hot tea to wash it down and then another, smaller bite.

I need to try and make sense of all of this. I make a mental inventory of what seems relevant—Walter asleep in Archie's bed, waking up in America, and going to Walter's surprise party, wakening back here and meeting Molly, seeing Doctor McKenzie and learning I might have a tumour, Scott thinking I'm dying, travelling to meet Walter in 1969, Alice chucking Sandy, travelling again to find myself as Walter's wife in the 1970s, speaking to Molly and Walter on the phone, travelling to the Merseyside Blitz and meeting Suzy, Gran's moments of lucidity. In the time it takes to list everything, I've already finished the first roll and taken a bite from the second.

My school reports have consistently referred to how highly analytical I am when it comes to problem-solving, which is definitely something I recognize about myself. I like to list all of the known facts and then try out different hypotheses. But that approach only works when there are sufficient data points to enable me to work things out.

And this is one of those frustrating times when I just don't know enough to work out the answer. I play everything I know over and over in my mind. It must have something to do with time. Less than a day has passed in 2019, but so much more time elapsed on my travels. And I've got actual years' worth of memories of my time with Walter. I gave up physics after Standard grade, but I suspect that if I'd kept it on, I'd be none the closer to understanding all of this. It's clear that whatever's happening, the normal rules that apply to time and space just don't count. My body must be in two places or times at once. When I was in Ethiopia, my body was obviously also still at the hospital, unconscious. Physical items seem to travel in both directions. Kia's button, the bandage safety pins, and Walter's jacket have all come back with me from the past. I can still feel the pain in my knee and shoulder from the blows in the Blitz. But the time I woke up in bed with Walter, I was naked, despite falling asleep and then wakening up back here fully clothed. There's no consistency.

Is it something to do with this bedroom? I keep falling asleep here, then wakening up back here after travelling. Except that wasn't the case when I went to Ethiopia. I don't think it's anything to do with this room.

I can feel my frustration growing as my failure to make any sense of it all continues. I need to stop myself from becoming irritated. I remember the advice that Mrs. Collins, my class tutor, gave me last year. She told me that I have good emotional intelligence. When I get frustrated that logic and rational analysis aren't working, I should simply go with my gut instinct. I pause and try to clear my mind of all the clutter. Then it becomes obvious. This whole thing is about me. Me and Walter.

The second roll is finished. I must've been starving. And I'm halfway through my tea.

The strawberry tart is a fantastic sweet treat to follow the bacon roll. Better brush my teeth now and change into my pyjamas. I'm suddenly exhausted. Will I sleep? Travel again? I close the curtains, climb into bed, courie under the duvet. So, so tired.

August 11, 2019

41.

THERE'S A PERSISTENT, INSISTENT tapping. It's intrusive and unwelcome. I'm warm and comfortable. I don't want to be disturbed. But it continues, then stops. There's the sound of a door handle turning. "Eilidh?" Mum's voice.

"Yes?"

"Sorry to wake you, but I was wondering if you would want some lunch."

"What time is it?"

"Just coming on to quarter to twelve." It can't be! I sit up, blink at the light streaming round the edges of the curtains, and rub matter from my eye. Mum's head and shoulder come into focus, the rest of her hidden behind the door. She's studying me, trying not to look concerned. "How're you feeling?"

"Fine. I feel fine." I shake my head gently from side to side. "No headache at all." And there isn't one. There was a twinge in my shoulder as I sat up. But it was just a twinge. I push the duvet to the side and swing my legs round to put my feet on the floor.

The smile on Mum's face disappears as she looks at my legs below my pyjama shorts. "What happened to your knee?"

I glance down at the furious purple around my right knee. "Oh, that? I'm not sure. I remember banging my knee off the chair." I nod toward the chair by my desk. "But it barely hurt at the time. I can't believe it's come up like this."

Feeble and implausible. Incredulity is writ large on Mum's face, but she chooses not to challenge. "Okay. Now, what about lunch? There's a roast that'll be ready in about three quarters of an hour. Or would you like something lighter? A sandwich, or something like that, brought up to you?"

Bless her. She's worried sick about me and trying so hard to hide it. "A roast sounds brilliant, Mum. I'll be down and looking for a healthy portion." Her expression doesn't change, but I see in her eyes that she's pleased.

She's about to say something when the sound of the doorbell downstairs interrupts. "Don't tell me that's another one."

"Another what, Mum?"

"You should know, Eilidh." She can see I haven't got a clue. "A delivery. There have been two already for you this morning."

"Oh, yes. I remember. I indulged in a bit of internet retail therapy when I was feeling sorry for myself." I need to change the subject before she asks what I've been buying. "Is there enough hot water for me to have a shower?"

"There is. But didn't you have one yesterday?"

"I did, but I fancy another one to properly waken myself up."

"Okay, then. I'll see you downstairs for lunch." She's satisfied and heads off.

I brush my teeth, shower, get dressed, and go downstairs. On top of the bookshelf by the front door is a bundle of three envelopes and a parcel all addressed to me. I scoop them up and take them back to my room for opening in private later. Then I join Gran in front of the TV and pass the time chatting about nothing in particular until lunch is ready.

The meal is lovely. Mum's obviously been up at the crack of dawn to slow roast a leg of lamb—my favourite. And she's made a real effort with the roasties and the veg. I know it's the height of summer, but I love a good Sunday roast whatever the time of year. The conversation all seems to flow easily enough, although I get a sense of brave faces being put on, probably for my benefit. I'm happy to go with the flow. Gran doesn't have the savvy anymore to pick up on any undercurrents, so she just responds to the general positivity round the table, helping to amplify it. Scott actually contrives to be funny and interesting. George makes a couple of cryptic comments in his usual clumsy manner that cause Mum and me to flash *what's he up to* glances at each other. But I don't go after him because I don't want to upset the mood.

At the end of the meal, the boys uncharacteristically offer to clear up and load the dishwasher. Mum escorts Gran back to the living room, and I head out for a seat in the garden to get some fresh air.

There's a gentle breeze, and the beautiful perfumes of the climbing rose and sweet peas are a joy. There's the faint sound of an electric mower in the distance, and the sky is as blue as it ever gets. A couple of gulls, almost as high as heaven, are heading toward the coast.

"Penny for them." Mum's hand's on my shoulder.

"Not a thought in my head, Mum. Just enjoying this beautiful day."

"And how are you feeling? Really."

"Honestly, Mum, I'm fine. I feel really well."

"Good." She takes a seat beside me. I can see she has something to say. "Doctor McKenzie phoned last night. After you'd gone to bed."

"And?"

"She's spoken to Elspeth Cooke. You've to go to the Beatson tomorrow at one o' clock to meet her."

"Oh! That's quick."

"I think she's doing a favour for a friend. I suspect she's seeing you in her lunch hour."

"Right. That would make sense."

"If we leave here at eleven, it'll give us plenty of time to get there, get parked, and maybe grab a quick bite before we see her."

"But Mum, you've got your work. I can get up there on the train by myself." Rather than actually tell me not to be so stupid, she allows her withering expression to deliver the sentiment. "Aye, okay, then."

"So are you going to spend some time out here this afternoon? Have you got any plans?"

"I thought it would be nice to catch up with the girls. I'll text Seonaid in a wee while to see what we can arrange. What about you? What're you up to?"

"I'm going to go in and reload the dishwasher. Then maybe take your Gran for a walk. Perhaps go and talk to George. He's up to something."

"Yeah. I spotted that too. Why are you reloading the dishwasher? The boys said they'd do it."

Mum gives me her most disdainful look. "There were already breakfast dishes in it from this morning. They'll just have piled stuff in willy-nilly. Not stacked it properly. I swear they do it on purpose so they don't get asked to do it again."

We both laugh and my phone buzzes in my pocket. I pull it out. "It's a text from Seonaid."

Mum gets to her feet. "I'll let you get on with it, love. I'd best get back inside."

I nod acknowledgement as she heads into the house. The text from Seonaid is short and to the point: *How are you feeling?*

Me: *Slept really well. Feeling great.*

Seonaid: *Good. Fancy meeting up with Alice and me?*

Me: Deffo. *Where and when?*

Seonaid: *Benches at Ballantyne Park. 3:00. Does that work for you?*

I check my watch. Quarter past two.

Me: *Perfect. See you then.*

I'm excited and pleased at the prospect. It seems ages—years—since I last saw them. And despite my new friends in Holland, I still think of Alice and Seonaid as among my oldest and best friends. I get up and almost skip into the kitchen.

"I'm meeting Seonaid and Alice at Ballantyne Park later."

Mum looks up from rearranging the contents of the dishwasher. "That's nice. What time?"

"Three o' clock."

"And will you be home for your tea?"

"I'm not sure. I'll text you."

"Okay. You won't be staying out late, will you?"

"No, Mum. I won't be staying out late."

We exchange smiles, and I make my way upstairs to my room. The courier company details on the parcel show it was despatched from Leeds, confirming what the contents will be even before I unwrap it. I fetch the nail scissors from my chest of drawers and cut open the bulky, heavy package. The shoes fall out on to the floor part way through cutting. I pick the right one up to examine it. Plain, black, chunky low heel, scoop-cut upper, with a narrow strap over the instep fastened by a simple buckle. This wouldn't look out of place today. I sit on the edge of my bed and try them on. Perfect fit!

Back to the package, which I decide to now tear open. My delight with the shoes is immediately counterbalanced as the coat becomes visible. I pull it out, shake it, and hold it in front of me by the shoulders.

It looks exactly like it did in the pictures, so I can hardly complain. But the feel of it is awful—horrible, cheap, lightweight nylon. I would *never* wear this—whether it's 2019 or 1969. It's hideous. I lay it down on the bed and return to the remnants of the parcel.

The muted-blue floral pattern shirt actually looks all right, and in good condition. The faded bellbottom jeans are, quite frankly, ridiculous. I'll pack those to take with me, rather than actually wear them. I don't remember seeing that many people dressed in such wide bellbottoms in either Holland or Belgium. Maybe Scotland was different, but I'm not risking wearing those back and sticking out like a sore thumb.

I fold the jeans and shirt and place them in the drawer at the bottom of the wardrobe, then put the coat on a hanger and place it inside. Now to check the contents of the envelopes. There's something curiously satisfying about opening a handwritten envelope addressed to yourself. Maybe the association with birthday cards from when you're a kid? I assemble the contents of the three envelopes and count the money carefully. The full £267 is there, denominated in £10, £5, £1, and ten shilling notes. They look so old-fashioned compared to modern banknotes. More than half the total is in tenners, so the wad isn't too thick. I'll need to be careful where I keep it when I go back—it's several weeks wages for most people. I place the banknotes under my pillow and gather the packaging and empty envelopes to take out to the recycling bin.

As I descend the stairs, I can hear Mum talking to Gran in the living room. "I'm just on my way out to meet Seonaid and Alice!"

"Okay, love. Have a good time and say hi to the girls from me."

"Will do, Mum. Bye!"

"Bye!"

I leave through the kitchen, out via the back door, pop the recycling into the blue bin, and then along the side of the house toward the front gate.

42.

BY THE TIME I get to Ballantyne Park, the girls are already waiting for me. We group hug, and I'm reminded of how much I love them. And how much I've missed them. Seonaid decides to shoot the elephant before it can follow us into any room.

"Okay, Eilidh. Do you want to talk about your brain and confide in your besties, or is it *verboten*? Your call—it's no sweat for us either way."

"You're going to be wasted in medicine, Sho. You should be in the Diplomatic Service." There's a nervous laugh from Alice. "I'm fine with talking about it if you guys are. I should warn you that I might sound a little bit weird, but you should both be used to that with me by now."

"You can say anything you like. You know we'll just talk about you behind your back anyway." Seonaid is grinning.

"And same question to you," I say as I turn toward Alice. "Is talking about you and Sandy taboo, or do you want to spill your guts?"

Alice pulls us both back into the three-way hug. "You might be worried about sounding weird, Eilidh. But believe me, you'll be referring me for therapy once I've finished."

We make our way to the shade thrown by a clump of trees and sit down on the dry grass. Seonaid produces a bottle of Sauvignon Blanc and three plastic tumblers from her bag. The next couple of hours shoot by as we discuss everything that matters and plenty that doesn't. There are some tears, but mainly laughter. I'm careful not to discuss locations or times when sharing my "dreams" about Walter, but I pretty much spill everything else. I catch a quick glance between the other two when I talk about Walter and know instantly there has been a pre-agreed pact to humour me. I'm cool with that. I understand.

Alice rehashes everything about her and Sandy, and we both feel her pain. The most intriguing insight is into her guilt and how painful it was for her. Starting to look at other boys. Wondering what it would be like to be with them. She'd been a girl of fifteen when she and Sandy first got together, and now she's a woman of eighteen. She says she didn't want to wonder about other boys, but she couldn't help it. And then she hated herself for it. The mood lightens when we speculate about all the other boys who fancy her who will be on the prowl now that she's single again. There's loads of laughter and denial, but she's enjoying the guessing game and the relief of being with friends. I deliberately don't mention George.

Seonaid completely wrong-foots Alice and me by announcing that she's going on a date with Harry Miller. After the ritual whooping and accusations of secretiveness, the interrogation begins. Apparently she was walking down Wellcroft Brae, and he pulled up beside her in a beaten-up old Vauxhall Nova. He offered her a lift and refused to accept no for an answer despite her protests that she was two minutes from home. Alice pointed out that the protests could hardly have been that strong. Anyway, then he asked her out for a meal, and they're going to Capaldi's in Ardnahuish next Saturday night! I'm chuffed to bits for her. It's her first-ever proper date, and although she's pretending to be chilled about it, she can't disguise how pleased she is. He's a tall, quiet boy. Hangs about with Kenny Marshall and Bobby Caldow— that crowd. All nice guys. He's going to do engineering at Strathclyde. Alice teases her about "examining her patient" and making sure she uses her best "bedside manner." The two of them end up play wrestling on the grass.

The wine is long since finished, but we're having too much fun to call it a day yet.

"The Tassie will be open. We could go there, grab a bite, and have a few more drinks." Alice demonstrates her genius!

The pub is quite sparsely populated when we arrive, and it's easy to get served. Two bowls of chilli, one lasagne, and three large dry white wines. We go to the table in the corner against the back wall—great for people watching and not easy to be seen. I text Mum: *Won't be home for tea. Getting some lasagne at The Tassie with the girls.*

Mum: *Thanks for letting me know. When will you be home? You're not planning on staying out late?*

Me: *I won't be late, Mum. 9:00 at the latest. Probably earlier.*

"Who're you texting?" Seonaid always needs to know what's going on.

"Just letting Mum know where I am. Not to make any tea for me."

"Okay. Now, wait 'til I tell you who Chelsea McDaid was seen in here with last night."

The conversation just flows. You know those nights when everything just comes so easy? When it's perfect? Well, it's like that. The food comes, and it's decent. The pub gets a bit busier, and there's a nice atmosphere. We each have another glass of wine, the chat remaining effortless. I'm laughing at Seonaid's description of the numpty that interviewed her when she applied to Newcastle, when Alice taps me on the arm. "Is that your George waving at us?"

I look up and there's George at the bar. Pointing and beckoning us to come over. Fuck's sake! What's he doing here? I point to my chest and mouth the words *you want me to come over?* along with an expression that makes it clear that is the last thing I want to do. He shakes his head and points emphatically at Alice. What the actual fuck?

Alice turns to me to state the fucking obvious: "I think he wants me to go over to him."

"Ah. After all these years! Finally, love's young dream fulfilled." Seonaid is laughing so much that her wine almost spills.

Alice is up and heading toward him without another word, surprising me. At the bar, they're immediately in animated discussion. Both faces very earnest, and then hers blooms into that spectacular trademark smile as she casts a look in my direction.

"What on Earth are they talking about?" Seonaid is no wiser than me.

"Not a clue, Sho. But I'm going to kill him."

The pair are as thick as thieves. I'm just about to go over to investigate what they're up to when Alice signals to me to do just that. She's gesturing for me to go to her, just as George leaves her and heads for the main door back out into the pub car park.

I get to my feet grumpily and make my way to Alice, with Seonaid close behind. "Okay, Alice, what's going on? What's my daft bastard brother up to?"

She doesn't answer. Just turns her head and nods toward the door. I follow her direction, ready to tell George exactly what I think of him for interrupting me when I'm out with my pals. But it's not George standing in the doorway. Of course, he looks like George, but with longer hair and a passable beard. Arms outstretched and grinning right at me.

"Archie? Archie! Is that really you?" Stupid question! I run into his bear hug, and his embrace lifts me off the floor. He's squeezing me so tightly I can hardly get my words out. "When did you get back? I thought you weren't due back for over a week?"

"Got back this afternoon. I would've stayed away another week, but I ran out of money."

That sounds like bullshit, but I don't care. I was away camping when Archie came home at the end of term and then went off travelling. I've not seen him for nearly four and a half months. "I can still hardly believe it. And what's with the beard?"

"Somebody has to uphold the family's hipster credentials. And it's certainly not going to be him." He nods behind me, and I turn to see George has reappeared and is grinning like he's won the lottery. He's flanked by Alice and Seonaid, and I swear they both have a tear in their eye.

"I don't know what to say." And I don't.

"Don't say anything. Come to the bar with me and help me get the next round of drinks." Archie looks at the others. "And you lot grab an extra couple of chairs for the table."

I follow Archie to the bar, my hand on his shoulder to confirm that he really is here.

"And are you getting the drinks in?"

"Certainly am. What are you and your friends drinking?"

"Two large dry white wines and a lemonade for me."

"Laying off the booze, then, are we?"

I can tell from the way he says it that he knows. "I've had a couple already, but that's enough for me today."

"Very sensible." He orders the wines, lemonade, and two pints of lager.

"So you ran out of money, but you're buying a round of drinks?"

We lock eyes. He smiles. He knows I know that he knows. "George phoned me yesterday and told me. I was in Bangkok. Plenty of flights. Caught one on standby to London and then a connection to Glasgow. Got to the house an hour ago."

"Archie! You didn't need to do that. Cut your trip short."

"That's right, Eilidh. My twin calls to tell me my favourite sister might be seriously ill, and I'm just going to continue swanning about in Thailand?"

"He shouldn't have called you. I'm going to kill him."

"If he didn't call me, and I found out later, I'd have been furious. I'd have called him if it was the other way round. I'm here now, and glad to be. Don't have a go at him. You don't want to make him look bad." Archie nods toward our table in the corner. Seonaid is texting, and George is chatting to Alice, his head tilted in close to hers.

"Oh my God! Promise me you won't let him make more of an arse of himself than usual. I don't think I could stand the embarrassment."

Archie just grins at me as the barman delivers the last of our order. "You take the two wines, and I'll bring the rest."

We make our way back to the table and take our seats. All four of them know each other well enough for it not to be uncomfortable. Archie is sufficiently socially adept that he can keep things moving by telling tales from his trip without even the suggestion that he's monopolizing the conversation. He's good at telling funny stories, not necessarily jokes, which are usually at his own expense. He's the charmer in our family, and I've missed him. The evening continues in a lighthearted vein. Even George manages not to be a prick, and I sense just a sniff of interest from Alice, although too subtle for George to spot—despite the fact that it's exactly what he'll be looking out for.

A quick look at my phone, and I'm surprised that it's quarter to nine. "Oh, look at the time! I said to Mum that I'd be back before nine."

Everyone else expresses their surprise at the time except George, who looks utterly crestfallen. Normally, I'd expect someone to suggest having another, particularly when the company is as good as it is tonight. But they all know I've the appointment at The Beatson tomorrow, so no one advocates staying on.

It's still bright sunshine when we get outside the pub, although George says, "The night's starting to draw in."

Jesus! He's utterly transparent. He knows that Alice lives on the other side of the park, and he's positioning himself to "gallantly" offer to walk her home. But Seonaid lives in the same direction, and he's obviously forgotten that.

"Well, we'll head off through the park now," Seonaid says, smiling. "Good luck tomorrow, Eilidh. It was good to see you again, Archie."

"And it was good to see you too, George." Alice's smile is on super-radiant setting. "Let us know how you get on, Eilidh."

Goodbye hugs all round, and the two of them are off. I take one brother on each arm, and we turn in the opposite direction.

"I hadn't realized what an absolute beauty Alice has turned into," Archie says to neither of us in particular.

I'm onto it immediately. "You're right, she's totally gorgeous."

"And she's not just a looker. She seems like a really nice person too."

"She is, Archie. One of the kindest, most generous people you could ever meet."

"Did I get it right back at the pub? Has she split up with Sandy Waddell?"

"Yes, just recently. So that's her young, free, and single again for the first time in years."

There's as much bait as possible on the hook, and Archie and I pause to see if it works. But George isn't biting. "Aye, very good, you two. I'll tell you, you need to polish up your act a lot. You're really rusty. You must think I came up the Clyde in a banana boat if you think I'm walking into that one."

The rest of the walk home is filled with laughter, mock recriminations, teasing, and daft banter between the twins. I love it and join in. I'd forgotten how much I miss the pair sparking off each other.

When we get back to the house, everyone is waiting. Archie's surprise return has got everyone buzzing. Mum's as happy as I've seen her in ages. Scott's got both his brothers and is like a dog with two tails. Gran doesn't really understand the excitement but is caught up in the positivity and joy. We all sit round the kitchen table, drinking tea and eating biscuits. The chat is good. Archie repeats some of his Thailand stories—the ones that can be shared with Mum, Gran, and Scott—and George and I are happy enough to hear them again. Archie makes everyone laugh. It's nice to see Mum happy, distracted from the worry I know she has about my appointment tomorrow. Scott throws in a couple of quips that hit the spot and keep the mood going. I can see how pleased he is to make a table full of adults laugh. There's a lot of *remember when* stories flying around, most of them funny at the expense of one of us siblings. The only thing missing that would make this night perfect is Dad.

It seems like we've only been chatting twenty minutes when Mum points out that it's half past ten. A bit like at the pub, there are no protests, and everyone accepts that it's time to call it a night. I wonder if I can manage things so that George, Archie, and me can carry on after the others have gone to bed. But I reckon that wouldn't be fair, particularly to Mum. She hasn't said so, but she wants me to get an early night.

Everyone wishes everyone else goodnight. Automatically, we fall into the established pecking order for pre-bed ablutions. Gran first, then reverse age order, with me following Scott, then Archie, George, and Mum. I lie on my bed listening to the latter three coming up the stairs to the bathroom one at a time, each with their own distinctive pace and step pattern. I hear Mum switching off lights as she goes.

43.

MY PHONE BUZZES. Who's messaging me at ten past eleven? Molly: *See what you think of these. I'll call you during the week.*

There are two attachments. The first is a head and shoulders shot of me in front of some kind of flowering shrub. It's really grainy, but it's obviously me. My hair is much shorter than I've ever had it, and I'm holding my arm out, pointing at the photographer, as if to say "Don't you dare take this picture." It's strange to see a picture of my future self from the past. I don't look that much older than I am now. Was this in Belgium? Or Holland? Or after that? Or before?

I click on to the next photo, and my heart misses several beats. Walter and I are in profile, holding each other close and staring into one another's eyes. My hair is pretty much the same as it is now, and I'm wearing a red top. The picture is only from the waist up. But I must be wearing heels because there's only about six inches height difference. Although his head is tilted, looking down at me looking back up at him. He is so good looking. So wonderful. God, I love that man.

I get up from the bed and go to the wardrobe, fetch Walter's jacket and my school rucksack from inside, and then the blue shirt and jeans from the drawer below. I retrieve the old banknotes from under my pillow, count out ten pounds worth—a fiver, four singles, and two ten-shilling notes—fold them in half and put them in my pocket. Then I roll the rest of the notes into a fat cigar, go to my desk drawer, and get an elastic band to hold them together. I go to my laptop and send the screenshot of Patience Smith's birth certificate to the printer, delete it, delete it from deleted items, and then delete all browsing history. Carefully, I fold the bellbottoms and place them in the bottom of the rucksack, take the printout of the screenshot, fold it, and place it over the jeans. I place the roll of notes on top, neatly fold Walter's jacket and pop it in, then place the rucksack on my bed.

I take off my top and put it in the washing basket. A quick glimpse in the mirror, and I'm persuaded the bra should follow the top. I go to the chest of drawers and select another bra to put on, grab three more bras and a handful of knickers and stuff them on top of Walter's jacket in the rucksack. Then I put on the shirt. It fits really well, and I'm pleased with my reflection. I'm going to stick with the jeans I'm wearing. They're straight legs and will go with the shoes, even if they might look a bit out of place in 1969. The shoes are still at the foot of my bed, and my feet slip into them easily. Shit! Socks! I go back to the chest of drawers and grab a couple of pairs of socks and a pair of flesh-tone tights, then stuff them into the rucksack as well. Finally, I sit down on the end of the bed so I can easily reach the shoes to fasten them.

I get up and draw the curtains, retrieve the envelope from my sock drawer, and shake Kia's button out into my palm. I look at it for a long time, press it gently against my cheek, and look at it again. Then I put it into the opposite pocket from the one with the money. It'll be the first week of November. It was cold enough on Hallowe'en. I can't go back in just this shirt. I rummage in my drawers and find a black wraparound cardi, with a belt that ties at the waist. I put it on, then check the mirror—it looks okay. Then back to the wardrobe and take the coat out. Reluctantly. It looks all right. But the feel of it!

I step back to my bed, lay the coat out, and fold it over twice. I plump up the pillows then lie down on top of the duvet, folded coat resting over my waist. My hand reaches for the rucksack, and I place it on top of the coat, take my phone from my pocket and place it on the bedside table. Then I reach up with my right hand and flick off the light switch.

Okay. This is it. What was it Suzy said? Focus on where and when I want to be. The Silver Tassie on Saturday, November 8, 1969. Early evening. I need to sense it. The building hasn't changed in at least fifty years, and possibly never. If the Ladies is still in the same place as it was, then I could try to sense myself into being in one of the two cubicles. I just need to hope that there's no one else in there! It's a Victorian pub, and the floor and wall tiles in the toilets all look original. So do the sinks—they'd be the same in 1969. I'd be able to hear the noise from people in the bar and the lounge. Maybe the toilet in the next cubicle flushing? There would be that pub smell. Mixed with the smell of soap, probably. And almost certainly cigarette smoke as well back then. I just need to imagine it all. Then sense it.

Am I sure about this? Do I really want to do it? Do I really want never to see my family again? Not ever? I know that if I go back to 1969, I'll be dead in 2019. Can I put them through that? Gran said that losing Suzy almost killed her. And she said that a parent losing a child would be even worse. Can I really put Mum through that? Especially so soon after losing Dad? And what about George? And Archie? And Scott? Tonight's reminded me of how good we are together as a family, even though we're forever bickering with each other. And Gran. What about her? Would she know what happened? Would she remember that I travelled? Or would she have no idea at all what was going on?

And how about my pals? What about Lindsey and Seonaid and Alice? Seonaid and Alice are more like sisters than friends. We all look out for each other, want the best for each other. I know that we'll all be friends until our dying day. Except that this would be my dying day. Not their friend any more. Just a memory. A memory that would fade. I'd never be able to talk to them again. To comfort and be comforted. To share secrets. Can I really choose to never see them again?

And what if I do go back, and it doesn't work out? Even if I make it back, it looks like I die pretty young. I was dead by the time of Walter's fiftieth. Where was I meant to be when Walter was in Ethiopia? How do I die? Walter doesn't have any children. Does that mean I die before we're ready to have any? Do I even want kids? Am I giving up everything in the here and now to go back for just a few short years? Maybe those years in Belgium and Holland I've already lived are all I get. Maybe I get to relive those and then die suddenly. Do I give up all of my prospects in 2019 to relive a few years in 1969?

But Suzy said that … what was it she said? That what I experienced when I travelled before were just possibilities. Glimpses of what might've been—that's what she said. What I choose to do can change things. She said that what I do when I travel has an effect. So maybe I don't die. Maybe Walter and I have a family and grow old and happy together. Maybe I can persuade him not to play in that match where he got so badly hurt. Perhaps he could get his transfer to a big Spanish club after all. Maybe I should be being less selfish about all of this. Perhaps I should go back to Ethiopia a week earlier and save Kia. Or maybe I could go back and warn Dad about his illness earlier somehow, giving him enough time to get treatment that could save him.

But I know that's not going to happen. This is about me and Walter. All of this is about me and him. Suzy said that when we travel, we experience love. My God she's right about that. And she said we have to choose. *Have* to. Between my love for Walter or for my family. I have to choose.

Walter in 1969 is young, handsome, athletic, adventurous, driven, and funny. He's also a product of his time—homophobic, unconsciously racist, and a bit sexist. But he's also the man with the potential to have a black best friend that he's willing to go to Ethiopia and risk being shot at for. A man who rescues and mentors underprivileged kids and works tirelessly for hospital and dyslexia charities. He has the potential to be the man who gives up everything to come back to the UK to look after his orphaned niece. He will love me unconditionally, and we will make each other complete.

If I choose Walter, we might live a long and happy life together. But then he'll get dementia. Physically fit, but with his mind gone—maybe for years and years. Do I want to spend the last ten or twenty years of my life married to the husk of a man?

Or what if Walter and me don't work out for some reason? Not like with me and Findlay—neither of us is a cheat or a liar. And I'd never, ever not love Walter. But what if he changed? Like Alice's feelings for Sandy? I know I've "lived" for over two years with Walter as my husband, and it just got better and better. But Alice and Sandy were together for the best part of three years before her feelings started to change. Can I risk going back and having a failed marriage? Stuck in the wrong time, not able to look to family or friends for comfort and support? Surrounded by people with prehistoric attitudes to so many things?

And what about Walter? Is it fair to him that I keep secrets? Is that really the basis for a sound and lasting marriage? What was it he said to me? That time when he said he worried about us? When he was recovering in hospital in Holland? He worried that he was holding me back. Not letting me fulfil my potential. He said that, if he thought he was making me unhappy, it would kill him. That it would be better if we'd never met. Better if I'd never known him. Is all this mystery and secrecy tormenting him? Am I sowing the seeds of my own marriage failure? Can I be sure that I'll never be frustrated that I didn't pursue my degree course? Maybe I should tell Walter the truth? But Suzy said I must never mention my original life.

I *want* to go back. I want to be with Walter, and I want to be *us*. I also want to be with my family and my friends in 2019. This thing in my head—in my brain—I sense that it's bad. Really, really bad. I could wait just until tomorrow, when I go to The Beatson, and get a proper diagnosis. But I don't need to wait for that diagnosis—I can sense that it won't be good news. If I stay in 2019, I'm probably going to die anyway.

Even if I do decide to try to go back, there's no guarantee I'll get there. Last time I travelled, I evaded the Chasers by the skin of my teeth. A shiver passes through me at the recollection. The last few times, they've seemed to get closer and closer to catching me. If I travel again, this could be the time they get me. Then I'd really be dead, both in 1969 and 2019. How can it be worth the risk?

I play all of this over in my mind. Time and again. Enough! I *have* to decide. I close my eyes. Tight.

August 23, 2019

44.

Extract from *The Brothmulloch and Ardnahuish Press and Argus*

TEEN DEATH RESULT OF NATURAL CAUSES

A post-mortem, instructed by the Procurator fiscal, has confirmed that Eilidh McVicar, 18, of 6 Brankholm Terrace, Kilmadden, died of natural causes. The cause of death was given as cardiac failure resulting from a previously undetected congenital heart defect. Eilidh was found dead in her bedroom on Monday, August 12. She was due to see a specialist at the Beatson Cancer Centre in Glasgow later that same day, but the cause of death was completely unrelated to that appointment.

Eilidh was due to start at St. Andrews University next month, where she was to have studied history. Eric Stewart, headmaster at Kilmadden Academy, Eilidh's old school said, "Everyone is devastated by this news. Eilidh was not only particularly gifted academically, she was also a big personality who was very popular with teachers and fellow pupils alike. Her death is a terrible tragedy."

No one from the family was available for comment.

November 8, 1969

45.

"ARE YOU EXPECTING someone, Wattie?" Davie Thomson, sitting further along on the opposite side of the table, is smiling as he shouts to make himself heard above the racket of the busy Saturday evening Silver Tassie. He's obviously spotted me checking my watch again.

"That'd be telling." I return his grin.

I need to be less obvious about checking my watch and looking at the door, or every other guy on the team will start teasing me about it. Everyone's having a good time, including me to an extent, despite being even more distracted than I thought I'd be. We've had a cracking result, winning 3-0 away to Thornlie United, and I scored two of them—the first and the third. I'm the subject of multiple toasts as the rest of the company look for any excuse to down another pint or spirit. I dutifully raise my orange juice and lemonade each time and try to play down my contribution to the result.

I've been thinking about Patti all week. I was even thinking about her during the match today, for God's sake! I had more butterflies in my stomach on the bus trip here after the fixture than I did before the game. I'm not really religious, but I found myself praying for all I was worth on that coach journey, promising whatever deity might care to intervene that I'd do anything for her to be at the pub.

Despite all that, I hadn't anticipated just how crestfallen I'd feel when we bowled into the pub just after six o' clock and she wasn't here. Over the next hour, the place filled up and I almost cricked my neck looking up every time the door opened and someone came in. When she hadn't turned up at seven, and then at half-seven, I told myself I'd been stupid to let my hopes build up so much.

Now it's nearly quarter to eight, and it's obvious she's not coming. The same bunch of lassies who're usually here when we come in after a game are sitting at the next table, and the blonde who's never made any secret of the fact she fancies me, Moira, is in the seat adjacent to mine. She spins round and slides on to the bench seat beside me. "If it's company you're looking for, I'm sure I might be able to help.' She fixes me with promising smile.

Even though she's got teeth like a Victorian graveyard, Moira's both pretty and good fun. I slide my arm round her shoulder. I might as well enjoy the here and now rather than mope about what might've been.

Then the world changes. The sounds of the juke box, the one-armed bandit, and several dozen alcohol-fuelled conversations seem to drop away. I'm staring, transfixed, at the figure who has just exited the Ladies toilet. Moira follows my gaze, looks back at my face, then gets to her feet as she mutters something about going to the bar for a drink.

Patti is peering through the cigarette smoke, scanning the bar until our eyes meet. My heart stops beating, then starts again at a thousand times its normal rate as she walks toward me. Absolutely, heart-stoppingly beautiful. She's carrying a bag and has my denim jacket draped over her arm. She gets to the table and hands it to me.

"I brought your jacket back," she says, smiling.

I think about telling her she should keep it in preference to the thing she's wearing that she must have got from a jumble sale, but all I can manage is, "Okay. Thanks."

She sits down on the bench right beside me. "Blondie won't be sitting back down here."

"I think that's probably right."

"I wasn't asking, Walter. I was stating a fact."

Acknowledgements

I'd like to thank the following people:

John Ballam for his wisdom, encouragement, and advice.

Maureen O'Neill, Audrey Slade, Theresa Black, Viv Moaven, Jo Pike, and Chris Wilson for their help and support.

Lucy Govan and Zoë Govan for providing inspiration.

David Govan for the provision of technical support.

Michael Mirolla for believing in the book.

Errol F. Richardson for his help designing the cover.

Paul Carlucci for his advice and help in navigating the editing process.

My wife Chris for her love and support, and for demonstrating more patience than should ever be required of any one person.

About the Author

Russell Govan shouts at politicians when they appear on his TV screen, irrespective of which political party they represent. He also gets annoyed by the Scottish national football team for its consistent ability to raise then dash his hopes. He started writing in 2015 and had two well-received thrillers published in 2020 and 2021. He has had entries shortlisted in a number of writing competitions, including an extract from an early draft of this novel which was shortlisted for the 2019 Grindstone International Short Story Prize. Living in Oxford, he remains married to his long-suffering wife and is a father of four.